The Song of the Skylark

BY THE SAME AUTHOR

The Miller of Carnac
Argentine

Antoine-Louis Duclaux,
Comte de L'Estoille
writing as "A. de L'Estoille"

The Song of the Skylark

translated, annotated and introduced by
Brian Stableford

A Black Coat Press Book

Acknowledgments: Thanks to Marie Duclaux de L'Estoille, Thierry Fraysse, Christine Luce and Jean-Marc Lofficier.

English adaptation and introduction Copyright © 2020 by Brian Stableford.
Cover illustration Copyright © 2020 Michel Borderie.

Visit our website at www.blackcoatpress.com

TABLE OF CONTENTS

Introduction

This is the second of three volumes translating the work of Antoine-Louis Duclaux, Comte de L'Estoille (1835-1894), the first volume of which, *The Miller of Carnac and Other Works* translated stories and prose poems published under the pseudonym "Louis de Lyvron" between 1865 and 1869. This volume contains a translation the first and longest of the works that he published during the second phase of his career, *La Chanson de l'alouette*, issued in three volumes in 1880 by Alphonse Lemerre under the signature "A. de L'Estoille," Antoine de L'Estoille being the name he employed in common usage. The third volume of the present set of translations, *Argentine and Other Works*, includes selections from the latter phase of his career as A. de L'Estoille.

The introduction to the first volume of the present set includes a synoptic account of L'Estoille's early life and career, to the extent that the information in question is presently recoverable, but it is sufficient to say here that he was a native of Renaison in the Monts de la Madeleine, between the Allier and the Loire, where he also spent the latter part of his life and where he finished writing the text of *La Chanson de l'alouette*. He attended the military academy of Saint-Cyr, then located in Yvelines, before joining a cavalry regiment of the kind known as spahis, in which French officers supervised native recruits from North Africa, and he spent the late 1850s in the region south of Algiers, before his regiment was apparently dispatched to Italy in December 1858 to fight in Napoléon III's campaign against the Austrian army. He seems to have returned thereafter to France, where he appears to have been stationed for a while at the Camp de Châlons.

When L'Estoille launched the first phase of his literary career in 1862 he based most of the material that he published on his experiences in North Africa, and the remainder on his lifelong interest in the ancient history and legendry of his homeland, following a recent tide in the fashionability of interest in the ancient history of "Gaul" and its supposed folklore and legends, particularly those associated with Bretagne. It is necessary to say "supposed folklore" because much of the material published by folklorists and historians associated with the French Romantic Movement was highly imaginative, often invented wholesale, sometimes described nowadays as "fakelore." L'Estoille took license from several significant examples of such eccentric creativity and became a prolific and imaginative "fakelorist" himself; *La Chanson de l'alouette* is one of the most extravagant and adventurous exercises in manifest fakelore produced in the latter half of the nineteenth century.

Although I have translated "*Chanson*" conventionally as "Song," it ought to be noted that the term was often applied specifically to the inventions of Medieval troubadours, themselves prolific inventors of fakelore and the parents of the genre of Medieval Romance, who were storytellers as well as versifiers. Their performances often combined poetry and prose, thus setting important precedents for what L'Estoille—following the example of Auguste Villiers de l'Isle-Adam, one of the editors who published his early work—called "*poèmes en prose*." Although most subsequent authors of *poèmes en prose* followed exemplars provided by Charles Baudelaire and Stéphane Mallarmé in producing short works of a lapidary nature, as L'Estoille appears to have done himself while writing in snatches during his time in North Africa—in work reprocessed in his first collection, *Haïcks et burnooses* (1865; tr. as "Haïcks and Burnooses" in *The Miller of Carnac and Other Works*)—when he began to refine that work for publication he rapidly began to produce longer works, sometimes building idiosyncratic literary "collages" and sometimes using a quasi-dramatic format.

La Chanson de l'alouette represents the culmination of that stylistic trend in his work, and it quite uncategorizable, the eccentric organization of the text defying classification as a novel, and its complexity stretching the notion of a book-length "poem in prose" to destruction. It is unique in the annals of French literature, although it has certain affinities with Edgar Quinet's *Merlin l'enchanteur* (1860),[1] which similarly attempts to fuse a transfiguration of the author's own life-story with a fakeloristic pseudohistory of France. Its peculiarity is enhanced by the fact that it recycles the material of two earlier works by L'Estoille, the quasi-autobiographical "Symphonie" (in *Poèmes en prose*, 1867; tr. in the first volume of the present set as "Symphony") and the historical fantasy *Vercingétorix* (1869; tr. as "Vercingetorix"), in which the author made a second attempt to reconfigure episodes reported in Julius Caesar's *Commentarii de Bellio Gallico* (tr. as *The Gallic Wars*) as a chapter in a kind of national epic.

Although the substance of those two works is extensively redeployed in *La Chanson de l'alouette*, it is considerably altered, on the one hand to reflect the elaboration and sophistication of L'Estoille's pseudohistory and imaginary prehistory of Gaul, which includes an idiosyncratic theory of serial reincarnation that he appears to have taken seriously, and on the other to reflect the fact that in between 1869 and 1880 France had suffered a catastrophic military defeat in the Franco-Prussian War of 1870-71. The second and third parts of the narrative are, to a considerable extent, a response to that defeat, in the course of which L'Estoille was recalled briefly to military duty. Although *La Chanson de l'alouette* and subsequent quasi-autobiographical writings make no direct reference to any participation in the Armée de la Loire that was hastily formed in the hope of stemming the Prussian invasion, he was certainly involved. The narrative voice of *La Chanson de l'alouette* does observe one episode in the Franco-Prussian War, but does so as a ghost, the character designated as "the

---

[1] Black Coat Press, ISBN 978-1-61227-303-7.

9

Poet," who is identified as the author of the inserted "Story of Ar-Braz" being deceased. Presumably, that poet was identified by the author with "Louis de Lyvron," of whom he imagined "A. de L'Estoille" to be a reincarnation of sorts.

Although it is impossible to be certain when the various parts of the narrative were written, the internal evidence suggests that the first part was completed before July 1870, whereas the second part—although it similarly recycles much of "Symphonie"—was only written some time thereafter; the second and third parts are provided with a frame narrative in which thirty years has elapsed since the conclusion of part one, and it becomes evident that the conclusion of the first part is imagined to have taken place in 1870, so that the frame native is set in 1900: a *fin-de-siècle* that culminates in a literal Judgment Day. The narrative voice of part one is explicitly said to be dead by then, although his relationship with the narrative voice of the second and third parts is evidently peculiar; it is difficult to resist the suspicion that in the mind of the author he had killed off his earlier literary persona and replaced him with another, as indicated by his change of signature.

In the dedication of *La Chanson de l'alouette*, which is appended to the third volume of the Lemerre edition rather than located in the preliminary material of the first, L'Estoille says that he had wanted to write such a work (presumably meaning a national epic of sorts) for twenty years, implying that some of his early works ought to be regarded as sketches composed in view of their eventual elaboration. He did, in fact, give the impression that he regarded his early work in that fashion while it was in composition, not only by titling the most eccentric of his collages, *Fusains* [charcoal sketches], but also in the rather ramshackle construction of "Symphonie." Although it is not strictly necessary to read those early works in order to appreciate *La Chanson de l'alouette*, they certainly make an interesting study in comparison and contrast, especially in terms of the strategic alterations made to the recycled materials. The dedication describes the latter work as an *ébauche* [sketch] itself and expresses the intention of continuing to work on it, and L'Estoille might actually have done so for the 1894 publication titled *La Chanson d l'alouette*, but that is not available on the Bibliothèque Nationale's *gallica* website, so I have not be able to compare the text with the 1880 version.

Because the 1880 version of *La Chanson de l'alouette* is now reproduced on *gallica*, and has been made commercially available as a set of print-on-demand books, it is easily accessible, but the same cannot be said of the other works signed "A. de L'Estoille," which are phenomenally rare; one of the most interesting, *Contes du Nord* (1896), whose contents are translated elsewhere in the present set, is not in the Bibliothèque Nationale at all, let alone on *gallica*, and although the editors of the BN's catalogue did figure out belatedly that Louis de Lyvron and A. de L'Estoille were the same person, nobody appears to have noticed it in the 1880s or 1890s, in spite of the fact that many of the publications of that era contained material manifestly recycled from works originally published in the 1860s.

It appears that by then, Louis de Lyvron had been almost forgotten, his significance as a precursor of the Symbolist Movement being noted only in a single article by Anatole France published in *Le Temps* in 1888, in which France remembers having met "Louis de Lyvron" in his father's bookshop when the latter was a spahi. That reference is slightly puzzling, the spahi having presumably identified himself by his pseudonym either without mentioning his real name, or doing so in such a fashion that France was unable to remember it a quarter of a century later. At any rate, France failed to observe that "A. de L'Estoille" was a current contributor to the Symbolist Movement, and had been even before that label was popularized in 1883; none of the subsequent historians of the movement deigned to recognize his contribution, or even his existence. Although *La Chanson de l'alouette* is saturated with symbolism, to a far greater extent than any other contenders

11

for a title of being a pioneering "Symbolist novel,"[2] that fact seems to have escaped notice almost entirely, at the time and since.

The absence of critical attention paid to the works of "A. de L'Estoille" partly reflects the fact that he was living and working in Renaison, a long way from Paris. He does not seem to have retained any of the literary associations that he had had during his former incarnation as Louis de Lyvron, which might have been slight even then. There was no clear distinction in the 1880s between what would later become known as "vanity publications" and the routine publications of commercial publishers, the latter routinely requiring "unknown" authors to pay for the publication of their works. It may be significant that Alphonse Lemerre was popular among *avant garde* writers, especially those associated with the Symbolist Movement, because he did not ask for cash up front when taking on commercially risky projects, but only required the author to promise to purchase a certain number of copies of the printed book. It is not improbable that he and other publishers employing the same stratagem only printed as many copies of some of their more esoteric publications as they had required the author to purchase. The unusual scarcity of many of "A. de L'Estoille's" publications might well result from the fact that they were only distributed privately, with no copies sent for review or marketed through bookshops. Whereas Pa-

---

[2] The notion of a "Symbolist novel" is somewhat oxymoronic, the Symbolist Movement being primarily, if not essentially, a movement in poetry; the production of long prose works greatly encourages, if it does not actually compel, the development of naturalistic narrative methods. Most novels produced by writers associated with the Symbolist Movement are therefore hybridized, only containing Symbolist elements within a fundamentally naturalistic narrative; *La Chanson de l'alouette*, by contrast, only employs brief sections of quasi-naturalistic narrative within a collage of sequences of prose-poetry and mock-dramatic dialogue, thus hardy resembling a "novel" at all.

risian authors usually distributed their compulsorily-purchased copies to friends in the literary community—copies that, notoriously, routinely ended being hawked by the *bouquinistes* of the left bank of the Seine and thus circulated within the said community—most of L'Estoille's privately distributed copies presumably remained in his abundant family and the libraries of friends who did not live in Paris.

How and why L'Estoille became such an ardent Symbolist before commentators like Stéphane Mallarmé, Jean Moréas and Charles Morice began to spread propaganda for such a literary *modus operandi* is a purely matter for speculation, but in his earlier work, written during the Second Empire during a time of relatively stern censorship, the lexicon of symbolism provided many authors with a useful means of representing sensitive subject-matter, just as it had in the days of Medieval romance, becoming blatant in such erotic allegories as the *Roman de la Rose*, and again in the seventeenth century in such inventions as the *Carte de Tendre* mapped out by the salon writers dubbed *précieuses* by Molière. L'Estoille was no exception; in the prose poems of *Haïcks et burnooses* erotic matters are addressed entirely in a symbolic language of flowers, insects, birds and imaginary creatures such as sylphs and djinn. As his work developed in the 1860s the last category increasingly took aboard *fées* [fays], who had a useful ambiguity, the word being applicable both to human enchantresses and to immaterial entities, and thus to individuals capable of transition between the two modes of being. When he came to write *La Chanson de l'alouette*, fays and their transitional ambiguity had become central to his metaphorical way of thinking, and the metamorphic faculties with which they were credited are also attributed to other imaginary beings, most crucially the two sphinxes who play a crucial role in the plot, in various guises, and who are specifically identified as Death and Sensuality or, collectively, as "the Enemy" or as "maidservants."

Erotic symbolism is not, of course, merely a literary artifact; the entire language of "love" and "romance" is inherently

13

symbolic, and so are the vocabularies of the most vulgar obscenity and the most clinical anatomy. Symbolism is everywhere in life and thought, and no matter how forthright the most determinedly "naturalistic" representations of human endeavor and ambition are, they cannot avoid it. There are, however, differences of degree and, more importantly, differences of conscious deliberation. The various Symbolist manifestos issued in the 1880s are not recommendations as to whether or not authors ought to employ symbolism, but prescriptions for how and why they ought to deploy it.

It is only in a crude way of thinking that symbolism is a mere matter of decorum and decoration; the theorists of the Symbolist Movement argued that the esthetics of disguise were much more sophisticated than that, extending far beyond tactical euphemism. Some argued that there was a special kind of "truth" in delicate and beautiful symbolic representation—and few individuals in quest of "true" love would want to disagree with them—and they also suggested that there is an essential esthetic appeal in ambiguity and mystery. Hostile critics of Symbolic poetry and prose, however, often contend that the element of transfiguration involved in symbolic representation is annoying, because of the frustration caused by problems of decryption that are sometimes insoluble. To say that *La Chanson de l'alouette* is vulnerable to such criticism is an understatement; to many of its readers it must have seemed unnecessarily and perversely gnomic.

Theorists like Mallarmé insisted that authors should never "explain" the symbolism of their works, because the implication that such explanations were possible by means of a simple substitution of the entity for its symbol was false and diminutive. He could also have suggested, as some later psychoanalysts did, that the processes of symbolism employed by writers—especially visionary writers—were not entirely conscious, often drawing material from the unconscious part of the mind that would be blotted out of ordinary conscious thought by some kind of internal filter or censor. If that is true, there is a possibility that even L'Estoille's understanding of what he was doing in constructing the extraordinarily elaborate symbolism of *La Chanson de l'alouette* was incomplete, and perhaps it was the fact that he did not entirely understand it himself that drove him to do it, not once but repeatedly, always striving for more complex refinements.

In the earlier versions of the narrative contained in "The Statue," one entitled "Symphonie" and the other contained in *Fusains*, the two metamorphic sphinxes do not appear in their ultimate guise, although a single Sphinx makes a brief appearance in both before being replaced by a multiplicity, the symbolism of which is much sketchier. Although the protagonist of *Fusains*, like the protagonist of the revised stories, similarly returns home from Africa following an episode of delirium—a delirium that never goes away completely, even when he appears to have recovered his health—no explanation is suggested for the causes of that delirium in *Fusains* except that an army doctor has diagnosed it as "cerebral fever"—a diagnosis the protagonist rejects. In *La Chanson de l'alouette* much more detail is provided, but the extra detail only serves to confuse the issue. Immediately before the crisis the protagonist is tempted by two Egyptian women whose names are subsequently attributed to the sphinxes, who are then transformed into a doctor and nurse who care for him before his return to France. His affliction is attributed by himself to a fall from a cliff, although one observer assumes that it was actually an attempted suicide, and his carers refer to it repeatedly as a "hole (*trou*) in the head."

The interpretation of that passage is crucial to a understanding of the story, and perhaps of its author; although the second part of *La Chanson de l'alouette*, like the second part of "Symphonie" and the whole of *Vercingétorix*, transfers its focus to the legendary history of Gaul, and the story of the embryonic nation's failed rebellion again the first Roman invasion, that story retains the substance as well as the texture of the delirium elaborately represented in part one. The fact that the frame narrative of parts two and three is set in the future adds a further dimension of exoticism to their hallucinatory quality and their vision of an Apocalypse. In "Symphonie," as in *Fusains*, the protagonist is eventually united with his "beloved," called Alona in "Symphonie," but in *La Chanson de l'alouette* that eventual union is infinitely more problematic, and can only be peculiarly posthumous as well as futuristic. How that relates to what happened to Antoine de L'Estoille in Africa, and what happens to his various fictitious alter egos, is profoundly unclear, and readers are free to concoct whatever hypothesis they like, just as they are free to decide for themselves whether or not that problem constitutes an annoying frustration detrimental to their appreciation of the work.

No psychoanalyst, so far as I know, has ever singled out *La Chanson de l'alouette*, or L'Estoille's work seen as a whole, as subject-matter for retrospective analysis, but they would surely have found it fascinating if they had, and the neglect leaves readers who are that way inclined free to fill in the gap. L'Estoille, whose fictitious alter egos are routinely sympathetic to the suspicion that they might be mad, would probably not have disapproved, although his real life following his marriage and the traumatic episode of the Franco-Prussian War appears to have been settled; he and his wife Marie had four children between 1873 and 1880 and remained on good terms with his parents and siblings, although apparently not with hers (her father had opposed the marriage on the grounds that Marie was marrying beneath her).[3] However puzzling L'Estoille's work might be in its strangeness and unorthodoxy, however, it is certainly not lacking in sanity, and its

---

[3] The latter point of information comes from an extract from a journal kept by Marie's aunt, kindly copied by one of her descendants, who observes that although he was not handsome, and was of lower social status than Marie, the latter was romantically inclined and was presumably attracted by his intelligence. It is interesting that "Louis de Lyvron" had published two fabular stories in the *Journal des Demoiselles* whose humble heroes achieve love matches with women of higher social status against the odds.

pathos is highly effective. It is a pity that it was so neglected at its time of publication, and it is fully deserving of the modern reappraisal that its reappearance in the twenty-first century permits.

The translation was made from the three volumes of the 1880 Lemerre edition reproduced on *gallica*, although they are not easy of access via search engines, which tend only to turn up the first volume unless specific precautions are taken.

Brian Stableford

PART ONE: THE STATUE

I

As a child he lived in an old château in a gorge in the Cévennes. He was as wild as a tercel; he climbed trees and walked barefoot.

In that château, in the depths. of a flower-garden—a wretched flower-garden if it had been new, but a beautiful flower-garden because it was old—between two yellow marble vases full of apples and pomegranates, a stone woman who had only one arm wept over a round basin.

That woman was, it was said, a statue, but do not believe it; she was a real woman who wept by day and walked by night.

She was a real woman—I can answer for that—and the child loved her.

She was a real woman; by night she could be seen passing through the hornbeams and bathing in the pond. More than a hundred times, by night, she had been encountered on the dark stairway or in the long corridor.

By day, her tears filled three large shells and then fell in a cascade into a little basin, a pretty basin under tall linden trees.

Do you like linden trees, trimmed linden trees? And high hornbeam hedges? And lawns bordered by box?

The child loved them; but above all he loved the statue that only had one arm and whose feet were dainty, so dainty that speckled ferns grew between their toes.

He was jealous of the ferns, the child, but they went so well with the little feet that he watered their velvety leaves every morning.

He was also jealous of a yellow wallflower whose perfume rose as far as the pale woman.

Perhaps the child has become a man, but it might also be the case that his soul sometimes sleeps in the leaves of a fern or the yellow flowers of a wallflower..

I know which, but what does it matter to you?

He was, as I have said, as wild as a tercel, and as lazy as a lizard. Any unfamiliar face made him flee; every bed of moss attracted him.

How many good places there were under the service trees, near the lilac! Lying on his back, his hands behind his head, at the bend in the canal, how well-placed he was to see the gilded palaces of the clouds!

They were good times. Perhaps, today, he is rolling his stone in the hot sun; then, in the sage, alongside the crickets, under the tall lindens, when midday chimed, his eyes half-closed, his blouse open, he gazed at the serious face with the tousled hair in the water of the basin.

He gazed into the water because, in that water, the statue opened her casket full of charming jewels, of bracelets of pink anemones, or earrings of buttercups.

How the child loved her, that white woman with the sad smile!

But only the grandfather knew that.

In the sunlit vineyards where the cicadas sang on the twisted peach-trees; in the shady meadows where the glistening walnut-trees extended their roots into the depths of clear ditches, when the grandfather brought the child, the child spoke to him in a whisper about the white woman with the long lowered eyes.

"When you are grown up, never forget her," he replied to him.

They loved one another, the child and the grandfather.

Those were good times. In the wooden bench of the great hornbeam hedge they chatted like two friends, and when the old man fell silent, the child pressed the large hand with swollen veins to his lips.

In the evening, by the fire of woodchips, the grandfather talked about what a man ought to believe: about sprites and fays, about Morgane and Merlin, the knights of Arthur and the peers of Charlemagne.

Then he said: "March straight and look upwards; too bad if you fall; the strong man who falls gets up proudly."

The grandfather is sleeping today in the little cemetery in the middle of the vineyards; the child has traveled so far that he is weary of it; he has seen so many men that he is saddened by them; but...

What does that matter to you? You only want to know why the child never stopped before the two sphinxes that warmed their granite rumps in the sun.

He did not approach the sphinxes lying on the sand, which guarded the door of the drawing room because one night, in a treble dream, he had seen the monsters crush the woman with lowered eyes beneath their claws.

"Was he dreaming?"

"If it had only been a dream, why was a marble arm lying between the smiling monsters, outside the drawing room door, the next morning?"[4]

---

[4] Interpolated couplets of dialogue like this one, which sometimes extend to much longer exchanges, are one of the idiosyncratic features of the narrative. Because of the way that dialogue is signified in French texts, with a prefatory dash rather than quotation marks, if is not always obvious that the couplets are couplets rather than the following paragraph being a continuation of the second speaker's observations. As to who the speakers might be at any point in the narrative, readers will have to make up their minds about that on the many occasions when they are not clearly identified. It might be relevant to note that the protagonists of some other quasi-autobiographical stories by L'Estoille conduct dialogues with

21

Perhaps he was dreaming, though; he dreams every night.

As soon as he hides fearfully under the serge curtains of the big square bed, the stone woman leans over his beside, put a kiss on his forehead, and his soul flies away to strange lands where the flowers are alive, where the mountains sing and where blue gods bathe in rivers of milk.

"Is he still dreaming today?"

"Who can tell?"

II

It is the night of the summer solstice. A bright fire is burning on the Plateau de la Madeleine and the mountain-dwellers are circling and singing: Saint John! Saint John! Girls, come and dance at the fire of Saint John!" Girls and boys are dancing in a circle.[5]

The crescent moon, as thin as a sickle, gazes eastwards. Tears are no longer falling from the eyes of the statue into the granite shells. The leaves are motionless, the nightjar is flying soundlessly, the silent owl is putting his head outside his hole and the guard dog lying in front of his niche is wagging his tail slowly.

The statue descends from her pedestal.

The violets open their wide eyes in the grass; in order to see better, the narcissi sand up on their stems; a rose who loves a glow-worm calls to her sleeping sisters; and the bells of the hyacinths say to the stars of the jasmine: "Look at the statue walking in the path alongside the hornbeam hedge; the

---

characters that turn out to be imaginary internal voices, notably the dialogue between Jean Philibert and the parrot in the episode in *Fusains* rewritten as "Hélène" in *Les Amoureuses*.

[5] The feast of Saint John the Baptist (23-24 June) replaced pagan celebrations of the summer solstice in the Christian calendar, but local celebrations often retained pagan elements.

old trees are saluting her and the snakes of the canal are making emerald and sapphire bracelets for her."

She is walking slowly, a diadem of ears of wheat retaining the heavy tresses of her ash-gray hair and a belt of vines tightening her green robe decorated with golden reeds.

Blackbirds are whistling in the ivy. The druidess has put on her fay's robe, her bright robe of the past.

On the sand turning pale outside the door of the drawing room, the two sphinxes extend their granite paws

"He has gone," says the more handsome, "the one who had a lotus flower on his brow. Is it necessary to follow him?"

"No," replies the pink sphinx, the one that has an asp with an inflated neck on its forehead.

But the fay came down from the high hornbeam arbor by the path bordered by box.

"Shut up, maidservants," she says, touching them with the tip of her sickle. "It is to carry my bed, out there on the banks of the Ganges, that his chisel carved you in the formless block.

On the reddened sand the monsters stretch out under the golden sickle, blood having flowed from their porphyry flanks.

Leaning on the perron, the grandfather listens to the sound of the carriage descending the avenue. He says:

"The old man will die alone; the child has gone. It was time to make a man of him.

"These old hands will no longer hold yours, child, but this old heart will beat faster tomorrow in a broader chest, for loving you more."

The mountain-dwellers are singing in the depths of the valleys: "Saint John! Saint John! Bring faggots of broom and holly to the fire of Saint John to chase away the evil spirit."

The fire goes out and the stone woman, the fay of the round basin, emerges from the great beech wood.

She is as white as a daisy, as blonde as an ear of wheat, as supple as a rush and as beautiful as a rose.

Her sickle lowered and her eyes upraised, she stops before the extinct fire.

"Have you pardoned the proud man?" she says, with a sob.

Under the fir trees a voice responds: "The man is the master of his destiny; you have not wanted to die."

The druidess collapses and her tears fall on to the still-warm ashes. In the depths of the valleys the mountain-dwellers sing: "Saint John! Saint John! Come and dance, Fayolles at the fire of Saint John; midnight is about to chime."[6]

The tears of the druidess fall on to the still-warm ashes; as she watches the sparks rise she says: "Die! I haven't wanted to die? Oh, yes, but he wanted when he awoke to find my soul in a body similar to the one that he loved. Forgive the proud man, Master.

"Your people, like germinating wheat carrying in its leaves the mud of the earth, was born under the sun of India under flowers with intoxicating perfumes, but it went to die, blinded by the sun, asphyxiated by the flowers; wanted it to carry ears of wheat; you put your billhook and your hoe in the hand of the Potter.

"You said to him: 'Like the plants they are living, like the flowers they are loving; to the laws of matter alone they are submissive, and in the tender arms of matter their souls have gone to sleep; awaken them by crying my name to them.'

---

[6] Les Fayolles is a mountainous region in the vicinity of the commune of Roanne in the Monts de la Madeleine, where L'Etoille was born; the term is being applied here both to real imaginary inhabitants, with an element of wordplay, more evident in English than in French, that links the Fayolles of the story with the alternative spelling of *fées* (fays.) employed in Medieval romances featuring Mourgue la Faye (L'Estoille's Morgane; Morgan le Fay in Malory).

"Your name had too many letters for the tongues of children; the syllables were cut up and each of the syllables became the name of a god, but in pronouncing them, all were pronouncing your name.

"In the granite of Elora he carved them, colossal, vague and monstrous.[7] He put flames in their hearts and poems on their foreheads. Master, pardon your worker, who, in an hour of folly, after having given a body of bronze to your poem, wanted to give a body of mud to his song.

"Pardon; when, your people having grown, you wanted to show yourself to him in your dazzling unity, you said to the potter who as dreaming up above in his luminous pantheon: 'Get up!' Free, he responded: 'I am your slave; command.'

"And he said to me: 'Before us the road will be long; it will require an ax, and no longer a chisel; you shall be the Voice and I shall be the Arm. If life reunites us we shall love one another as we love one another today; if it separates us, we shall find one another again at death.'

"And without plaints and without regrets we have closed our eyes to the light from above, and your hand has thrown us into human darkness

"Pardon your soldier! Pardon your druidess!

"But you have pardoned; you have enabled him to be reborn near me, and during his sleep my soul talks to his... He is your worker; what have you commanded him to do? I don't know; but he has come because you have sent him. Let me help him; I am still the druidess and I will not forget my oath."

A breath of wind passes over the ashes; sparks spring forth and smoke rises.

---

[7] The reference is to the carvings in the subterranean temples in the caves of Ellora in India; in L'Estoille's imaginary prehistory they represent the primary Indo-European culture whose migration to Europe originated the culture herein originated by "the Celt" (he had previously called them Gaels), one of whose subdivisions became the Gauls.

The smoke dissipates... Where is the druidess? Who is that pale child with golden hair and lowered eyes?

The mountain-dwellers are singing in the depths of the valleys: "Saint John! Saint John! Dance at the fire of Saint John, Fayolles, midnight is chiming.

Like dry leaves over the flowery heath a breath of wind carries them away, the white Fayolles; midnight is chiming.

Like swallows around the great rock they are twittering. Listen! "We were druidesses when the woods talked; we are Fayolles among the baptized. Priestesses without altars, widows without fiancés, we are the beloved of the heaths, the incense of the forests."

The fire revives. On its ashes the child sleeps; like a flock of swans they circle. Listen! "The flame revives, the druidess sleeps; we have divined. The prison is open, the sin expiated. In the hollow oak let us hide the sickle that injured his hand; widows without fiancés, we love those who love one another; priestesses without altars, we bear all the way to the Master the incense of kisses."

Around the broad heath their dance unwinds; the child sleeps. Listen! "Forget, the Master forgives. Forget the starry belt that only death can untie. Forget the golden sickle that only death can break. No longer be, on awakening, the queen of the Ganges, the beloved of the great potter."

The sun rises. Like dry leaves on the flowery heath, a breath of wind cries them away, the white Fayolles.

Over the canal a blue vapor floats. Slowly, it rises all the way to the branches of the lindens, whose crowns are silvered; then, abruptly, like a falling veil, it falls on to the flower-garden.

In their niches in the hornbeams, one might think that the marble vases were leaning over on their granite pedestals, and that the two sphinxes were standing up.

The Orient is reddening, the mist falling.

They are no longer two monsters on watch before the drawing room door but two women smiling on their granite pedestals.

The crowns of the linens quiver. Three sunbeams tint the plain crimson. The mist flies away. The vision vanishes.

Is she not pretty, with her wide eyes open and her hair tousled, the child that the foresters bring to the grandfather?

"We found her on the ashes of the fire of Saint John."

"She does not have eyes like our women; she has the eyes of the women painted on Egyptian sarcophagi, eyes that give the impression of having seen the commencement."[8]

"She speaks a language that we don't understand; what is it necessary to do with her?"

"Leave her with me. I understand her. She is from a long away from here. Go, lads, and have a drink in the kitchen."

"Where do you come from, child?"

"From a land where the flowers talk, where the mountains sing, and where the blue gods bathe in rivers of milk."

"When did you leave that beautiful land?"

"I don't know. I awoke up here, next to a fire that was going out."

The grandfather smiled. *When the child comes back*, he said in his soul, *he'll no longer find the statue that he loved on the edge of the basin, but on the wooden bench of the larger hornbeam hedge, I believe he'll find the love of the past.*

"Do you know your name, child?"

"I've forgotten it."

"If you like, we'll call you Alauna."[9]

---

[8] Roanne has an important archaeological museum, nowadays known as the Musée Joseph Déchelette, in which many Egyptian artifacts are juxtaposed with ancient artifacts excavated in the locale; it was inaugurated in 1844, and L'Estoille surely visited it as a boy.

"I'd like that very much."

Look at her, but a little further on. As wild as a swallow, she will be fifteen years old tomorrow.

"Is the statue no longer on its pedestal?"

The gardener said: "It has been stolen for the messieurs from Paris.

"And the arm that was found one morning outside the drawing room door. Between the two sphinxes?"

"That has been stolen too."

"Ah!"

III

"Where is the carriage taking him?"

"To Saint-Cyr;[10] the child is becoming a soldier. But that is of little importance; what happened had to happen."

"And at Saint-Cyr?"

"He was, as I have sad, as wild as a tercel and as lazy as a lizard; he still is. He smokes, alone, along the walls of the noisy courtyard, and at his desk, chin in hand and his eyes half-closed, her thinks about the hornbeam arbor where the blackbirds whistle and he vineyards where the cicadas sing. On days of leave he sometimes walks for long hours, straight ahead, in the woods of Versailles or Ville d'Avray..."

---

[9] Alauna was allegedly a Celtic river goddess, although the name is derived from the Latin, where it was applied to the river Aulne in Bretagne by Roman colonists. The Romans also applied the name to a fort in Cumbria, in association with which it was sometimes Anglicized as Alona, the name given to the equivalent character in "Symphonie."

[10] The École spéciale militaire de Saint-Cyr, usually known simply as Saint-Cyr, is still France's foremost military academy, but it is now located in Bretagne rather than Yvelines.

"He's a dreamer. I suspected it, but now I'm certain of it."

"Since you're certain of it. I won't tell you where he goes when he isn't following the straight avenues of Versailles and Ville d'Avray. But if you think he's sad, you're mistaken; he has broad shoulders, shining eyes and red lips."

"On days of leave, then, when he isn't following..."

"You won't make me say what I don't want to tell you; but since you want to know everything, I'll tell you one of the stories that the grandfather told so well when the beech-logs were burning.

"Would you like to know why the wrens always hide their nests in the ivy?

"The story of the wrens is a fine one, but the story of the statue is even finer. Listen, and you'll know why she weeps by day and walks by night."

"Is she still weeping in the house of the monsieur from Paris?"

"The gardener claims that she was stolen, but the blackbirds say that she has put on her fay's robe again, her bright robe of the past. Either the gardener or the blackbirds must be mistaken, but that doesn't prevent the tale from being as true as a tale can be.

"A long time ago, a very long time ago, a silent forest intercut with marshes and heaths, covered the entire plain of Roanne on both banks of the Loire.

"In those days herds of elks grazed under the oaks, aurochs bathed their black manes in the marshes and eagles soared over the heaths. A few wicker boats moored under the willows, a few blue-tinted clouds rising from the forests and a few soft and guttural strophes rolled by the breeze over the flowery heath were the only indications that humans were there.

"It was the time when France was called Gaul; the time when men were ashamed of dying in their beds; the time when women only loved the brave; the time when the druids remembered what scholar search for today.

"On the banks of the Loire there was then a chief who had come from the Orient, and in a grotto in the Fayolles there was a druidess as white as a daisy, as blonde as an ear of wheat, as supple as a rush and as beautiful as a rose.

"The grotto in the Fayolles is to the right in the ravine that rises from Renaison to Murcins; enormous walnut trees shade it, a spring oozes into it, and speckled ferns carpet it.

"So, the druidess was as beautiful as a rose. She was so beautiful that the chief loved her; but in those days, like roses, druidesses belonged to God; he alone could enable the former to flower and give away the latter.

"The druidess commanded the clouds and the lightning, but she could not command her heart, and she loved the chief.

"She loved the chief, and, as she could not lie, at sunset one evening, on the Pierre-Grosse,[11] she told him so.

"The Loire scintillated; the forest, at their feet, vibrated like a lyre; under the crimsoned sky the mountain was blue.

"The eglantine of the woods could not lie; her soul was as clear as spring water; she also sad to the chief: 'My life is no longer my own, I have given it freely; but death will unbind me and I shall be yours. Bridle your mare, and when you give our people other rivers and other plains, I shall pray there. The Master will be as good to his servant as he is to the lilies.'

"Then the chief said: 'I love you entirely; I love your body as I love your soul. Your soul I shall rediscover, but death will take your body from me.'"

"Permit me to say that you seem to have ideas about death..."

"Which are not yours? That's quite possible; I don't have the same ideas as everyone. I'm not a Frenchman, I'm a Gaul;

---

[11] The Pierre-Grosse in the Auvergne, which gave its name to a hamlet which is now the site of a ski resort, was listed in several early nineteenth gazetteers as "druidic stone."

I regret it, but I accept it. What the Druids taught, I believe. For me, life is not an end but a means. For me, death is a commencement and not an end."

"But..."

"Admit, for an hour, that what I believe is true; if not, as I am a very poor preacher and as I want, in any case, to tell you a tale and not a sermon, let us shake hands and part good friends."

"Let's not fall out; you're a Druid, that's agreed, and I'm your disciple. Under the flowering apple-trees, speak to your young boar, old boar of the woods."

"Where was I?"

"The chief was saying to the druidess: 'In the star up above our lips will lack kisses.'"

"He didn't say that at all; but the druidess replied: 'Depart, friend, I cannot give you what is no longer mine.

"The chief descended from the mountain, but instead of bridling his mare he searched along the river for clay. When he had found some he made a statue out of it."

"How could he make a statue, that chief with bloody hands?"

"Perhaps you'll know that later. So, he made a statue, the warrior with the bloody hands; it was as white as the eglantine of the woods, it had her pensive forehead, her large eyes and her soft smile.

"When he had finished it he drew away slightly in order to get a better view of it. Dazzled, he closed his eyes. When he opened them again he saw beside the statue a woman who resembled it, but who was even more beautiful.

"The woman said to him: 'Come; I am even more beautiful than your dream, and my heart beats and my lips burn.'

"'You are not her,' the chief said. 'Go away.'

"The woman disappeared, and the chief took the road to the mountain again."

"You're a druid and I'm your disciple, but I no longer understand. Had she also lived before, the lovable woman who disappeared?"

"That woman was not a woman; she was the Enemy."

"The chief's enemy?"

"The chief's enemy and mine. She is the one who shrinks, who crushes, who rivets feet to the ground...but you'll see her again later.

"So the chief returned to the mountain and said to the druidess: 'Descend with me to the bank of the stream.'

"The soul of the druidess was as clear as a mountain spring; she followed the chief to the bank of the stream.

"Before the statue the chief said: 'I shall march straight before me, in order to give our race other rivers and other plains. I shall not return again, but if you wish, when you are free, hide your soul under this face; I shall find it again when your soul and your body awake.'

"'I want what you want,' replied the druidess, 'but can you create, like the Master, and if you can, do you have the right to do it?'"

"The chief was a strange man, of whom the bravest were afraid; he mounted his white mare and departed at a gallop."

"I can divine the end of the story. The druidess allows herself to die, and as, according to you, one is as free after death as before, instead of hiding her soul in a star she hides it in the statue. Ever since she walks by night in search of the chief, and she weeps by day because she has not found him."

"You haven't divined anything. A long time ago, a very long time ago, the chief had departed; the oldest of those who had seen him fall in the plains of the south were dead, and the druidess was still beautiful and still young. The sun of summer and the snows of winter had blackened the face of the statue but they had not hollowed out a wrinkle in the face of the druidess.

"However, she still prayed, and often wept. 'Pardon me, Master, she said, have pity and left me die.'

"The oaks died of old age, moss ate away the flanks of the statue, but the druidess was ever more beautiful and ever younger.

"The moss has eaten away the flanks of the statue until it is no more than a formless block of stone, but the druidess is still young.

"One winter night, frost breaks the block; the druidess is still young."

"I no longer understand. I no longer understand."

"A tale that one understands is no longer a tale.

"Before the broken clay, the druidess is weeping. A gentle hand touches her shoulder; she turns round and sees a beautiful young woman. 'Who are you?' she says.

"'I am the one you summoned. Your sickle is sharp; you have only to wish it and you can rejoin him.'

"'No, my body is no longer my own.'"

"And she disappeared: another woman who was not a woman! Druidism is a fine thing! It was the Enemy?"

"No, it was the Enemy's sister."

"Perfect. Is she also your enemy?"

"No, but if we continue like this you'll have forgotten the beginning of my tale before knowing the end. I'll cut it short.

"The beautiful young woman disappeared and a voice spoke under the oaks, which said: 'I am the power and the light; my road is the straight road.

"'Unknown person,' replied the druidess, 'I love him and I have kept my oath; my hand has not touched his.'

"'Let it be as he has wished; a man is the master of his own destiny. Death would have set you free; he did not wand that; live, suffer, and seek.'

"The voice under the oaks fell silent and the body of the druidess became a body of marble."

"And consequently, the Master did what the chief wanted."

"No."

What, no? The soul of the druidess isn't, as he wished, hidden under the face of a statue?"

"The chief had said to his lover: 'When your soul quits your body—which is to say, when, having been released from your vow, you have the right to be mine—hide in this imperishable body, a faithful image of your own, in order that I might, when I m reborn, rediscover you under the form that I loved.'"

"So he hoped to reanimate that body of clay?"

"Certainly…he had already animated many others."

What are you saying?"

"Nothing. I am saying: the Master had not done what the potter wished. In giving the druidess a body that the centuries could not wear away, he prevented death from releasing her from her oath."

"I hadn't thought of that."

"The soul commands its destiny. The druidess had wanted to be a statue; she was a statue.

"Sometimes, in the morning, in the densest of the thickets, woodcutters glimpsed that body with white gleams. Sometimes, when the midday sun lowered their eyelids, little pastors saw her gliding between the rocks. One day, she was no longer encountered in the ravine of the Fayolles; she was weeping in the old flower garden under the tall lindens."

"And now she's in the home of a monsieur from Paris?"

"So the gardener says."

IV

With a belt passed over his arm and a shako on the back of his head, he is running rather than walking along the avenue still moist with dew.

At the round-point he stops, astonished; he is not there. He was, however, to meet him at eight o'clock; that was agreed. Why isn't he here?

Finally, here he comes.

Is he a man? Is he a child? He is as thin as a girl, his black hair is curly and his eyes are blue.

"You're early."

The voice has a crystalline timbre; he's a child.

"But I have many things to tell you today."

He clasps the Saint-Cyrian's hand; he's a man; the mountain man shakes the fingers, smiling.

"I clasp as I love.

"And the statue? What has she said this week?"

"Laugh at me, but don't laugh at my dream."

"Me, laugh at the statue, after the portrait you've made me of her? I laugh so little that I take on your commissions for her; life bores me, I want to see something else."

"Madman!"

"No, I'm speaking seriously; life bores me. What do you find droll about life? Do you hope to amuse yourself a great deal in two months?

"We both know that it's necessary to think about death; it doesn't frighten us. We've come too soon or too late; let's go elsewhere."

"Elsewhere, are the woods as green, are the friends as devoted, are the dreams as sweet?"

"But it's to the land of dreams that we're going? Before knowing you I didn't know them, those beautiful lands, but since you've spoken to me about them, I find the earth cold and life stupid. Come with me."

"Come and have lunch."

"Let's have lunch together, if it amuses you."

"You wrote to me: *Come*. Here I am."

"What's the matter with you, child?"

"I have blood on my hands: read this."

"I read: 'In the beautiful country that you have made me love, since you don't want to follow me. I'll wait for you...' So?"

"He killed himself."

"He was stupid; but you're not telling me for no reason."

"Since I'd been telling him my dreams, he said, he found the earth cold and life stupid."

"Have you, by chance, a desire to imitate this monsieur who had a indigestion before sitting down at the table? If you did that you'd be a coward; life is a battle, a rude combat, and only a coward flees the battlefield. Remember that well, soldier.

"Ah, the petty monsieur found the earth cold and life stupid! He had nothing in his head or in his heart."

"Grandfather!"

"Shut up! When I was your age, with a sack on my back and a rifle in my hand, with no shoes on my feet and not a sou in my pocket, I followed Masséna[12] in paths where the air was keen and the stones icy, but I didn't find the earth as cold as that.

"Ah, he found life stupid! His own was stupid; life is stupid when one yawns, but when, on the evening of a fine battle, one feels one's bones and finds them all in place, one doesn't find life as stupid as that.

"Come, child; let's sit down on this bench and chat as we chatted in the hornbeams. You're a man now, I no longer have any need to choose my words.

"Imagine a stairway cut by landings, of which you can't see the first steps or the last, and on that stairway, at different heights, everything that has a soul. On that stairway everything is climbing and yet, having set forth on the same day, they're not at the same height; some have stumbled on the steps, others have sat down.

"Every landing is a place of repose. In human languages those places of repose are called the tomb. There, some linger and others hasten.

"That is life.

---

[12] André Masséna, (1758-1817) the military commander during the Revolutionary and Napoleonic Wars whom Napoléon called "the greatest name of my military Empire," eventually making him a duke and a prince.

"The bottom of the stairway plunges into infinite darkness; the top is bathed in infinite light. Between those two infinities there is God.

"A man is not free to put or not to put his foot on the steps of life; he has been created by the Master. He is not free to climb or not to climb all the way to the top, he belongs to God, who created him for a reason. But on the steps, he is free.

"Ignorance and dolor are down below, happiness and science on high; one who does not fear trouble climbs without stopping, the idler sits down.

"Before the foot of the valiant the steps lower incessantly. Before the man who finds the step too high, the step becomes ever steeper, and it is still necessary that he climbs it; but he climbs it alone, without support, and his guides are already far away.

"The madman who has killed himself will get up again exactly where he fell, and although he will certainly find the earth cold and life stupid then, it will be necessary for him to march, lost in a crowd who do not know him.

"Have you understood, child? The man who kills himself is a fool."

Large black clouds are gliding over the red moon; thunder is rumbling dully. A heavy warm wind is passing through the jasmines. The sphinx, the one that the druidess had wounded in the flank, quivers; its paws stretch out, its breasts stand up; then, stiff, its eyes fixed, it falls back on to the porphyry plinth.

Then the other sphinx, the one that has an asp with a swollen neck, says to it: "Where have you come from, my sister? Why have you left me, in this prison that is crushing me?"

"Our prison opens for the battle alone. I have commenced the combat. Has my blow carried? I'm waiting."

"You were near to him?"

"Yes; he found me so beautiful in the caverns of Elora. I said to him: *reality will never be worth as much as your dream; life is cold and somber; but death has luminous se-crets*."

"The ancestor has rejoined him."

"Then I've been vanquished again, my sister. I can struggle with the son, but I can do nothing against the ancestor."

"Who is that old man, then, stronger than death?"

"He's the acorn sown by the one who calls himself the Master. From that acorn an oak has emerged, whose branches elongate westwards. He's the father of the accursed family that calls you memory and calls me hope. He's the Celt with the broad forehead, the red blood and the strong arm.

"Against him we can do nothing. Let's wait, my sister."

On the edge of the round basin, Alauna is sitting on the lawn where the cricket no longer sings, gazing at the gray clouds shredded by the wind in the dull sky. She has folded her arms and large tears are falling from her somber eyes.

She is regretting the beautiful land where the flowers are alive, where the mountains sing and where the blue gods bathe in rivers of milk.

It is a mild autumn evening, the sun is reddening the hornbeams, the leaves are falling one by one from the crowns of the lindens and the last chilly roses are turning toward the sunset.

Slowly, the grandfather approaches, the grass muffling the sound of his footfalls. He loves the one that the foresters of the Madeleine brought him, the one whose dormant soul he had awakened,

A smoke had passed before he child's eyes; she did not remember where she came from or why she had sat down in the still-warm ashes of the Saint John fire in summer. She only had the soul of a flower. Gradually, the grandfather dissipated the cloud; now she is has the soul of a woman who dreams, behind the broad forehead framed by her golden hair.

The grandfather knows that souls, before quitting our earth, must pass through many bodies. He knows that death is only a portal, and that life makes that portal of glass or bronze.

If you live like the grass that grows, or like the serpent that crawls, if you learn nothing, a thick barrier will hide your past; you will be reborn without memories, without hopes, as if you had never lived. But if you have sought, if you have struggled, if you have loved, the veil of death will be so light that a sigh can lift it.

The grandfather knows that, and he says: "She is a soul with broad wings; she has crossed all the steps. She is floating over the summit, before her is the azure, the azure without barriers, the infinite azure. The angel with caressant arms, who lulls and puts to sleep, the patient guide, the gentle guardian of the threshold, seeing his mission terminated, has gone to wait for her in the green star. On departure, his hand has released the veil, and the veil has fallen back over the cradle.

"That is why she does not know what she was yesterday, why she dreams about a distant land where the flowers are alive, where the mountains sing and where the blue gods bathe in rivers of milk."

"You're weeping, Alauna," the grandfather says to her. "What's wrong?"

"I would like my beautiful palace on the banks of the Ganges, grandfather. I'm cold."

"You have a beautiful palace on the banks of the Ganges, do you?"

"Yes, grandfather, a beautiful palace of yellow marble with perforated balconies, a palace full of birds. In the isle that the waves lick, under the green mountain, the rooms are higher, he carpets softer... I remember... But in that palace the soul is lacking. On the balcony, over the bank of the Ganges, until evening, I would wait for him, and at night we would go together under the green mountain, into the crystal hall, where the monsters with the heads of women support the great nacre bed.

"Take me to the land of the sun, grandfather; I'm cold."

"We'd get lost on the way, darling; you've forgotten the road to your palace."

"No, the palace is on the bank of the river, between a cabin and a temple. The temple is so high that its roof disappears in the sun's radiance. The cabin is so small that a magnolia hides it entirely..

"A long time ago...was it a long time ago, or was it yesterday?...in sum, before I went to sleep...when the women with bare arms mingled the blue roses that grow on the rivers out there with my hair, in the temple a god was dreaming, and in the cabin a potter was working, who as making clay pitchers to draw water.

"One morning, without knowing why—it was spring time—the potter wept. His tears fell so large that they stained the white clay, so he left the sketched pitcher on the turntable and he went into the temple whose roof disappeared in the sun's radiance.

"I have never seen that god, but those who have seen him say that he has the head of a woman and the body of a lion. As soon as the sun sets he plunges into the forest, and when he returns to the temple, the immense vault is filled with an acrid perfume of flowers and blood. Those who cross his path in the forest love, languish and die.

"No one dared enter the temple.

"I have never seen him; the women who braided my hair only let me go out in the sunlight, on my white elephant.

"That god had, it's said, a companion who resembled him, but a black veil hid her, even from the eyes of the priests.

"Grandfather, what if the two monsters who keep watch at the drawing room door weren't made of stone? What if they were the god and his companion?"

"Who knows, darling? Tell me what the potter made in the temple."

"When the potter went into the temple, the god said to him: 'So you want to die, potter?'

"'I want to be loved.'

"'But after the kiss comes death; you know that, potter.'

"'God, take me before the kiss ends.'

"'The one who will love you will love you. Go.'

"'Before the kiss ends, I shall die? You've promised that, God, have you sworn it?'

"'Have no fear; I shall be there.'

"'Swear it, God. Between the two kisses, as if I were the master and you were the slave, you won't forget your oath; will you promise?'

"'Yes.'

"The potter went back, joyfully, to his little enclosure. *Who will I love?* he wondered. He searched for a long time, and then his eyes fell upon the magnolia. He sighed: "Only a flower can love a potter." He returned to the pitcher he had begun, but as he was still weeping, his tears diluted the clay and it became so soft, so very soft, that it took the form of a magnolia flower between his fingers..

"He had only ever made pitchers for drawing water. The sun was setting; he went to sleep.

"'The one that I want will love me,' he said as he fell asleep, 'but only a flower can love a potter. Until morning, fresh flower, let your breath flutter over my lips. Lie down beside my bed, God, and tear me apart before I wake.'

"And the god lay down at the foot of the bed of dry leaves.

"That night, the potter dreamed that a woman was hidden in the clay flower. He woke up and ran to look, but in the white calyx he only saw a drop of dew. The god was no longer at the foot of the bed of dry leaves.

"'Only a drop of dew can love a potter,' he sighed, 'and he picked up a handful of earth. But in thinking about the woman he had seen during the night his tears started to flow

41

and the clay became so soft, so very soft, that between his fingers it took the form of a woman.

"He had only ever made pitchers for drawing water. The sun was setting; he placed the clay flower on the head of the woman and he went to sleep.

"'The one that I want will love me,' he said as he fell asleep, 'but only a drop of dew can love a potter. Until morning, brilliant pearl, refresh my thirsty lips. Lie down beside my bed, God, and tear me apart before I wake.'

"And the god lay down at the foot of the bed of dry leaves.

"That night the potter dreamed that the queen was hidden in the clay flower. He woke up and ran to look, but in the white calyx he only saw a sunbeam. The god was no longer at the foot of the bed of dry leaves.

"'Since a sunbeam can love a potter,' he sighed, "a queen might be able to love him,' and he went to sit down at the door of the palace. A loud noise shook the vaults of the temple; the priests cried: 'The god of love has taken the form of a sunbeam.'

"The potter heard the cries of the priests; the queen emerged on her white elephant. He lifted the cup and said: 'Queen, I am only a potter, but I made this cup while thinking of you.'

"The queen took the cup, and a sunbeam sprang out of it.

"Then the women who were braiding my hair in the room sanded with silver twisted their naked arms. They cried: 'Amour was hidden in the cup; she is going to die! She is going to die!'

"Was that a long time ago, or was it yesterday? It was before I went to sleep. Have I been asleep for a long time, Grandfather?"

"The longest nights are sometimes the clearest; what does it matter, darling, if you remember. What did the potter do then?"

"He ran away."

"And you haven't seen him again?"

"Oh, yes, Grandfather. I've searched for him in the forest and in the plain, on the mountain and on the river; I've found him again in the crystal hall of the isle that the waves lick. Take me, Grandfather, to the land of the sun; I'm cold. What does it matter whether the palace has collapsed, whether the waves have eroded the isle; in the little enclosure, the magnolia is still flourishing."

"Who told you that?"

"They are not stone, the monsters guarding the door of the drawing room. Look at this magnolia flower; I found it a little while ago, between the claws of the pink sphinx, the one that has an asp with a swollen neck on its forehead..."

It was a beautiful autumn evening, the sun was reddening the hornbeams, the leaves were falling one by one from the lindens and the last chilly roses were turning toward the setting sun, and the old man's soul flew away in a sunbeam.

The old man's soul is rising in a sunbeam.

Like an eagle held captive for a long time, whose cage is suddenly opened, dazzled by the ardent radiance, it hesitates; but light is its domain, and it extends its powerful wings and soars in the azure...

You are beautiful, land of the west; land of the most beloved of my sons, you are beautiful...!

You are beautiful, globe with green valleys and scintillating summits; the Master has given you a necklace of sapphires, a diadem of opal...

You are beautiful, radiant stars, dazzling islands of the shoreless Ocean...

Your work is beautiful, Master, may your name be blessed!

May your name be blessed, the name that you have told to the daughter of my old age on the mountain of the Arie,[13] the name with a thousand syllables that the son of the blonde virgin has written in letters of porphyry on the banks of the Ganges.

May your name be blessed; from the veins of the Celt a vermilion river has flowed, from the narrow valley all the way to your throne it growls. May your name be blessed, Master, my sons have string arms; they plow your furrow broadly. My sons have sonorous voices; in the dense wheat the birds sing.

It was a beautiful autumn evening, the sun was reddening the hornbeams, the leaves were falling one by one from the lindens and the last chilly roses were turning toward the setting sun, and the old man's soul flew away in a sunbeam.

"She is alone in the old château."

"But he will come?"

"No. The ancestor had divined, perhaps he had remembered, and he knew that one day dries up the flower of amour if a tear does not sleep in the depths of its calyx. In the courtyard of the École he had said to him: "My hand will no longer squeeze yours, child; you will return when brambles have flourished on my tomb.""

"Alauna is alone in the old château near the great cadaver whose mouth smiles, whose forehead no longer has wrinkles. Between the crossed hands she has put the last rose, the chilly one that turns toward the sun, and she is weeping, on her knees."

"She believes in death, then?"

"No, but she is weeping all the same."

---

[13] Mont Arie in the Pyrenees, overlooking the Garonne, is also known as the Cap d'Arie, hence the odd formulation of the phrase.

She is a woman, a true woman; she kisses the forehead of the dead man and, in order that the moon might caress him one more time, she moves aside the curtain of the drawing room door. On the threshold she hesitates; then, slowly, she goes up to the big hornbeam along the path bordered by box.

Then the more handsome of the sphinxes, the one that has a lotus flower on its forehead, turns its heavy head toward the pink sphinx. "Do you remember," it says, the bed of nacre in the crystal hall under the mountain of Elora?"

"I remember. Like a young wife under her husband's gaze, the earth quivered in the ardent sunlight."

"We were the only gods. In our scintillating temple, near your cup, which was always full, my scythe, which was always red, gleamed. We had erected our altar near the palace of that queen, under whose brow a soul with broad wings said to come from a distant world grew up,. And in spite of her maidservants, one evening, on the banks of the Ganges, she would have drunk like the others from the cup in which, after the given kiss, the soul of a man dissolved in the immense soul."

"Who could have divined a master in that potter?"

"With his chisel that potter came from the embalmed isle where I filled my cup and where you tempered your scythe. Like soft clay he carved granite, and the gods, as tall as mountains, were born. How handsome he was, my sister."

"When the sparks flew, his chest bare and his hair in the wind, he sang the amours of the gods that his hand created."

"He was singing one evening, close to where we were sitting; do you remember how your scythe shone like crimson lips, how my cup overflowed like a full teat?"

"Had he not recognized you already, my sister? Was he not thinking about the promise made in the scintillating temple?"

"Who could have divined a master in that potter? When he had finished singing he said to us: 'You are as beautiful as the rising moon, as a star that is falling asleep; but you are less beautiful than the queen who will come when I have finished my task... I have finished... Listen! It's her. And the queen of the Ganges came in. She was holding the clay cup in her hand."

"Then you held out the emerald cup to him, you remember? He took it with a firm hand, and after having drunk a draught, he broke it on the crystal pavement. Then he said to you: 'Between two kisses you shall be the slave and I the master; you have sworn it. Your cup was colder than snow, your liquor was more insipid than the stagnant water of a marsh. Here, take my cup, my cup of clay; fill it with the flame of your eyes, the perfume of your breath and the blood of your heart, and if it burns my lips, if I drop it, we shall be yours. You filled the clay cup with the blood of your heart.' And then he entered the crystal hall with the queen of the Ganges."

"We followed them. 'Maidservants,' he said, 'at the foot of the bed of amour, both of you lie down; when the cup is empty, you will take both of them for us...'

"From the cup of clay he drank long draughts, and then he said to the queen: 'I will love you forever; our eternal love will see the world crumble, and in the star where we are going, my queen, in order to bless that amour, I shall carve gods even greater than the great gods of India. When the cup is empty, maidservants, you can take us,' he said as he got to his feet."

"With his powerful hand he took blocks of stone from the granite ceiling, and his chisel carved monsters. Then he said: 'Hide your maidservants under these stone foreheads.'"

"And the centuries fall into the blue abyss, and our prison is always harder."

"The ancestor is dead; let's fight."

Alauna comes back down the path bordered with box, and the two sphinxes fall silent.

V

He has a house of marble and faience in an oasis, under palm trees, next to a spring, but he is sad.

46

When the women of the ksour come, after sunset, to listen to the flute- and derbouka-players under the pomegranate trees, he flees the laughing groups.

Wrapped in his burnoose, a cigarette in his lips, when he passes with slow steps, the gazelles of the desert say to one another in whispers: "That's the kébir who only loves his horse, the kébir with gray eyes."

You are mistaken, gazelles; he loves, the kébir. When Allah's angel places his finger on your blue-tinted eyelids, his mistress comes to his tent. But his tent is too low for his amour; he loves, gazelles, a pale peri.

When the moon rises in her bright palace of clouds and flowers, the peri takes him away, and the clouds are so brilliant, the flowers so fresh, that sometimes, in the bright palace, his soul forgets itself all day long.

That is why, in the evening, he passes by without looking at the gazelles lying under the pomegranate trees.

Alauna is leaning on the mossy rump of the pink sphinx.

"I would like to see him," she says. "If he were the potter, I would carry him to my palace out there."

"Do you know him, handsome sphinx, who brought me the embalmed flower from the land of the sun? You must know him; by night you are not stone, as in the daylight, since you flew one night to the regretted land, where the flowers are alive, where the mountains sing and where the blue gods bathe in rivers of milk.

"It is mute! And you, do you want to respond to me? They are both silent; I am no longer in the land where the potters enclose the souls of gods in heir statue. These two monsters have nothing behind their stone foreheads.

"On this pedestal a word is engraved: *Sensuality*. What is there on the other? *Death*."

The moon rises over the hornbeam arbor. Alauna climbs the path bordered with box.

Then the more handsome of the sphinxes, the one that has a lotus flower on its brow, turns its heavy head toward the pink sphinx.

It says: "She has forgotten that an oath binds her; she is dreaming. She will fall, we are going to be victorious. The spark will be extinguished and the superb couple who braved the great laws of eternal matter, with their gods and their dreams, will dissolve in my breath."

"And humans will fall under my scythe without hope, to be reborn without memories."

Alauna comes back down the path bordered with box, and the two sphinxes fall silent.

Alauna climbs the somber staircase where, it is said, the statue passed when the screech-owl mewled at the moon in the old walnut trees. She sighs, clutching her heart, which is beating too rapidly: "You leaned over his bed, white fay of the hornbeams, lean over mine. Where you take his soul, take mine; if he is the potter I shall recognize him.

"But when I sleep, where does my soul go? One might think, when I awake, that it ought to have sand on its wings, and I think, vaguely, that I hear the refrains of strange songs, mingled with the powerful voiced of the waves on the rocks.

It is the night of the summer solstice. On the Plateau de la Madeleine the fires are going out, and the mountain-dwellers are singing in the valleys: "Saint John! Saint John! Come and dance by the fire of Saint John, Fayolles; midnight is chiming."

There they are, the white Fayolles! From the fissures in the rock, from the crevices of the fir trees, from the basin of the spring, from the calices of the furze, from the urns of the myrtles, with a spark on the forehead and a flower in the hand, their hair undone, their scarves floating, they escape, laughing. Like a nacreous mist they pass over the heath. Listen!

"We were druidesses when the woods spoke, we are Fayolles among the baptized, why? Why? Do you know, heather? Why? Why? Do you know, furze?

"We fly, altogether, into the ever-green forest of the star on high, as the swallows arrive with the sun one spring morning; so, when death unbinds our souls, our souls have reason to fly away, in order to await their sisters who are hidden in the flowers.

"Virgins without fiancés, why do we hasten? We are Fayolles among the baptized, we shall be druidesses in the green star. Do you know that, heather? Have you divined it, furze?

"Today we are awaiting the one who put the sickle in our hands and the vervain on our brows. We are awaiting the only druidess who will rediscover a fiancé in the green star. But the sin has been committed and the sin must be expiated; it is necessary that the chief recognize the druidess in the one who is now dreaming where she has wept for so long.

"That is why, every night, we who are rocked by a ray of light, who are lifted up by a breath, while his body sleeps, carry her soul into the woolen tent. Do you know that, heather? Have you divined it, furze?

"But the sin has been committed, and the sin must be expiated. One lives while the other dreams; one remembers while the other forgets. The chief is searching for a druidess, the queen is searching for a potter. Who will say to the potter: you were a chief. Who will say to the queen: you were a druidess? Our lips are sealed; will you say it, heather? Will you say it, furze?

"Saint John! Saint John! By the fire of Saint John you are dancing, Fayolles, midnight is chiming.

"Dance, white sisters, on the flowery heath, in order that the bees can collect their honey until autumn. We are going, before the night ends, to the land of palm trees, to carry the druidess into the woolen tent."

"Beware of the monsters who are on watch on the sand of the flower garden; once the soul has flown away, they could—they have done it before—crush the body devoid of a guardian."

"When one carries the soul away, the other watches near the body. The celestial sickle in our hands is still gleaming; we are Fayolles among the baptized, but in the green star we shall be druidesses."

His tent is outside Boghar, the town of palm trees.

At Boghar the Tell finishes and the Sahara commences; a great many people pass through it, and gladly pause there. Those who pause in Boghar are going to the land of death or coming back therefrom; they all have a terror or an amour to forget, so Boghar is a town of flute-players and almahs.

But, as in the oasis, at Boghar the peri slips into the kébir's tent. His soul flies every night toward the palace of clouds, and the wild turtle-doves from the blue mountains say by day when he passes by: "When his dream ends, how thirsty the kébir will be!"

But his dream does not end. Ever sweeter and ever brighter, always new and always the same, like a limpid river, it passes over heaths and through forests.

Yesterday, he is on the edge of a blue pond, florid with nenuphars and fringed with purple loosestrife. The moon is rising, a nightingale is singing, and a fay launches forth from a nenuphar.

The mist dresses the oaks with satin mantles, glow-worms spangle the grass, and roe deer, their necks extended, trample the moss with their yellow feet.

"Come," the fay says to him. "When I was a druidess I cut the mistletoe, today I sow pale violets on the woodland paths.

"Come; enlaced like the bindweed that hangs from the maples, we shall glide by night over the silvery meadows; we shall drink the dew from the lips of periwinkles and we shall sleep by day in a nenuphar rocked by the blue waves.

"Come, I am Rose-des-Eaux, the undine with the soft lips..."

"When the kébir's dream finishes, how thirsty he will be! Let me lift the flap of his tent; perhaps he is awake.

"Look over the plain, at the center of the crescent that his cavalier form behind him; perhaps he is awake. Can you see him?

"Can you see his horse flying, like a partridge, toward that hill of sand, above which crowns of blue smoke are trembling? Can you hear what Ahmed the chaouch is singing as he reloads his long rifle? Listen..."

"I was picked up on the sand in a bloody burnoose; then I guided caravans now I'm a cavalier. I love to feel warm heads, like open pomegranates, bleeding over my bare thigh; the warm heads are the pearls of my fiancée's necklace."

"Can you see the rifles lowering? Can you hear the horses crying under the spur? The bullets are humming like a swarm of bees; can you hear them?

"When the smoke flies away, how thirsty the kébir will be! I shall hold out a fresh cup to him, his foot in the stirrup. With my perfumed tresses I shall wipe his red hands..."

"Can you see him on the hill of sand? He has wiped his saber on the mane of his horse; his gaze is extinct, his brow furrowed, and, immobile on his great horse, he watches he stars lighting up in the west."

"When the kébir's dream finishes, if he is thirsty, let him come under the palm trees; I am the wild turtle-dove of the blue mountains..."

But his dream does not end. His curious cavaliers slip under the tents; he is asleep on the sand and his soul is far away, at the foot of a dolmen in the land of the Arvernes.

Around the dolmen, shadows are ranged. Some have wolf-skins on their shoulders, others burnished breastplates. They are, the fay says, the souls of those who died for Gaul.

They have come to our wedding, the wedding of the poet who seeks and the fay who remembers.

They both climb on to the table of lava; the crowd gathers at their feet and the druidess lifts the sacred cup. She says:

"Drink from the emerald cup, my beloved; drink, your lips are pure. Intoxication will never empty it, disgust will never break it, death has left no lees in the cup of our amour."

"When the hawk seeks a gazelle, it looks at the esparto-grass and not at the sun. Come with me, kébir.

"After the evening prayer, while the camels are ruminating, their heads on the sand, while he great mares lick their meager flanks, while the orient tells its necklace of pearls, while the fires blaze before the brown tents, a flute-player leans against a pack-saddle and an amah hidden beneath a red haïck crouches at his feet.

"The gazelle is in the esparto-grass; come with me, kébir. Listen..."

The son of the Beni-Mzab draws a few vibrant notes from a reed, and the believers approach one by one. He extends a carpet on the sand, the believers sit down, and the almah rises to her feet.

She gets up slowly, her arms folded. Her haïck rises as far as her eyes and falls all the way to the ground. She enters the circle, her arms folded, and she stops, motionless, in the middle of the carpet.

Vague noises, trailing notes, like fearful kisses or distant appeals emerge from the flute. The believers stroke their beards.

A note hisses like a serpent. The haïck falls and the almah rounds out her arms above her head.

"Come; I am the one who leads to the land where dreams commenced are concluded; I am the turtle-dove of the blue mountains.

"You are thirsty, come; I am the golden cup, the cup of snow, the cup into which you can put a honeycomb today and a sunbeam tomorrow.[14]

"Come and see the almah dance."

She rounds out her arms above her head. Her hair, braided with wool, is wrapped around her temples like a ram's horns, her eyes, elongated by kohl, are devoid of gaze, her teeth are shining between her parted lips, the nape of her neck touches her shoulders, her pointed breasts are erect. She is naked to the hip. She has a blue star on her foreheads, he palms of her hands are red, and beneath the white muslin, her legs have the color of honey.

The believers stroke their beards.

"You are thirsty, come; I am the ripe grape-cluster, the pated pomegranate, the embalmed orange of Allah's paradise. I am on the nielloed platter in order that I might be eaten while dreaming of the future and thinking about the past.

"I am not a woman, I am the houri, and envoy of Heaven. Look, Kébir and read on the sand the great word that the almah's foot is writing."

Come; the flute sighs, a derbouka resonates. The almah flexes her back and slowly, slowly she rotates. She spins slowly and her hips quiver slowly. Her eyes reflect the light of the stars; stifled sighs inflate her neck...

The kébir follows his dream; death has left no lees in the cup of their amour.

Then, from the cup that is always full, a cloud emerges of velvety wings, luminous scarves, loose hair, pink legs and bare shoulders.

That cloud has the form of a cone which is spinning on its point, and at every turn a couple falls from the swarm, like an over-ripe cluster of vermilion grapes.

The cloud whirls, and at every turn a couple falls from the swarm; the fays of the woods, with their green scarves; the

---

[14] There is an untranslable play on words here, linking "*rayon de miel*" (honeycomb) to "*rayon de soleil*" (sunbeam).

fays of the heaths, with their crowns of rushes; the fays of the springs, with irises in hand; the fays of the rivers, with glaucous eyes; the fays of the waves, with blue-green eyes; and he fays of battles, with open wings... Then the follets, with bodies of flame; the sprites, with inflated cheeks; the sylphs, with wings tinted by flower pollen; the gnomes, with large heads; the chilly dwarves in heir mouse-fur mantles; and the kobolds and the korrigans... At every turn, a couple falls from the swarm, like an over-ripe grape from a vermilion cluster...

"When the kébir's dream ends, how thirsty he will be! I would like to be the spring that sings in the paradise of Allah."

It is a clear summer morning; quail are singing in the clover. Sitting at the foot of a linden, the bare-headed Alauna is listening to the awakening garden.

"Why is the blonde young woman sitting under the linden? Why is she passing her delicate hand over the grass white with dew?

"Because... because quail are singing in the clover; because she will be sixteen years old tomorrow."

"She will be sixteen years old tomorrow? It's possible, but is she sure?"

"Is one sure of anything in this poor world? But she is speaking, poor thing. Listen."

"When I go to sleep, where does my soul go?"

"To the land where the blue butterfly flies, blonde girl."

"It is said, when I wake up, that it has sand on its wings, and I think I can still hear the refrains of strange sings."

Algiers, the white gull, is bathed by a clear gulf, as you know. Under the palm trees of Boghar, where the camel-drivers sing, a horseman sometime passes, returning from the land of sand, as you know."

"I know that on the bank of the Ganges, the potter, in order to guard out nuptial bed, created gods; in order to guard the cradle, I know that he ought to create gods even greater than the great gods of India."

"She is dreaming. Where are you going?"

"I'm going to tell the jasmine that is sleeping over there to wake up. I'm going to tell the hyacinths to open their cassolettes, the roses to lean over, the linden to sow its flowers, and the lavender to wither."

"Why?"

"You shall know. How the flies are buzzing in the hornbeam arbor! How the swallows are twittering in their nests! How the snakes are slithering in the canal! Sing, turtle-doves, on the service trees. Sing, quail, in the clover!

"Why?"

"Now listen to the virgin with golden hair, and you shall know why it is necessary for virgins not to dream on summer days, when the lavender is withering, when the turtle-doves are singing in the service trees.

"What if he were the potter? I need to know; I'm afraid and I'm cold in this great château."

"If he were the potter, darling, you'd say to him: 'Potter, shape for your queen gods even greater than the great gods of India.'"

"I'd say to him: 'I love you.'"

Leaning on the parapet of the high terrace, she passes her hand beneath her thick tresses, and in a low voice she repeats: "I'd say to him: I love you."

She gazes without seeing a the russet plain. A man is at the foot of the wall, but she does not see him.

In the midday sun the lavender is withering and the jasmines are opening. Her breast swells, her nostrils quiver, but she does not see the stranger setting up his easel at the foot of the wall.

She does not see him smile as he gazes at the white canvas, and she sighs in a low voice: "I'd say to him: I love you."

THE STRANGER

I'd like to be that man... Stay! Please stay; I haven't said anything, I haven't heard anything.

ALAUNA

Monsieur!

THE STRANGER

One can talk before me. One can dream aloud; I'm not a monsieur. I'm a madman who goes where the road goes. A dream pushes me, and only beauty stops me.

You're beautiful and I was weary; that's why I sat down on this stone.

Tilt your head slightly. Everyone sees his dream at the end of the road. Your dream... I haven't said anything! I haven't heard anything!

So, everyone has a dream. Personally, at the end of the rod, of all the beauties glimpsed, I shall make the supreme beauty.

ALAUNA

And you will be a great painter...certainly.

THE STRANGER

I shall be a great madman, since I shall love this painted head.

Oh, don't move; I have been search for such a long time for those bright eyes, in which something akin to smoke is passing. Look at that holly bush. You resemble the blonde nymphs born of the flames of pyres in the sacred woods of India.

ALAUNA

Have you encountered them...often?

THE STRANGER

Very often. But you are even more beautiful than them. Are you Sita, the daughter of the furrow? Ganga, the daughter of the foam?

ALAUNA

Ganga, the exile of the luminous palace?

THE STRANGER

Ganga, the daughter of the Ganges, whom the East wind carried away and whom the tigers seek out there is the ruin of her palace.

I go where the road goes, but, my heart being mute, I listen and my heart is so mute that I can hear the roses laughing and the lilacs whispering. Would you like to know how Ganga, the blonde queen, was born one summer day? It's a pretty poem, which the roses love to sing in that land out there when the moon rises, when the blue gods bathe, when the great elephants, which support the domes, lament dully.

Would you like that? It will pass the time. But lean over a little.

Out there, on the bank of the Ganges, I've seen the veiled virgins throw their necklaces to story-tellers, but I make them pay more dearly... smile. Smile and I'll tell you how the blonde queen, the great love of the great potter, was born.

The wall is so high and my canvas is still blank! For one whom only beauty stops, smile.

ALAUNA

A poem is well worth a smile; tell the tale.

THE STRANGER

It was in the time when the flowers opened more freshly, when the trees grew more rapidly, when the most beautiful women and the strongest men only stammered one word—the word that was worth as much as all the others. It was in the time when life, like a river of milk, overflowed in plains that were always florid, under the ardent sun; in the time...

ALAUNA

When the heavens were empty. I remember.

THE STRANGER

She remembers! She's Sita, I was sure of it. No, she's Ganga, the blonde queen.

ALAUNA

But you're no longer painting.

THE STRANGER

I too believe that I remember.

So, the heavens were empty. In his bottomless gulf, dreaming alone, the one who said he was the Master...

ALAUNA

The one who said he was the Master? Like the stork in autumn, my dream is flying away.

Daughter of the foam of the shoreless gulf, the torrent is carrying you away.

THE STRANGER

Madman! Madman! In the desert thirst burns you, and you believe that you can see a spring, but it's only sand. Keep walking, on and on.

ALAUNA

What if it were him?

Out there, on the banks of the Ganges, when the veiled virgins have thrown their necklaces to the story-teller, their elbows slide on the silk of the cushions, their eyes close and the story-teller draws away silently; but we're not on the bank of the Ganges... I've paid and... I'm waiting.

THE STRANGER

On roads devoid of springs I've been walking for a long time, you see, and I'm thirsty; look at my lips.

When a pebble glints, I take it between my teeth, I'm so thirsty. Oh, the snow, the white snow, reddened by the sun of amour!

But the pebble isn't snow, and my lips are bleeding. Look!

Like the nymphs of India you're beautiful; like them, love the flower that shines, he bird that sings, and in the dust flying over the road seek a cavalier, and not the potter of the Ganges. Let amour smile at you! Forget the one who has gone astray.

ALAUNA

And the promised poem?

THE STRANGER

I no longer know it.

ALAUNA

Near the tent of the Celt on the mountain of the Arie, the virgin dreamed, as beautiful as the dawn, as sad as the night. As she pulled the petals off the marigold of the sands she said: "Like the mountain, my heart is made of ice; the summer wind had enabled nothing to germinate there.

THE STRANGER

Oh, the snow! The white snow that the sun of amour reddens!

ALAUNA

Then a cloud hid the mountain and the daughter of the Celt, in a block of snow, found herself changed. In the block of snow, when she was changed, the virgin said: "Like the mountain, my heart is made of ice. When will the summer wind come?

Then a warm wind tore apart the cloud, and that wind melted the snow, and the virgin, ablaze with amour, found herself changed into a limpid river.

THE STRANGER
You know it, then, the beautiful poem of the queen and the potter?

ALAUNA
Perhaps? But what are you doing? Come down.

THE STRANGER
Personally, I've forgotten that beautiful poem; far from the regretted land, I've been walking for such a long time.

ALAUNA
Under the breath of the Master, the virgin has changed into a limpid river.
Like the mountain, my heart is made of ice. When will the wind of summer come?

THE STRANGER
In the green forest, I can already hear him. From the plain he is rising... here he is!
His wing caresses the block of snow; the snow melts. How clear the water is!
It sings on the grass. On the holy mountain, how blue the stream is!
In the gorge it foams; it bounds over the rock; here it is in the immense plain. Where is it going?
Thunder rumbles, lightning flashes. Under the lightning bolt, the plain fumes. From the smoke a cavalier emerges, as red as a furnace and as tall as an oak.
The cavalier departs at a gallop; the stream follows him. Before him, the forests pen, the hills are cleft; the stream follows him.

Before the foaming flood the black antelopes stop, aston-ished; the elephants think, the tigers flee. Above the racing flood, cranes circle and swans soar. The cavalier gallops on, and the forests open and the hills are cleft.

Before the cavalier the blue gulf hollows out; he launch-es himself into the waves, and all the way to the somber abyss the Ganges follows him; the Ganges of the triple course, which sees the three domains: the sky, the earth and Hell.

ALAUNA

Why are you there?

THE STRANGER

I'm there, then? The Ganges follows the cavalier and I follow...

ALAUNA

What?

THE STRANGER

White foams glistens on the river; the wind carriers it away into a field of rice. Straw is woven into a cradle, and the foam falls into that cradle.

Then, under the summer wind, as under the plow, fur-rows open up, and from the fuming earth, women with bare arms emerge.

They crowd around the cradle, the brown maidservants; on the white straw, a queen smiles.

Do you remember? Like a blue nenuphar, a palace had spring from the limpid river. In your cradle of rice, the women carried you there.

ALAUNA

But the Master's breath had pushed a fleck of foam fur-ther on than the field of rice, under flowering magnolias; that fleck fell on the clay...

THE STRANGER
And the clay became a child, and that child was the potter, and the potter loved the queen. You remember, my...

ALAUNA
And what did the potter say to the queen, as he held out the cup to her in front of the door to the palace?

THE STRANGER
I know that, but in order to tell you, I want your hand. You're beautiful, my blonde queen, even more beautiful than you were out there. Like a bird, my dream is singing; shall we follow it under the lilacs?

ALAUNA
What did he potter say to the queen?

THE STRANGER
When the chisel weighed in my hand I said to you: 'Sing a poem, my beloved.' Then I wound your tresses around my neck and I dreamed. Do you remember? The chisel is weighing in my hand...

ALAUNA
No... Not yet.

THE STRANGER
Sing a poem, my beloved.

ALAUNA
While holding out the cup, what did the potter say?

THE STRANGER
As today, he said: "I love you."

ALAUNA
You are not the potter. Go away.

"Flies are buzzing in the hornbeam arbor; swallows are twittering in their nests; snakes are slithering in the great canal; quail are singing in the clover, and yet the stranger is going way, head bowed. Why?"

"Why is he going down toward the flower garden by the path bordered with box?"

ALAUNA

Who has seen him wind my tresses around his neck?

Them! No one but them! In their granite bodies, they were lying at the foot of the bed of nacre; but their eyes of stone could see.

Their prison is open! He has forgotten, then?

Like the mountain, my heat is made of ice. When will the wind of summer come?

The women are so beautiful, it's said, out there under the palm trees…I want to know! Maidservants!

Pardon, pardon, my beloved; both of them came. They were alive, the sphinxes.

In those bodies of granite, why are you crawling, maidservants? As beautiful as in the temple, as beautiful as in the cavern, stand up before me.

You're obeying? He loves me still, then, the potter? You don't want to respond? Your hand has touched mine; go fill your cup in the water of the basin and empty it over my soiled hand.

And you! On his bench your sister has unbound my hair, as my servant on the bank of the Ganges braided it.

DEATH

Today I'm your servant, but tomorrow…

ALAUNA

Tomorrow. perhaps I'll say to you: "I'm tired; make my bed."

Like a lotus with a golden heart, it shines on the great river, our amour.

SENSUALITY
Into the cup I put mistletoe, sage and vervain; before plunging my hand into it, druidess, put blood into it.

ALAUNA
Your road is the straight road; but have pity, Master, my feet are bleeding!

DEATH
Oaths bind, druidess.

Around the hayricks the haymakers are singing; before their oxen, the herdsmen are singing. Alauna is lying on the grass, weeping, with her head in her hands.

ALAUNA
Your road is the straight road, but your road is narrow; hold out your hand to me, Master. My head is spinning, my eyes are troubled; hold out your hand to me.

The sin has been committed, and must be expiated; but the breath that inclines the fir tree shreds the anemone; measure your justice to my weakness....

Forget my words, Master; I am waking from a long sleep; my lips alone have spoken. I am your maidservant and your daughter; I will always obey you, and I will always love you. Light or heavy, I will kiss your hand, and tranquilly I will go to sleep in your arms, like a sparrow in its nest.

Her head lies on her folded arm. She is asleep, the druidess; to the white anemone, the Master has measured the wind.

She is asleep, and two tears are still trembling, at the ends of her lashes. The two iridescent pearls roll down her cheeks, but when they arrive at her lip her mouth is already smiling, and a sunbeam, filtered by the ash trees, drinks them. To the white anemone, the Master has measured the wind.

"But I can hear something like a sound of wings. One might think that spangles were scintillating in the gold of the sunset."

"Shut up; they're fays. Listen; they're fays that are speaking, fays descended from the great woods."

THE FAYS

She's asleep.

THE CRICKET

She's been weeping.

THE ASH TREE

She said to me; "In autumn your leaves fall, but in spring your buds open, and laves are born where your leaves died. In the winter wind, my dreams swirl like our dead leaves, but in spring, my heart will become verdant, like your crown.

"With my dreams, the winter wind will shred my crown of vervain."

THE FAYS

Her crown of vervain! Who, then, has been able to re-mind her of the past?

Last night again, when her soul, with us in the woolen tent, spoke to the one she loves, it said: "I'm a fay."

By rendering to the marble hair its silken reflections, by rendering to the eyes of marble their soft gleam of old, before the fire of Saint John, the Master had pardoned her.

It's him who said to us: "Hide her sickle, hide her belt and her starry robe and under the heavy agate tombstone, go to seek the golden necklace that the potter of the Ganges carved for his queen. The druidess has fallen asleep, but the queen will awake.

The Master had pardoned; it's him who said to us: "By day she will be a woman; by night she will be a fay; it is necessary that amour fills in the abyss that it has hollowed out; it is necessary that she brings back to my path the one who has strayed.

Who, then, has been able to remind her of the past?

THE WREN

In my hole, where I was nestled, I saw everything and heard everything; but I have not understood everything.

A man with blond hair, dark eyes and a soft voice sat down next to her; he said to her: "I love you." He caressed her hand and I was joyful, for we love those who love.

I said to myself: "At midday, they will often come into the hornbeams, holding hands, speaking in low voices without turning their heads; and I shall hop behind them gaily."

We love those who speak in low voices and walk at a slow pace, holding hands.

THE FAYS

What did she reply?

THE WREN

"Go away." And he disappeared.

THE FAYS

How?

THE WREN

Probably as those to whom one says "go away" disappear. I don't know, myself. Then she said: "Maidservants!"

Then two stone monsters came; but they were not two monsters... I've talked too much; I'm thirsty. I'll get it in a moment.

THE FAYS

The eternal enemy is recommencing the struggle; she alone was able to speak.

The sin was committed; it must be expiated. On the steps, a man is free; if he falls he must get up by himself because nothing has bumped him. But if, when he bends his knee, he extends his hand toward the Master, the Master cries: "Courage! You will get up stronger and more valiant."

From the azure sky you have not fallen, turtle-dove; your wings have all their feathers. If you are bleeding in the brambles it is because you want to extract your beloved from the brambles. We will help you, blonde queen; we shall not fly back up to the green star without you.

If only she could believe, on awakening, that it was a dream! You would not want her to weep, you whose voice she can hear; tell her.... Hush! She's waking up.

ALAUNA
He carved the cradle in the purest ivory. It was a great lotus borne by two dolphins. At the head, to guard the expected, a stork was perched, its wings open over the white calyx. At the feet, to cheer him up, between two crumpled leaves, a laughing monkey was gazing.

In the winter wind my dreams fly away like dead leaves. Druidess! I am a druidess!

THE WREN
Oh, the lazybones, who sleeps all day.

ALAUNA
I really am a druidess; I understand their voices.

THE WREN
One understands everything when one is in love. When you come into the hornbeam arbor I'll follow you and if you lie...

While you were asleep I've been working hard, look; I've built my nest for my summer marriage and—why were you sleeping with your head on your arm? My fiancée had said to me: the ladybird had a golden bed in the daisy; I want a golden bed too—I stole a hair from you. Come and see whether there's a golden thread shining in my nest.

I cut it very gently there, very close to your ear, but my wing brushed you and I almost woke you up. You said to me then: "Like my maidservant on the banks of the Ganges, braid my hair." I laughed.

ALAUNA

Poor little thing.

Your breath brought the fleck of foam into the field of rice; today, as on the bank of the Ganges, where you want me to go, Master, push me.

THE NIGHTINGALE

Under the palm trees of Boghar, in a pomegranate bush, I have my winter house. The nights are becoming cold; I'm going to quit you.

THE CRICKET

If you leave, you won't see the vines gilding, and dewdrops listening in long necklaces of pearls on the silver threads extended by the fays.

THE NIGHTINGALE

But I'll see the virgins with peach-colored cheeks dancing under the pomegranates.

When the kébir passes the wind disturbs their veils; I don't know why. It's for me, brown gazelles, that your veils lift; the kébir is following his dream and doesn't look at you.

ALAUNA

He's in Boghar!

That's why, when I wake up, I think I can still hear the refrains of strange songs... When tears flowed from my marble eyes every night into the round basin, near him, my soul flew away; now, when I sleep as before my soul escapes... I'm not a woman.

But I sense that your hand is light upon me, Master. I sense that the sin is expiated, that death is imminent; I know that he is the potter.

THE NIGHTINGALE

And I know that he loves you.

When the sun is hot he reads the Bible, the Koran and the fantastic poems of Arabia, in which indefatigable horsemen pass by without saying where they have come from or where they are going.

He reads in order to find a remedy for his sadness, but as he has drunk with avid lips, he has only found thirst at the bottom of the divine cup. Now he no longer reads, he dreams.

He searches in the stars for the one he has not been able to find in the poems

He can dream at his ease; the three rooms of his house open on to a gallery sustained by twisted columns. A hand with six fingers, a talisman against spells, is sculpted at the points of the swollen arches, and in his whitewashed rooms a thin pale red garland runs beneath the joists.

He can dream at his ease; to perfume his dreams, the enameller had covered the walls of his gallery with blue roses; to carry them away he has covered the walls of his staircase with blue ships.

Blue roses, perfume his dreams!

He can dream at his ease; his garden extends from the stream escaping from the collapsed aqueduct to the crest of the white cliff, whose vertical flanks bear a few lentisk bushes and clumps of geraniums. His garden is planted with orange trees and pomegranate trees.

When a warbler sings in the pomegranates, when a fine vapor rises from the broken aqueduct, when the stars spangle the dormant bay, he sees the one he would love if she were a woman passing between the sky and the earth.

Blue ships, bear away his dreams!

Now he no longer reads, he dreams. He lets the bridle float over the neck of his horse and he dreams, in the shady gorges of the Boudjareah, on the slivery dunes that tremble in the sunlight like a linen veil, the green date plantations of Hussain-Dey and the yellow cliffs of Cap Matifou.

One day, at noon, in a ravine that opens to the sea, his horse stopped in the shade of two lemon trees before the iron-clad door of a white house with barred windows. In the glittering wall, at the back of a narrow niche, clear water was falling, drop by drop, from a copper pomegranate into a marble basin.

The sirocco was blowing.

He left the horse to drink from the basin; then, the shade of the lemon trees being cool, he sat down on the stone bench at the foot of the glittering wall.

He watched the balancelles gliding like gulls over the azure bay. He watched the sunlight setting the white cupolas of the terraces of Algiers ablaze... But on the perforated balcony above his head, silk quivered and a penetrating perfume mingled with the perfume of the lemon trees.

He is no longer gazing; motionless, he listens. Perhaps he is waiting,

Two bursts of fresh laughter ring out, like a gold coin in a silver bowl, and a grave voice says, emphasizing the words:

"It is close to Allah and far from sultans, the land where we erect our tents!

"By night it sparkles like the sea. It quivers by day like a crimson veil fringed with diamonds and clusters of emeralds. Its hills undulate like the veins of racehorses, and its motionless lakes are deeper and more limpid than he azure-tinted eyes of houris.

"It is close to Allah and far from sultans, the land where we erect our tents!"

The grave voice falls silent and a clear voice responds:

"Like a vulture, my heart has two sharp wings; it rises toward the sun... It has risen so high, so very high, that it will never descend again!

"Does your black horse have wings, handsome cavalier?

"Like a swallow, my heart has two wings, two silken wings; it has flown toward the Orient... It has flown so far, so very far, that it will never come back again!

"Does your white camel have sings, handsome cameldriver?"

With the perfume of the lemon trees a penetrating perfume mingles.

In a low voice, without raising his head, he says:

"In a garden lived a sylph and a rose: a sylph with somber wings and a rose with a golden heart.

"'I'm in love,' said the sylph, 'I'm dying of love.'

"'I'm in love too,' replied the rose, 'I'm in love with a beautiful butterfly as brilliant as a flame.''

"And the rose smiled at the sylph flew away.

"The next day the rose said: 'The daughters of the sun love sparks... Poor fool, your wings are black.'

'My wings are made of darkness but my heart is made of flame. I divine what the butterfly cannot see, I dream what he does not know, and in my dreams you tell me what you do not tell him. He opens your lips, but I alone have your kisses.

"The sylph shook his somber wings over the rose and he died.

"The next day, the rose was inclined on her stem; the butterfly was only a man, the sylph was a poet..."

Two bursts of fresh laughter rang out, like a gold coin in a silver bowl, and the clear voice said:

"I would like a philter that gives death, a philter that kills like lightning; I would rub her lips with it and this evening, I would have her last kiss.

"A beautiful blue bird is nesting in the cedars. Fly over the snow, little blue bird!

"I have chosen a flyssa as sharp as a glance, a flyssa with a solid hilt, a flyssa long enough to go from my heart to hers, and this evening I shall drink her last breath.

"A beautiful blue bird is nesting in the cedars. Fly over the snow, little blue bird!

"I am searching for a stone heavier than the mountain and wider than the sea, in order to place it on our tomb, and on the Day of Judgment we will hear the angel's trumpet together.

"A beautiful blue bird is nesting in the cedars. Fly over the snow, little blue bird!"

The sirocco is blowing, and a fine dust descends on the road bordered with aloes.

He puts his hands under the water that is trickling from the copper pomegranate.

"While bathing his hands in the icy water, des he raise his head?"

"Probably, but as he passes his hands over his face he says:

"'My babouches weigh as much as a bronze cannon, my burnoose is heavier than a tombstone. My temples are throbbing, my eyes are troubled.

"'Agitate the fan with the silky plumes; make sprays of icy water spurt from the nacreous basin.

"'Bring me flowers of jasmine... no, roses. The perfume of jasmine is as soft as a smile, but the perfume of roses is as sweet as a kiss.

"'Enlace your naked arms, flex your ivory flanks! Turn, turn more rapidly; my tent is as wide as the plain and as high as the palm trees.

"'Let your veils fall; I am the voice that commands, I am the hand that gives. My horses are stronger than the desert wind, my spahis faster than a speeding bullet. Enlace your naked arms... I am the emir... the sultan... the caliph! Flex your ivory flanks... I am the arm of Allah, the saber that touches and kills!

"'Bring jasmine, jasmine and roses; the sand fumes where I have passed. I am the devouring flame, the fiery vapor that glides toward the Occident. The course of the earth is less rapid than mine, the clouds cradle me and the moon opens her snowy crescent in order to embrace me.'"

The grave voice replies:

"Our tents emerge from the sand like gilded breasts from an open haïck, our large tents grouped in a circle on the sand that reeks of musk. They are cool by day and warm by night, and the demon does not approach them.

"O you who live and die in cities of mud, you who respire air that others have already soiled, you who, like the tortoise, never quit your house; if you saw our blond palm trees, you would believe that the paradise of Allah was awakening you.

"Our brothers only know how to sing and fight, but their verses are so sweet that they make your daughters pale, and their spurs are so long that they bear away, as they pass, your carpets and your wives."

Without turning his head, he gets to his feet slowly. He has the stirrup in his hand and he says:

"The calices of roses require vermilion leaves. Human amours require embalmed evenings and bloody mornings. Shake your silvery mane, El-Biod, your nacreous flanks will be blue-tinted. Fly like a pigeon toward the sister of my soul, toward the sister who is waiting for me in the land of palm trees.

"The man with the narrow heart, the man with snow in his veins, loves in closed rooms, behind bolts and sabers; but the swallow of the plain, the bearer of spurs, loves in the open air and he sunlight. Fly southwards, El-Biod, to the land of palm trees."

He is in the saddle. His horse rears up and he says:

"My flyssa is losing its edge in the sheath, the powder has whitened the copper basinet of my rusty rifle, and my heart has swollen in solitude like a cadaver neglected on the road.

"Where are you then, sister of the stars? Half of my soul, where are you? I have searched near the spring; I have asked the partridge and the gazelle for you in the esparto-grass. The sand is sticking to my lips, but I want you and I shall have you."

The stallion launches forth on the stony road.
He blows a kiss at the balcony.
Two bursts of fresh laughter ring out, like a gold coin in a silver bowl.

"How pale she is! Why is she so pale?"
"I don't know; but let's follow her behind the hornbeam hedge and perhaps we'll know. She has been as pale as this since the day when the unknown painter stopped under the terrace."

"He departed, leaving his easel, and on that easel, a strange painting. At close range it is Alauna lying dead, smiling on a heap of flowers; from further away, it's only a trees with dazzling flowers."

"Listen. Like the warbler, which sings in order to hear itself singing, the solitary blonde speaks in order to hear a voice."

ALAUNA

One evening, when men were camped in the plain down there, on the bank of the Loire, a Gaul on a white mare appeared. He had a woman on the rump of his mount. He said to the chief: "Salut, Brother."

The woman said to me: "Salut, sister."

They were Ar-Braz and the Skylark: Ar-Braz, the son of the Celt, and his immortal companion, the daughter of the first day.[15]

Ar-Braz said to the chief: "In the valley of the irises, the Purs have separated.[16] While our horses marched toward the sunset, you drove your cattle in the direction of the Orient. Why, Brother, have you quit the river of the blue lotuses for the land of oaks?"

The chief replied: "I go where the Master wishes. You are the plow and I am the sower; you open the furrow and I cast the wheat; behind me, perhaps, the harvester is marching,"

Then the Skylark said: "Over the sown grain I shall sing, Brother. But do you want us to push the furrow further forward? My sons have strong arms, blood flows in their veins. The Gallic hive is full; do you want a swarm to depart?"

The chief replied: "If you wish, let's depart. The Master knows the limits of his field; where the plow has to stop, the oxen will lie down of their own accord. But over your furrow, divine Skylark, the druidess ought to remain; to spell out his name and teach his secrets, the Master has chosen our daughters."

How long ago that was! It was a long time ago, and yet the flower, then opening in my heart, barely blossomed... I believed I loved you then; but today, I love you.

---

[15] Braz in a Breton word meaning "great." In the first part of "Symphonie" an apparently-equivalent character is introduced as Boun, but the fictitious mythical hero Ar-Braz is extensively featured in the second part, and further elaborated in *Vercingétorix*.

[16] L'Estoille's readers would probably have construed "Purs" as if it were French for "Pure Ones," but the greater likelihood is that Duclaux derived it from *pur*, the syllable attributed by French linguists to a rune that resembles (accidentally) a capital P, and which was thought to mean "giant."

Then the sin was committed and the chief departed. Ar-Braz followed him with the Skylark.

"I never saw them again.

When I took my pain into the ravine, I did hear once, behind a fleeing army, cavaliers with loud voices shouting: "Ar-Braz! Ar-Braz! Ar-Braz is born!"

But I did not hear the Skylark singing.

Then, slowly, the centuries fell away, and one evening, a man descended from the mountain, as handsome as a handsome god of India. The woodcutters in the forest said: "That's Vercingetorix of the clan of the Monts Dore." The shepherdesses, standing on the rocks, while waving flowering furze, shouted: "O mistletoe! O mistletoe! Ar-Braz is born!" But I didn't hear the Skylark singing.

How long ago that was! And yet the blue bird, which my heart was brooding like a nest, is scarcely beginning to flap its wings today... I believed that I loved you then, but today I love you.

How long ago it was! Today, when my heart is heavy and tears rise to my eyes involuntarily, I would like to see the Skylark, the beloved of the first day, the fiancée without sadness, the spouse without anger, her voice soft and her gaze clear. I would say to her: "I am suffering, Sister. Sometimes I doubt; I am always afraid. Tell me whether the chief will only love his druidess, when the laborer has pushed the furrow all the way to the plains of the Ebro."

But I am the druidess, she who knows and commands. Clouds, stop! Where is the daughter of the first day? Where is the Skylark of the Gauls?

Without stopping they pass by. How can you expect still to command the clouds, you who cannot command your own heart? Your sickle is broken, only your oath remains.

The hay has been brought in; the meadow is deserted. Over her pale forehead she passes her emaciated hand.

ALAUNA

And now, does he only love me? The women are so beautiful, it's said, in the groves of pomegranate trees.

Nightingale, you have told me: "He loves you." Tell me again.

THE WREN

The nightingale has already departed; he's chilly. How pale you are again! Sit down on the bench; a warm wind is rising from the vineyards. Sit down; the wind that gilds the grape-clusters will also gild your cheeks. You're not one of those delicate peaches that a sunbeam cracks, you're a beautiful grape-cluster that the ardent sun velvets.

While you trembled in your bed, all white, did you hear a *tap tap* at your window? That was me.

What did you want to ask that nightingale?

ALAUNA

What he has seen in his winter house.

THE WREN

He's a little loquacious... he boasts readily. What you want to know I can tell you myself. But do you know why I love you?

It's a family secret... the secret is perhaps not entirely mine, but what isn't mine is yours.

When you were a druidess...

ALAUNA

When I was a druidess?

THE WREN

That's exactly what, in the secret, isn't mine.

The fays will be annoyed, but I'm not afraid of the fays. When the snow is swirling they're very content to find my nest and warm their hands under my wings.

So, when the fays were druidesses with you—for you have been a druidess and the greatest of the druidesses—one of your ancestors...you're laughing? Laugh, laughter is good; good for the cheeks, good for the heart.

Would you laugh if you were sure that he loves you? Then laugh heartily; he loves you and he has told you so a hundred times.

ALAUNA

What should I do? Where should I go?

THE WREN

I'm a wren; no one listens to me, but they listen to the nightingale.

Perhaps you'll believe them. Can you see them coming, along the path?

You can't see the fays? You can't see Myrtle, who accompanies you when you go out there?

I know everything; they talk in the great hornbeam arbor, and I follow them; I move without stirring the leaves and I hear them. They talk about nothing but you and the skylark.

Do you know her, that skylark?

ALAUNA

Yes.

THE WREN

Well, she's with Ar-Braz in the funereal grotto in the land of the Orient.

I don't know her myself, that skylark. When they talk about her for too long, I go *frou! frou!* in the foliage. They're afraid, they look around, and they talk about you.

I know everything. I know that by night you become a fay like them. I know that you were the stone woman who wept over the round basin, and that you were already a fay by night then. I know that before the summer fire of Saint John your marble body was exchanged for the body of a child.

I know everything. I know that every night, when you were a statue, you spoke to his soul. I know that now, you go into his tent... Oh, fays can go in anywhere, and by night, you're not a woman.

They talk in that big hornbeam, they talk. Yesterday they said... They didn't say anything yesterday.

ALAUNA

What did you hear?

THE WREN

Nothing interesting. They said: "She's still too weak to go so far... in her poor broken body it's necessary that her soul sleeps..."

I can't lie; they said... there they are, speak to them.

ALAUNA

Myrtle?

THE WREN

Instead of weeping, Myrtle, reply.

ALAUNA

You're weeping, friend? Why do you no longer come in search of me, to go out there? I haven't violated my oath.

Why haven't you come for a long time? My poor soul is so thirsty that my lips are cracked and my blood is burning my veins.

THE FAYS

You're only a woman; you can live, suffer and love.

ALAUNA

Does he love me?

THE WREN

Like thistledown, a breath carries them all away.

In winter, when you come to say: "Little wren, your nest is so soft! You're nest is so warm…!"

ALAUNA

Does he love me?

THE WREN

Go ask him. Since you're no longer anything but a woman, it's necessary to live, suffer and love.

In his white room, around which a thin garland of pale pink runs, he goes to sleep, and as he closes his eyes he says:

"Only Moorish women have those voices, simultaneously dull and soft, that make you dream of blue wood-pigeons. They alone have the secret of those strange perfumes that bite you in the temples.

"I'd like to see them. The balcony is barred, the door reinforced with iron, and the master, doubtless an old pirate, when he goes to dream on the harbor wall, hides the key to his door in the folds of his turban.

"If I were a believer, the djinni who flies by night from the beautiful garden where, like a chaplet, the Prophet tells his necklace of houris, the djinni with soft wings sown with velvet eyes would bring me a dream...

"I'm not a believer; the djinni has not shaken his wings with velvet eyes over my head.

"They're two foolish girls; at midday I'll see them. I'll see them, even if I have to… do something stupid. I need to do something stupid; it's necessary for reality to kill the dream. It's necessary that the phantom who haunts my dream vanishes forever.

"Is it really necessary to expel that beautiful phantom entirely? No, for too long it has cradled me in its opal arms, the beautiful beloved phantom.

"If the fay, last night, had leaned over my bed and if the djinni had come, I would have said: 'Go back, djinni, to Mahomet's paradise.

"Strange! Strange!

"I'm not capable of carving the head of a stick, and as a child, I loved a statue. I loved it as I've never loved a woman, and as I probably never shall love one.

"I only read the poets of the Orient, but as a soldier, under the palm trees of Boghar and the orange trees of Boudjareah, I dream about druidesses of whom I've never even read the name.

"Strange! Strange!

"But what if I dream by day and only live by night? Nothing can prove to me that it isn't the case, and if so..."

"*Mon capitaine*, the horse is saddled, the pistols are in the saddle-holsters."

"Put the pistols back on their nails and wait for me at the bottom of the stairs with two bunches of violets. If I haven't come back this evening, I probably won't come back tomorrow."

The sirocco is blowing, the sun is burning, the road is deserted; all the believers are asleep.

He climbs the stony slope at a gallop. There's the white house. He slows his horse to a walk and without looking at the windows, like a man who is letting his soul follow a dream, he says in a low voice:

"Why are you stopping, El-Biod? We haven't found her; it's only a vermilion rose shining under the lemon-trees."

"Roses have the souls of women," responds a softly grave voice on the perforated balcony. "Roses have the souls of women in the shade of great lemon trees; but sometimes, cavaliers pass by, and those roses let their souls follow the cavaliers who pass without stopping."

The clear voice continues: "Like the sea, my heart has waves, blue waves and green waves; but the wind alone lifts them, and its kisses make me weep.

"Why does my heart have waves, if the galley with the white sails does not float on them?"

He attaches his horse to the trunk of a lemon tree, he lies down in the shade and rolling a cigarette, he says:

"O you who know what the bullets say, you who have slept over braided hair, but who do not know the sister of the stars, my beloved Yamina, children of the powder, listen!"

On the perforated balcony, two fresh bursts of laughter ring out like a gold coin on a silver tray.

He says, as he watches the blue smoke rising:

"I could show the bee where he honey is sweeter than in asphodels; Yamina is a bean-flower that the Eternal has perfumed. Yamina has no sister among the daughters of the desert.

The grave voice responds:

"Look at that cloud gliding over the plain, more rapidly than a partridge flying toward a spring, darker than the smoke of esparto-grass. It is not the wing of the simoom that is lifting the sand, it is our cavaliers returning from a raid.

"Put the crimson aatatiches on the camels; put tufts of white feathers on the aatatiches, arrange your camels in a line, daughter of the Ouled-Aïad. Throw your necklaces to the chosen of your heats, but smile at everyone, daughters of the Ouled-Aïad. Pour balm where the bullet has passed.

"Hasten! Hasten; the burnooses of our brothers are red, their hands are black. It is pleasant to kiss hands blackened by powder, it is pleasant to place one's head on a bloody burnoose."

He has stood up. He leans his elbow on his saddle and he says:

"Yamina, you have no sister among the daughters of the desert. Your neck stands up like the standard that braves the enemy. Your bosom resembles a cluster of grapes swollen by the dew and sugared by the sun.

"Your shoulders are two blocks of snow; your ribs are rounded like Damascene sabers. Butterflies mistake your fingers for rosebuds and your feet for lily-pads. Yamina, my heart has melted under your gaze and you have drunk it in a kiss."

Listen to the clear voice:
"In the desert devoid of water the great palm tree stands, alone. Its trunk crackles in the sun and plaints fall from its calcined palms, next to which amber-colored clusters have never swayed.

"Open your wings, beautiful pigeon, open your blue wings and carry my song where my heart wants to go!"

But the wind blows from the sea and the great palm tree shivers. "I am the kiss," says the gust, that your beloved is sending you from the land where fresh springs sing in great woods."

But he responds, his foot in the stirrup: "Open your blue wings, beautiful pigeon; take my kisses to where my heart has remained."

Two branches of jasmine fall from the balcony and the ironclad door swings silently...

The room opens on to a gallery. It is white, high and square. For a ceiling it has a blue cupola; its walls are bare and on the marble paving-stones there is only a round bright red carpet with cushions embroidered with gold.

The carpet is scarcely larger than a lion-skin.

He stops on the threshold of the square room.

They are lying on the carpet, a cushion under the elbow. A haïck hides them entirely; their eyes shine between the fissures of the veils. Motionless, they gaze at him, standing on the threshold.

"Open your wings, beautiful pigeon," he says, pressing the jasmine branches to his lips, "open your blue wings and carry two kisses to where my heart has gone."

Then, slowly, he walks toward he round carpet, and sits down gravely on a cushion embroidered with gold.

He passes the jasmine flower over his lips, and the same fresh and sonorous laughter that fell from the balcony a little while ago rises to the blue cupola. Gravely, he extends his arm toward a nielloed tray and takes a candid fruit.

"You're a poet, cavalier," says the dull voice. "Your verses gleam like a flyssa and ring like a spur."

"Then they are engraved on the portals of paradise."

"And are they also engraved in Yamina's heart?" the clear voice continues.

"My verses do not have claws like a vulture, they have wings like a partridge. If you want to rediscover traces of them in the morning, seek them on the lips and not on the heart."

"You're not in love, then?"

"Me! But I'm nothing but love; I love all dark eyes..."

"And blue eyes?"

"Perhaps..."

The woman with the grave voice is named Meyrin, the woman with the clear voice Aïchouna.

Meyrin's eyes are dark, like a moonless night; Aïchouna's eyes are blue, like a Saharan pond.

Meyrin's hair has tawny reflections of copper, and when Aïchouna lets her heavy tresses fall over her bare shoulders, one might think that they are two black snakes drinking from two bowls of milk.

They are two daughters of the banks of the Nile, whom the hand of Allah has pushed across the land of sand all the way to the house in Algiers.

In the evening, when the coffee is fuming in vermilion cups, when the nargilehs starred with gold are extinguished, when her pale head falls back on the damask of the cushions,

Meyrin takes her three-stringed guitar and Aïchouna sings cheerful songs and dulcet poems in her clear voice.

"He has already heard them many times before, those strange poems, why is he having them repeated while his head sinks back on the damask cushions?"

"Because Aïchouna has a fresh voice. Because her lips, when she sings, vibrate over her white teeth. Because her eyes flash. Listen."

"While awaiting the night, Aïchouna, my dove, what if all three of us were to make an excursion on the sunlit gulf where the old Pharaohs, in order to guide their triremes, had black sailors with the heads of hawks, where golden scarabs with emerald wings alighted on the forehead of the sphinxes whose brown flanks were bathed by warm waves."

Aïchouna parts the gauze the adapts its folds to the marble contours of her sharp breasts; she lies back on the cushion and, her hands crossed behind her head, her lips moist and her eyes looking heavenwards, she says:

"On the edge of the gulf, where the stars sow sparks as they twist their hair, a palace of bronze is flamboyant. It is the palace of Saba, the eternal city that men no longer see. It is the palace of the queen who speaks like a prophet and sings like a bird.

"In the palace of Saba, Solomon built himself a room without windows, the iridescent vault of which is sustained by a thousand silver palm trees. It is the chamber of the queen with lips as soft as a dream, a brow as high as a poem and eyes as clear as a pool.

"In the room without windows a swallow with great wings soars under the iridescent dome, a panther with meager flanks watches her fly, and Solomon, the poet king, who collects flowers in sheaves and puts pearls in necklaces, has been spelling the same word for three thousand years without tiring.

"When the swallow opens her lips the waves sing in the round gulf, and when the panther roars, kisses sing on lips in Saba, the eternal city that men no longer enter, in Saba, the city sought by those whose lips are dry and whose kisses are fiery.

"But in the room without windows, when the queen closes her eyes...

"Listen!"

"Do you hear her brothers coming, Meyrin? May Allah be blessed; thee powder is about to speak. Human amours require perfumed evenings and bloody mornings; may Allah be blessed, Meyrin. If I had a rifle, bullets would spring from my hand like sparks from a fire of dry wood; but as I have no rifle, dance, Meyrin, my turtle-dove."

"*Mon capitaine! Mon capitaine!*"

"What the devil do you want?"

"The battalion's march is being sounded in the Kasbah."

VI

The sun is setting. On the horizon, the sky, reminiscent of a steel doe, is resting on a uniform, dry, naked plain. To the South, a large cloud of dust is flowing. To the North, thin threads of vapor are rising. The Orient is blue-tinted, he Occident is violet, the sand is russet.

A huge vulture with a bald breast, its neck bent and its wings trailing, is seeking to maintain its equilibrium on a camel's skull.

In the background of the plain, the column appears. It is marching slowly. The day has been rude; water was scarce, the packs are heavy.

Two cavaliers, their red burnooses lifted, their arms bare, their rifles across the saddle, arrive at a gallop.

The vulture takes flight heavily. The cavaliers stop. Standing up in their stirrups, they look, and then they rejoin the column at a walk.

They say a few words to the general and mingle with his escort.

He general extends his arm. A company of chasseurs stops; its members put down their sacks, unfold their cloaks, divide into three groups, post sentinels, and lie down.

The general and his escort retrace their steps. The column breaks up silently. The horses' heads are lowered; the men drink.

The captain has visited all his sentinels; in the guard-post he unbuckles his belt, plants his saber in the sand and sits down on a sack.

"Do you recognize him? He is crumpling a dried flower between his fingers and throwing it away."

"I recognize him, but what is he saying?"

"Listen."

"They're very beautiful, but they're not as beautiful as my dream, and since I set foot in the white house, the fay no longer returns.

"It wasn't a fay that leaned over my head; it was the statue in the garden, the one that Grandfather didn't want me to forget.

"Grandfather, brambles must be flourishing on your grave; when I return from Algeria I'll go to see you. You never speak to me; your soul must be waiting for me back there."

The tents loom up whitely behind the fires. A trumpeter hurls three shrill notes at the gallop. The cloud coming from the South increases. The sky is blue-tinted, the sand silver.

The wind brings a vague rumor. Spahis, their heads over the necks of their horses, pass by and are lost in the shadow riding slowly from the horizon to the zenith.

The rumor swells, accompanied by a dull rumble. A star lights up and a spark springs from the tip of a lance, from which a blue pennant is floating; the general descends from his horse. Large flags flutter around him.

In the guard-post, the captain and his sub-lieutenant are drinking coffee from two battered metal mugs.

"But you'll come back to us, *mon capitaine?*"

"I don't believe so. That will change your epaulettes."

"Wait another two or three years; you have such a fine future ahead of you. But perhaps you want to marry?"

"Yes, I have a desire to marry History, that beautiful girl you have disdained, lieutenant."

"You won't have me for a rival. But why wouldn't you bring that proud spouse to the battalion?!"

"Go and see whether those two fellows are asleep; I'll reply to you when you return."

The rumor swells. Camels are heard bellowing, sheep bleating, horses whinnying, women screaming and children wailing. Rifle fire crackles out there in the darkness. The flames of the fires twist redly.

The spahis of the escort empty sacks full of heads. A confused mass appears. Soldiers run before it and return with sheep, which they butcher as they march.

The clarions sound the appeal; a great silence falls. Pieces of flesh are roasting over the embers. Butter is running from split bladders.

The ranks break up. Soldiers return to supervise the smoking meat. Others, lying on carpets, are playing with jewels. Others are breaking the heads of sheep with sabers and throwing the tongues and brains into mess-tins. Others are rubbing their feet with grease.

Naked children emerge from the confused mass, slip between the sentinels, drink from a water-bottle and flee. The fires go out; the camp goes to sleep.

The moon shines and the confused mass brightens. Here, camels are swinging their necks, anxiously. There sheep are massing together. Elsewhere, in a circle of spahis, crouching men with their hoods pushed back are gazing at severed heads whose lips are pursed.

Behind the sentinels he passes back and forth slowly.

"Is he thinking about the white house in the ravine of the Boudjareah?"

"No, he's thinking about the statue. He's thinking about the grandfather who said to him: 'Love her forever.'"

"On your feet!" cries the sentinel hidden in the bush.

The large white mares are turbulent; the darkness is striped by flashes; heavy carbines are lowered. Bayonets are lifted again, bloody; white forms are gasping on the grass. Like a vision, everything disappears.

In the camp, a turco is playing the flute in front of the last fire to go out.

The swallow has followed her sisters to the land of the sun, but will she return with them in the spring?

Perhaps.

Beware; on the beach out there, black crows are watching for weary swallows.

"The wind from the sea has crumpled your wings, poor thing. Chilly, you hide in a hollow in the rock..."

"Look at that shadow passing. Beware."

"It's not a crow passing over, it's a hawk. But beware, swallow, it's returning from the land of sand."

At the foot of the high cliff, under an overhanging rock, she watches the waves play with the shingle and she says:

"Like those pebbles, life is rolling me; like them, I'm lamenting under the impact; like them I don't know whether tomorrow will be a day of calm or tempest."

It was the shadow of a horseman that was extending over the sand. He passes along the narrow path beside the cliff at a gallop, and he does not see Alauna.

But she has seen him. The blood rises to her pale cheeks. It's him.

We were waiting for you, as the plain awaits the sun.

"You're as beautiful as the rising moon and the star that is going to sleep. Under your gaze, Aïchouna, a frisson runs through my bones. When I hear your voice, Meyrin, as when the bullets whistle, the blood seethes behind my brow.

"Look, here's your place. Your nargileh is still there. Your doves are beating their wings in order to follow you, my handsome wood-pigeon, to the blue land of dreams or the red land of kisses."

"Come, we'll put our cheeks on your feet, and you can mingle our long tresses, as you did yesterday."

"No, this chamber is too low; its cupola is crushing me, its walls stifling me. Come into the grove of lentisks; the waves are caressing the cliff and the perfume of the bean-fields is mingling with the perfume of the laurels."

"We come here often; from here you can see the road; but the wind from the desert only brings your sad doves thirst."

"Here's the dew! The sand will be verdant and my heart will flourish! Sing nightingale, sing; here comes the beloved on her white mare. Sing, nightingale, sing; my heart is a rose-bush and its vermilion roses are for the beloved."

Give me your hand, Aïchouna; sit down here, Meyrin.

What do you say to that, my sweet gazelles?

One day, without looking for them, a cavalier found a sapphire and a ruby.

"Where shall I put them?" he said. "On the brooch of my turban? No, the caliph has none similar, and they'd be stolen while I'm sleep. On the hilt of my saber? A bullet would smash them. In my heart no one will see them; I'll hide them there.

But his heart was full of the ashes of a distant amour; he was afraid of tarnishing the stones and, not knowing where to hide them, he took the road to the desert. He went toward a mountain where men never went; he climbed the highest summit, and here, on a rock on which only angels could set foot, he put the inflamed ruby next to the cloudless sapphire.

"I was the ardent cup! Get up, Meyrin!"

"I was the fresh cup! I'm following you, my sister..."

Over the jagged rocks at the foot of the cliff the sea is foaming.

The blue gulf takes the two sisters.

At the foot of the cliff, which is crowned by a clump of lentisks, she is dreaming, while listening to the waves playing with the shingle.

On the dormant bay the stars are mirrored, and in the breeze blowing from the land, the perfume of the bean-fields mingles with the perfume of laurels.

"It's necessary that he loves me," she sighs. "Amour must fill in the abyss that amour has hollowed out! It's necessary, but I've broken my sickle and I've lost my crown, and I'm only a woman, who only knows how to weep... and to love. Once, I believed that I loved you; now, I love you!

"I've lost my crown; I'm no longer anything but a wisp of foam. Celestial daughter of the holy mountain, nymph beloved by the sun, I was born of your fresh breath; give my eyes the tender hue of the gulf where you bathe, put the perfume on my lips of the embalmed forests where you pass slowly to the regretted land.

"I am no longer anything but a woman; it's necessary that I be beautiful in order to be loved.

"I am no longer anything but a woman; I've broken my sickle. But when I commanded under the fir trees up above, I kept the kite away from your nest, warbler and I kept the lightning away from your wing, kite. Warbler, teach me to sing; kite, give my tresses the reflection of your wings.

"I am no longer anything but a woman; it's necessary that I be beautiful in order to be loved."

Two vague forms pass before her eyes... and then a black shadow. What is that muted sound?

"The black shadow is a man who has fallen over the cliff. He is gasping on the shingle. Alauna runs forward and bumps into a woman that I did not see coming."

"She leans over the dying man."

ESTHER

He's dead, leave him.

ALAUNA

No, no, Help!"

ESTHER

Is he young?

ALAUNA

I don't know... I can't see... Help! But who are you, you who are saying that he's dead?

ESTHER

A stroller, like you. Do you know him?

ALAUNA

Yes.

A SERGEANT

What's all this noise? What is it?—let's see. A dead man! Hey, Corporal, four men, and quickly.

What are you doing here?

ESTHER

He fell from the cliff in front of us.

ALAUNA

He's going to die.

THE SERGEANT

IF he fell from up there... Let's see—you others, carry him away... Gently.

A CHASSEUR

It's the captain!

THE SERGEANT

Damn! A lantern! Why don't you have a lantern, imbecile? *Mon capitaine!* Damn! Damn! Run and fetch a doctor, Jacquin. Run to the Place Charre... Hold his head up higher, animal.

The chasseurs lie him down on the camp bed of the battery post.

THE SERGEANT

There! Put the sack under his head. What a hole! My God, what a hole!
He isn't dead!

ESTHER

He isn't dead?

ALAUNA

No.

THE SERGEANT

We have hard heads. A hole in the head kills you, or it's nothing... *Mon capitaine!* Do you recognize me? I'm Guillaumet. He's recognized me... That has an effect on me, *oof...* Give me something to drink.

ALAUNA

He's opening his eyes.

THE SERGEANT

Good! To her now. Well, what? It's nothing, my little lady; he hasn't broken anything, he isn't spitting blood. A hole
in the head, that's nothing; I've had a good hole in the head
myself, me who is speaking, and it wasn't anything.

ALAUNA

It wasn't anything?

THE SERGEANT

No. Leave him be. Come on, come on! Don't get upset.

You'll drop her! Throw water in her face. Gently, damn
it, gently! Lay her down…lay you mantle underneath him.

Pierre, come and replace me; my arm's numb. Sit down,
like this. Hold her head on your knees, like this. Prevent the
compress from falling off, and with your other hand, moisten
it, perpetually. What a hole!

This is an affair!

They're both asleep. If they'd been asleep like that yesterday, next to one another, the disaster wouldn't have happened.

Do you know this little lady?

ESTHER

No.

THE SERGEANT

Your misfortune.

THE SENTRY

Sergeant? The doctor.

THE DOCTOR

Is he dead?

ESTHER

No.

94

HIM

Meyrin!

ESTHER

He's delirious.

HIM

Aïchouna!

THE DOCTOR

Everybody out; he needs air. My sister will suffice. His wound isn't serious.

THE SERGEANT

Get out, the rest of you. I'll stay.
Why didn't you bring the battalion doctor, Jacquin?

JACQUIN

I found this monsieur, who said: "I'm a doctor." As I had encountered Jean, coming back from duty I'd said to him, "Run and fetch the doctor," and I brought this monsieur myself.

Jean wasn't drunk, he won't waste any time.

THE SERGEANT

So much the better.

My little lady. My little lady! Corporal, one soldier on sentry duty outside the window, and the rest of you get some air outside the door, on the bench. My little lady... It seems to me, *Monsieur le docteur*, that your sister would have known, better than me, how to undo these buttons

That's better. The wound isn't serious... I undid those; perhaps I broke the button-hole.

THE DOCTOR
Don't worry, Madame, the wound isn't mortal, it isn't even very serious; but you have a fever. You'll have to be taken home; the walk will put you right.

ALAUNA
I don't want him to die. Do you hear?

THE DOCTOR
She doesn't want it!

VII

That doctor, a savant Jew, lived with his sister not far from the battery in a little house with a shady garden. The wounded man was carried there.

For two weeks, Esther and Alauna cared for him.

ALAUNA
He's calmer now, but he still doesn't recognize anyone.

THE DOCTOR
I'll answer for him. You said: "I don't want him to die." He won't die. If you always commanded, you'd always be obeyed.

It will be necessary to care for him for a long time, perhaps until the end. Would you like him to be my own son as well? We'll enable him to live very gently, and if we can't reignite the torch that is going pale, we'll at least remove the brambles and stones from his route. Would you like that?

ALAUNA
I want him to live entirely. I want that.

THE DOCTOR
She wants it!
I'll find out why he tried to kill himself.

ALAUNA

Don't say that to me.

THE DOCTOR

In order to cure the malady it's necessary to know what caused the malady.

This summer, on top of the cliff, in a white house, there were two women, two sisters.

ALAUNA

Meyrin and Aïchouna?

THE DOCTOR

Yes, and he loved them.

ALAUNA

He loved them! The potter only loves once.

THE DOCTOR

What's that?

ALAUNA

And when he came back, they said that they didn't love him anymore? They lied. They'll always love him.

THE DOCTOR

They've gone.

ALAUNA

They'll be back.

I'm tired! I'd like to sleep, but I'd like my soul to sleep with my body.

You must know a philter that puts the soul to sleep with the body.

THE DOCTOR
Yes, but when one sleeps that slumber, the body sometimes doesn't wake up again.

ALAUNA
He'll revive entirely?

THE DOCTOR
He'll live entirely. You want it.

But how do I know that you'll want to drink the philter then?

ALAUNA
I know what you want. Keep your promise and I'll keep mine. Put the soul to sleep and take the body. My body weighs me down and my soul will reawaken.

When one has seen you, one doesn't forget you; I recognized you as I recognized you on the terrace. Go on, oaths bind.

The Jewess is sitting at his bedside.
"Where have I seen her before?"
"You'll find out; but she's singing, Listen."

ESTHER
Every night the roses fade in the boscage of Jericho.

HIM
Why have you flown away, my doves?

I wanted to follow you, but my wing is broken. Will you not descend any more from the blazing sky, turtle-doves?

ESTHER
Your turtle-doves are flapping their wings in order to follow you, my handsome wood-pigeon, to the blue land of dreams, to the red land of kisses.

THE DOCTOR

Well?

ESTHER

Shut up.

HIM

I can hear wings in the blue sky. But the whitest one doesn't come...

Both of them! There they are, both of them! Oh, what a terrible dream! It can't be...but what if it must be?

If it can be, let the Master judge; the man must not lie.

Give me your hand, Aïchouna. Sit down here, Meyrin.

What do you think of that, my sweet gazelles? A cavalier one day... The fay! There's the fay!

Why, my blonde fay, have you no longer come, for such a long time? They're very beautiful, look—but I only love you.

ALAUNA

You hear, maidservants?

DEATH

I've kept my oath, will you keep yours?

ALAUNA

Whenever you wish.

HIM

What have you promised her?

ALAUNA

My body.

HIM

Your body to Aïchouna? But your body, beloved, is a drop of dew, a wisp of foam, a ray of starlight.

You want to give your body to Aïchouna? But I have already given it to her myself, and I was wrong to do it; a body is only a prison. I don't want to cage my swallow.

"Sweet gazelles, leave me; I'm one of those whom the sun blinds in the blue mountains, one of those who drink from springs devoid of water. At the breath of summer, open your vermilions, embalmed roses; the nightingale is seeking you. Forget the somber nocturnal moth whose wings have brushed you.

ALAUNA
He must live entirely.

HIM
My temples are throbbing! Where am I? Why is this linen bloody? I remember! I remember!

In the blue sky, the moon trembles like a swan's feather on a woodland pool. The buds are turning green on the boughs of the hornbeams, and clumps of primroses are opening golden eyes.

"For what are your golden eyes searching in the blue sky, flower of spring"

"I'm searching for the swallows. The one who departed with them ought to return with them. I was only a bud yesterday, but tomorrow I shall be withered; tell him that he is coming back if you see her..."

"Like the swallows with the sun, tomorrow she'll be here."

THE WREN
They'll be here tomorrow; the fays said so yesterday. Their breath has pushed the ship, gently. They will both return.

I don't know any more; they were in a hurry. They were going out there, to the funereal grotto in the land of the Orient to search for the Skylark that I don't know.

That Skylark is their queen, it appears, and she's also the sister of the one who is coming back. But that's a great secret; don't betray me.

Here they come! Here they come! Hide in the dry leaves. But you can't! Go back to the drawing room quickly; the door is open. I'll tell you everything tomorrow.

She's very beautiful, that Skylark. She isn't a fay like the chilly ones who shelter in my nest on winter nights.

Is it necessary, in order to listen to her, to hide in the foliage? I daren't.

THE SKYLARK
The grass is green, the sky is blue! Spring is sowing white daisies on my bosom.

The grass is green, the sky blue! Apple trees are snowing on my head.

THE VALKYRIES
Sow violets on the pathways, blonde druidesses, sow violets. It is the flower of husbands with red betrothals; sow pale violets in the meadow, sow them on the heath.

THE SKYLARK
Sow white roses, sow buttercups; for my soldiers the tomb is only a bed of sweet dreams. As soon as my song rises into the sky, they awake, smiling and proud. Sow roses, druidesses, for the soldiers of the Skylark.

Snow, branches of the apple tree; snow, boughs of the hawthorn; snow, snow on my hair; tomorrow I shall have a diadem of lightning and steel, which my soldiers will have forged.

THE CRICKET
On their black mares with quivering nostrils and coral hooves they are beautiful, those fays, but the one that speaks is more beautiful still. While dancing, our fays do not buckle the

grass, but that one! Sparks fly under the hooves of her mare; she is not a fay.

Since the first suns I have deafened everyone. This one calls herself the Skylark, but she is the queen of whom people speak in evenings by the fireside. She is the queen of the Sunset, whom the Roman walled up with her soldier and her bard, in a marble prison, under the steps of her palace.

THE SKYLARK

The grass is green, the sky is blue! The sun has crumbled its golden radiance over my eyelashes, and the sylph of spring has burned the sweet incense of forests on my lips.

For the husband to come she has ornamented the bride,

Snow, branches of the apple tree, snow, boughs of the hawthorn snow, snow on my hair; the Awaited is awake and I want to be beautiful.

The grass is green, the sky is blue! Sing, sing, poet; I am the virgin with the azure eyes, the virgin with the fresh lips. I am the queen of the Sunset.

THE NIGHTINGALE

From the land where the jasmine and the lemon tree enlace; from the land where the blue pigeons call to one another on the date palms; from the land of evenings without lightning, mornings without mist and middays with clouds, I have arrived in order to love and sing.

I am the queen's bard, with laughter as soft as a dream and a gaze as tender as a kiss.

THE WREN

What you're singing to the skylark you sang yesterday to the panther.

Queen of the Sunset you summoned a bard; here I am. Would you like me to sing what the bush says when the frost changes into diamonds; what the rock says when December gives it a mantle of sapphires; what the meadow says when April strews rubies and pears on its glaucous leaves?

THE SKYLARK

My bard has a thousand voices, my harp a thousand strings.

Sing the spring, nightingale; sing the winter, wren. Sing also in the sky where you soar, hawk; can you not see from on high the cannons that are being harnessed?

Sing, sing, my bards; in the night of the tomb my crimson robe has paled, but the blood of my sons is red and tomorrow I shall have a queen's robe.

Sing, bards, sing; I need the crimson. Sing, nightingale, wren, sing. Sing, harp with a thousand strings; the grass grows greener where blood had flowed.

THE WREN

Cannons are being harnessed? Sabers are going to shine; clarions are going to sound gaily in the vineyards...I too want to depart with your soldiers... You're laughing? Why are you laughing, Fayolles? My friend will be there tomorrow... He's here. It's Alauna who is climbing the path bordered with box.

ALAUNA

O you who loved me when I was a druidess, show me the herb that soothes; tell me the word that heals.

In the whitening sky the pale moon is trembling. The nightingale is singing in the lilacs; the wren is running gaily in the green moss; the primrose is inclined over its leaves silvered by dew.

At a slow pace, he marches in the broad pathway. Fever gleams in his eyes; breathless and halting, words fall from his lips.

HIM

Nothing has changed. I planted these narcissi. It's me who dug this little ditch, where water cannot flow. This apple tree that I trimmed as one trims lindens is cured of its wounds. Nothing has changed.

But I have changed, myself. I stumble over a grain of sand, and the daylight dazzles me. I've been too far; I'm weary.

Where have I been? I no longer know. Why is the daylight wounding my eyes? I don't know. Tell me, great service tree; tell me, green laburnum; tell me, friends; I never forgot you.

No, don't tell me. I don't want to know; I'm too tired. I'm still the wild tercel, the lazy lizard; as you talked to me then, talk to me today.'

Old faun garlanded with ivy, when I told you takes, you smiled. What naughty sprite has broken one of your ears? The naughty sprites have cleaved my forehead, old friend; it will be necessary to remind me of the tales that I have forgotten.

In this mud the heather is dead. The serpents of its coves have killed it. On my forehead too the serpents have killed the heather, and now, where the bees collected pollen, the wind raises clouds of dust, black clouds.

But the snakes in the canal have no venom; but the naughty sprites don't haunt this flower-garden; the fay has expelled them, and tomorrow, as of old, I shall laugh; as before, old faun, I shall tell you tales.

I lost myself in the desert out there. The sirens of the sands, those who sing in the evenings and gnaw cadavers by night, had drawn me far from the road. I was about to die of thirst; the sun had already burned me lips and made my forehead burst; but yesterday the fay came; she laid me down on her scarf, and today, here I am on very green grass, in very cool shade.

I had not forgotten her, the tender friend of old, and if I am not already on the edge of the basin, it's because my feet are too bruised and my legs tremulous.

I'm going slowly now, and then, having searched for such a long time, I'm sure of finding her here, I'm so thirsty that, like a gourmet, I shall drink my joy drop by drop.

When I have gone around these bushes I shall see her.

In the old hornbeam arbor, in front of the Valkyries, in the midst of the fays, on the while mare, how beautiful she is, the queen with the broad brow! The Skylark of the Gauls, how beautiful she is!

The Orient is already reddening. Alauna is climbing the path bordered with box

ALAUNA
Show me the herb that soothes; tell me the word that heals.

THE SKYLARK
Salut, Sister.

ALAUNA
The Skylark!

THE SKYLARK
Over the field that he has sown, I have sung, my sister; but the crows have come, and they have eaten your wheat before it germinated.

Everything has to be done again.

Tell the sower to get ready, and the laborer to harness his oxen. Tell the sower to get ready; in the plains on high the ears are heavy, his basket will be full.

Tell the sower to hasten; proud bulls will pull the plow.

ALAUNA
Sister, you don't know, then...

THE SKYLARK
I know that the hour is imminent. I know that the sword of Ar-Braz is bright in its scabbard. I know that the great dead will be reborn tomorrow. I know that the clay is ready for the potter.

Listen, those who, lacking a guide, have gone astray; those who, lacking leaders, have been vanquished.

They are calling! They are calling!

You're weeping? Your breasts are bleeding? Come, my lips will dry your tears, my hands will close your open breasts.

Come, I have a fresh garland of gladioli and periwinkles; we will go into the reeds, under the willows, under the aspens, to listen to what the water is saying to the caressant branches.

Come; in the shadow of the rock, between the blasted oak and the flowering hawthorn. I will sing you the beautiful verses of the past, and your tears will dry up, and the blood will no longer flow from your open breasts.

Daughter of the light, you who know the secret, tomorrow I shall wait for you. In order to hope, it is necessary to believe, and my sons are weeping; listen.

Let the sower hasten, proud bulls will pull the plow.

THE FAYS

We were druidesses when the woods talked, we are Fayolles among the baptized; but tomorrow, at sword-point, we shall shine as sparks.

Oh mistletoe! Oh, mistletoe, the cup is full! Oh, mistletoe, the iron is forged! For tomorrow let us sow violets, roses and cornflowers

Tomorrow we shall wait for you, druidess. Tomorrow, the potter's chisel, in order to name gods, will only have to put a word on the tomb of our soldiers.

The sun is rising. With the last pleats of the veil trimmed with pearls, which the lazy night leaves to be torn apart on the poles of the vines, the blond swarm vanishes and the black mares fly away.

But the Skylark is not a Valkyrie, and is not a Fayolle. She is not a spark escaped before time from the great hearth; she is not a druidess waiting, in the green star, for Alauna the queen of the Ganges to be ready to rise again; she is a woman, the Skylark. She is a woman, whose heart is large enough to hide all our amours, whose brow is high enough to shelter all our dreams, whose hand is gentle enough to bandage all our wounds.

On her bosom, Alauna is weeping; but she is smiling as she caresses the poor frightened gazelle.

THE SKYLARK

He only loves you, he has never loved anyone but you. When, on the bank of the Ebro, struck by a spear one victorious evening, he saw death approaching, he took my hand and he said: "You are my sister and my mother, Skylark. Ar-Braz is like me, a son of the Celt, and I have become Gaulish. Your men will be the blade of the sword of which I am the hand-guard.

"Sister, you will aid me. Mother, you will advise me. I wanted to brave a law that I knew to be just. Punishment awaits me… I divine it. I no longer recognized what I wanted to render imperishable, neither on high nor, perhaps, thereafter.

"But when the sin is expiated I shall become again the Master's workman, the companion of Ar-Braz, your soldier, your bard or your priest. Then I shall be able to recognize her, but perhaps it will be necessary for me to search for her for a long time. Will you aid me, Sister? Will you guide me, Mother?"

I promised to aid him, and he died, confident.

Today, Ar-Braz is waiting for his companion, and I am waiting for my bard. He will keep his promise and I will keep mine.

ALAUNA

Oh, come!

THE SKYLARK

He will recognize you; he loves you. Listen.

HIM

When I have gone around these bushes I shall see her; but I'm going slowly. Like a gourmet, I am drinking my joy drop by drop.

Bonjour, wren. Do you have pretty chicks this year? You can show them to me, you know; I won't touch them, and I always have fine wisps of wool in my pocket for making curtains.

ALAUNA

Oaths bind, maidservant; render him to me entirely. You have sworn it.

THE SKYLARK

To whom are you speaking, druidess? Tell me, Sister.

ALAUNA

I'm speaking to the Enemy... Here he comes. I'm afraid!

HIM

She's no longer here!

She's no longer here, and it's finished. The earth is cold, life is stupid; let's go look elsewhere.

ALAUNA

Oh, my sister! My sister!

HIM

Don't be afraid, cricket; I won't trample your grass. Don't look at me like that, lovely salamander; I won't soil the water of your basin. I'm simply going to lie down in the shade of the linden, go to sleep, and never wake up.

Death has no need to sharpen her scythe; I'm only alive because I didn't want to die before seeing her again.

ALAUNA

He only loves me.

THE SKYLARK
He's no longer my bard; wake him up, Master.

HIM
She's quit me, like the others. With the broken thread I'll no longer be able to make a knot, and the captive will fly away.

How pleasant it is on this moss! Can one imagine a better bed? That busy cricket is my nurse; that salamander shaking its head is the doctor, who is saying: "Another one less! Another one more!"

ALAUNA
You swore, maidservant!

HIM
And the warbler that has alighted there, what does she want? Is it the forgotten prayer that you're singing, warbler? Sing, only my lips have forgotten.

What you say is true, warbler. What you believe, I believe. Before the fire of woodchips, in his wooden armchair, when Grandfather sat down, he put his hand on my head and he said: "Kneel down, child, and say your prayer."

Master, on your path, instead of marching I have slept; I do not merit a salary. But your bounty is infinite; to the tercel you will leave a azure corner your blue sky; you will warm up the lizard with a ray of your glory.

Master, I have done nothing. I have allowed the grain you have sown to be eaten by the birds; but Grandfather was a robust workman, permit him to share his sheaf with me. Master, instead of marching, I have slept, I do not merit a salary, but if you put an implement in my hand again, what I have not done, I will do.

THE SKYLARK

Snow, branches of the apple tree, snows, boughs of the hawthorn; my inspired bard will sing my youth, will sing my beauty.

Alauna is speaking to him.

ALAUNA
Enlaced, like the bindweed that hangs from the maples, we glided by night over silvery meadows, we drank the dew from the lips of periwinkles.

HIM
It's her! Sing, cricket, I'm loved!

ALAUNA
We went along sunken paths, hand in hand, and the campanulas rang joyously, and the honeysuckle opened its cassolettes, and the nightingales in the eglantine bushes saluted the chief and the druidess.

HIM
She's in the hornbeam arbor, but if I go there she might run away...
Let's try to respond to her.
We flew through the forest, hand in hand, and the birches said to the oaks: "Wake up! Wake up!" We were two sunbeams, to breaths of wind, and now...

ALAUNA
I'm a woman and I love you.

HIM
It's her! It's really her!
No, you aren't a woman, you're my fay, my beautiful fay. I'm only a wild tercel, a lazy lizard; a woman can't love me, only a fay can love me.

THE SKYLARK

Sing of the blue sword that loves the flesh! Sing of the blue sword!

O sword! O great king of the battlefield! O sword! O great king!

HIM

A head for an eye, an arm for a finger and a heart for a wound!

Once I sang that... Did I sing it? Did you teach it to me? Respond, my beautiful fay!

ALAUNA

It's the song of Ar-Braz; have you forgotten it?

HIM

Ar-Braz? I remember… and there's the skylark.

I remember. I was a chief with bloody hands; but today I'm only a wild tercel, a lazy lizard. Only a fay can love me.

THE SKYLARK

Salut, Brother.

HIM

But a woman can love the brother of the skylark...

I remember! I remember! Druidess, I have marched without stopping; we have pushed far beyond the furrow...

But it isn't clay that I have modeled. In this beautiful body that is leaning over me, I don't recognize the body that I kneaded in white clay on the edge of the stream when my cavaliers mingled with those of Ar-Braz, waiting in the plain.

And yet, those are the eyes that smiled at me on the mountain, that is the hand that showed me the path of the Pierre-Grosse.

The veil is tearing! O Master, you love him then, your workman? Like a father, who joins in with his son's games, smiling, with your powerful hand you have rounded out the heap of sand with which I had made my plaything.

No, you have done better; you are the Almighty, but also the Good. In order to chastise your proud son you broke his toy; but when you saw that he was weeping, you left him that of which he did not dare to dream.

This body, which was no longer yours, he has rendered to you, druidess; give it to me.

The veil is tearing! The living past is reborn! You are the queen of the Ganges and I am the potter.

ALAUNA
I will always love you.

HIM
Our eternal love will see worlds crumble... My beloved! My beloved, what's wrong?

ALAUNA
She has kept her oath... I'm keeping mine... I'm dying.

PART TWO: THE ONE WHO IS TO COME

Why bring me back to the garden of the old château? The château no longer has a master, the flower-garden no longer has a gardener.

In thirty years, how many trees fall, and how men change!

In the brambles of the path, the mossy sphinxes lie. The snows of winters and the sun of summers has blackened the face of the statue; the fays no longer pass through the big hornbeam; the wren is dead; why bring me back to the garden, from which the beloved souls have departed?

In thirty years, how many trees fall, and how men change! The man who called himself the potter the grave-diggers have carried away like the others, and thirty years have effaced the named on his grave,

Why bring me back to this garden? Would you like to re-read the tale of the statue in the shade of the linden? You'd be wrong; the frame that pleased us at twenty, because we were filled with our hopes and our dreams, can no longer please us today. It was only gilded; time has tarnished it. It had no back-cloth to sustain to nor a spike to support it; a gust of wind caused it to fall, and if we touched it, it would fall to pieces in our hands.

In this château without a master, in this flower-garden without a gardener, there is a poet, and I would like to hear a poet sing.

Reality is so sad that I would like, for an hour, to allow myself to be cradled by the impossible.

Come into the hornbeam arbor. Perhaps we shall encounter him on the wooden bench; he loves it.

He loves the wallflower of these ruins, the wild flower that the creator has made beautiful, that poverty has made proud and solitude has made gentle.

It is a strange château! It is a strange garden! One does not live there as one lives elsewhere; one sees there what one does not see elsewhere.

When the gravediggers had carried the captain away thirty years ago, the testament of the dead man was found on the drawing room table. That testament said: "Lock the gate, break the key. The two female strangers who will come and open the gate are those to whom I give this château and its garden."

Five years later, two female strangers came; they were both beautiful, and each of them was nursing a child.

Those children, when they grew up, loved one another. Today they are married. The woman is going to be a mother and the man is the poet that I would like to encounter.

Where the wooden bench was I do not see the poet, but I see a woman. Is that the flower of the ruins?

She is beautiful. She is very beautiful!

Her hair is as blonde as ripe wheat; her eyes are as blue as the sky after a storm; her lips are as red as the swords of old.

If savant philosophers had not shown me the naked truth. I would say: "That is not a woman, she is more than a woman."

We are living, friend, in unhappy times.

"We're looking for the poet who knows how to sing and the woman who knows how to love. Are you the woman we're looking for?"

THE SKYLARK
I'm not the woman you're looking for. I'm the skylark.

Ideas can live, souls can acquire a body; were the philosophers mistaken, then?

THE SKYLARK

For those who are mistaken heaven brings a ray of light, but for those who have lied...

Why are you marching head bowed? You seem sad and mute; why?

We are weary.

If you are really the Skylark, we are glad to encounter you. They said that they had crushed you in the plains of the East, under the iron shoes of their horses.

You really are the Skylark that sang when we were twenty; we recognize your voice.

They have burned your nest.

If the blood were still seething in our veins we would harness the plow and we would go, under a blue sky, far from the accursed, to cultivate a field for you; but we are weary.

THE SKYLARK

You wanted to fathom the bloody cloud of the evening; that is why you are sad and mute. Laugh, my sons; the somber clouds of stormy evenings are only a light mist, which the first star whitens and the first breath of wind carries away.

When the stars light up, when the wind has risen, we have only seen the abyss, the empty abyss. That is why we go about sad and mute.

THE SKYLARK

Lean over that bottomless gulf, my sons, and you will see infinity therein. Lean over that azure gulf without dread; soft voices are singing forgotten poems there, the poems that enable belief, that enable hope.

I have seen the heavy cavaliers coming from the East and my eyes are full of tears. The tears were so large that they were able to fall. Since that time, I can scarcely see my path, and you want me to look so far and so high.

The time has come, Skylark; like individuals, peoples are born, grow old and die. Gaul is dead.

Don't try to evoke the phantoms of the past with your songs; the sword that you would draw would fall back on us. We no longer have anything but the peace of the tomb; don't take it away.

Return to the green stars, Skylark; your soldiers are dead.

To the everyday task we return; it was to forget and not to weep that we came here to search for a poet. Your song is sweet but it is sad; if you are the muse of the unknown poet, take him with you to the green star. Today, when thinkers make us weep, it is necessary that dreamers make us laugh.

We are living, you see, in unhappy times.

THE SKYLARK
It is for the good of men that the Master has created eternal combat.

In order to fight, soldiers are necessary, and we no longer have any; the victor takes all our sons and mingles them with his own in the four corners of the empire.

You would like us to attempt, today, what we were unable to prevent when we had orders. We are unhappy people; but we are sane people; to launch ourselves into that adventure would be folly.

Yes, it would be folly.

But perhaps it is also you who pushes this dreamer, the daughter of a peasant woman, of whom we would like to make a scholar, and whose name is André.

If you were his inspirer, you were wrong. He slips into our workshops and into our schools; he only says foolish things, and if, by misfortune, the children believe him, blood will be shed and that blood will fall back on you.

We repeat, Skylark, that we no longer have any peace except that of the tomb; don't take it away. Go back up, in order not to descend again, to the green star. We would have liked to live in better times.

Above all, don't forget that your soldiers are dead.

THE SKYLARK

Pick white roses, pick buttercups; for my soldiers the tomb is only a bed of pleasant dreams! As soon as my song rises into the sky they wake up, smiling and proud.

They are not dead, my soldiers!

Pick roses, druidesses, pick buttercups, fays, for the soldiers of the Skylark. Snow, branches of the apple tree; snow, boughs of the hawthorn; snow, snow on my hair; tomorrow I shall have a diadem of lightning and steel, which my soldiers will have forged.

And you, my bard, awake!

My harp has a thousand strings; sing like the nightingale, twitter like the wren, cry like the hawk, they will all understand you; my sons have large hearts, red blood and strong arms.

On my head the apple trees are snowing; sing, bard of the Gaels, my eternal youth, my eternal beauty.

I am the queen of the sunset; sing, sing, poet. Tomorrow I shall have a diadem of lightning and steel, which my soldiers will have forged.

Sing, my bard, support on your arm the one whom you love; the sin is expiated.

Snow, branches of the apple tree, snow, boughs of the hawthorn; it will be beautiful, the poem that the queen of the Ganges and the great potter will sing between two kisses.

THE NURSES
We have already lifted before him the veil of the past;
would you like us to tear it?

THE SKYLARK
Who are you? I don't recognize you; you're not mine.

THE NURSES
We're the nurses of your bard.

We have struggled against your son for a long time, Skylark. We are those who were worshiped in the temple on the
bank of the Ganges, under the granite flanks of the pink
sphinxes, in the grottoes of Elora.

THE SKYLARK
Beware, maidservants.

THE NURSES
We are still his maidservants; he still loves and oaths
bind. But today, we are also his friends and his nurses.

When his body fell here, near the basin, under the lindens, we followed his soul all the way to the green star where
the druidess was waiting for him. There, he said to us: "You
are free, Aïchouna; Meyrin, you are free. I would have loved
you if I had not loved my fiancée. If you want to be my sisters,
how I would love you!

"I am the voice of the one who thinks, you are the voice
of the one who lives together, let us sing the glory of the eternal Creator. Everything is beautiful in his work, bodies as well
as souls."

We hesitated, and he said to us: "You are the living matter, I am the immortal spirit; but within your bodies, souls are
dormant, and my soul, a body obeys; between our two domains, instead of hollowing out an abyss, let us break down
the barriers, and the one who lives will think better and the
one who thinks will live better.

"Nature, your laws are holy; none of us wants to contest them, none of us wants to try to elude them.

"We live like the oaks; we ought to love and die like oaks. But what oaks do not yet have, we have; our immortal soul is one.

"Our bodies are yours, take them. Make oaks or roses of them. The oak will be tall, the roses embalmed; our souls leave something in the bodies they have animated.

"But our immortal soul is one; don't try to break it, in order to mingle it with the immense soul that ferments in the snow and boils in the Ocean."

And he returned the cup to us, and he returned the scythe, saying to us: "Strike without respite; the body is a shackle that, every time it is broken, is resoldered more loosely," and saying to us: "Pour without respite your intoxicating poisons, they will not burn our lips and our bright-eyed companions have large wombs and strong arms."

We believed him, and the oaks will grow taller and the perfume of the roses will be sweeter.

We are yours, Skylark; in their strength, your sons will fall, and when your daughters fall asleep, like ripe ears of wheat, they will leave behind them baskets full of blond grain.

THE SKYLARK

The Master has kept his promise to the daughter of the foam; amour is no longer a brutal intoxication, death has no more terrors.

Sing, sacred oaks! Sing, mossy stones! The promised day is dawning.

The reveille is sounding; get up, soldiers!

The grass is green; the sky is blue; in the field the ears of wheat are ripe. Sing, crickets, sing, cicadas; in the field, the ears of wheat are ripe.

Look, how beautiful my field is! The furrows with sharp ridges, very straight and very even, extend across mountains and plains. It was a good laborer who held the plow; his plowshare was well-tempered, and the bulls he guided were proud bulls.

Look, how beautiful my field is! How well it is sown! Look. Like a flock of sparrows, the seeds rise from the basket when the sower raises his hand. Like hail they bound when his hand plunges back into the full basket. He was a good sower, believe me. And the grain was healthy; look. Look at the gilded plain.

But the wheat is ripe; my two men want to bind the sheaves,

Look at the wheat falling under their heavy sickles.

The Master has given me two robust workers there. Sing, crickets, sing, cicadas, in the field the ears of wheat are ripe.

All three of them have turned toward the clump of lilacs. Will the veil of the past be ripped before the poet's eyes?

On the wooden bench of the big hornbeam, his hand on the shoulder of his beloved, he rereads the tale of the statue.

THE POET
There was a white lotus cried by two dolphins...

BLANCHE
He will not have been so well cradled.

THE POET
Why?

BLANCHE
You, friend, could sing like the potter of whom there is mention in that book, but I could not be the queen of the Ganges. All my estate would fit into the hall sanded with silver, and my maidservant wears clogs.

If you want a fine cradle it's necessary to ask the blackbird or the wren. In exchange for a song, they might make us a nest for the one that, like their chicks, will have nothing but a green branch on which to sleep and the vast sky to sustain his wings.

THE POET
What if you were the queen of the Ganges and I were the potter?

You are as beautiful as the one for whom the tigers weep out there in the ruins of her palace, and the most vibrant of poems does not rise as high in the heavens as the sound of a kiss; our life makes the dream pale. May your name be blessed, Master!

BLANCHE
And why should you not do for me what the potter did for the queen?

I want a poem.

THE POET
Yes, I shall say: I love you. There, the poem is done. On your lashes, my lips have drunk a tear; what's the matter?

BLANCHE
When he comes, it's not in French that his name will be written.

Ar-Braz, Ar-Braz, where are you?

ANDRÉ
We're searching for him, friends, and we'll find him.

Blanche, it's necessary that the name of our son be written in French. It's necessary that the west wind carries away the red-haired barbarians with the dry leaves.

THE POET
You come when she calls, Ar-Braz! Will you be the one for whom she calls?

ANDRÉ

Ar-Braz was a soldier and I'm only a dreamer; but sing, I'll speak, and the one who is to come will hear us.

I believe that the hour is imminent.

When he comes, it's necessary that everyone will recognize him, while, in the shadow, I murmur his name, sing his legend in the sunlight...

The wheat is cut, the grape-clusters are reddening; André has not yet returned, and while his beloved dreams of the angel with the blue eyes, the poet writes the poem of Ar-Braz.

THE POEM OF AR-BRAZ

It is for the good of man that the Master has created eternal combat.

(*The Mysteries of the Bards.*)

I

The star is illuminating; look! The wind is quivering; listen!

Look into the azure where the dreams of the past are gliding; the blonde fays are whirling, crowned with vervain. They are singing the forgotten poem as they twirl; listen.

THE FAYS

Blue water is melting from the snow; the oak is putting on leaves, the hawthorn is flowering, the sun of the first days is shining over the peak.

The sun is shining over the peak; its darts, piercing the dense foliage, fall into the flowing water, and beneath their golden points the foam becomes roseate.

The foam becomes roseate, and then rises, like a light smoke, into the cloudless sky.

In the cloudless sky, the sun's rays touch the pink vapor, and that vapor becomes a woman.

Neither flowers nor women; nor bodies nor souls, we are only the voice of the oaks, the mist of springs and the perfume of furze; but we see the future and we have seen the past.

In the splendor of the first day, we saw the foam of the sacred spring change into a body of alabaster. Then we saw a spark spring from the divine hearth and slide between the pink lips, and the beautiful body was animated. Our queen was born.

We saw her first smile, we heard her first song. Her song was so sweet that the rapturous stars stopped in their luminous circles.

Then, the voice to which the echo dared not reply said: "You shall be the skylark of the furrows of the sky. Soul with powerful wings, daughter of my smile, I give you to guard the race that is slumbering under the bark of the oak, the race that will be born, the chosen race."

And the divine Skylark, the soul with the great wings, touched the trunk of the oak, and the trunk split. Then she touched the hawthorn, and the flower bloomed.

That is how the Celt was born of the trunk of an oak. That is how his companion was born of a flowering hawthorn.

When the moon rises we dance!
Fortunate are those who listen to us, who know us.

Fleur-d'Épine had three sons, and then the long-haired Ar-Braz.

Amid his brothers, Ar-Braz was like a gladiolus in the midst of rushes, like an ash tree in the midst of willows. He loved the wide plains, the somber forests and the florid peaks.

He was a horseman. All day long he wandered, following his shadow over the sand.

One evening, he saw a beautiful young woman on the hill. "Would you like to love me?" he said to her. "I will always love you."

"Always?" replied the virgin. "Autumn withers the grass, winter blanches it."

"From the melting snow the grass emerges greener. Woman, I am one of those whom death takes only to rejuvenate them; you will always be beautiful, you will always be young, and I will always love you."

The virgin sat on the rump of the white stallion, and Ar-Braz only stopped in front of the tent of the Celt.

"O my son," said the old man, that is not a woman; look—behind her brow a star is shining. Look, she is not a woman; she is the Skylark."

"I will always love her."

"Always!" replied the immortal soul, disappearing into the crimson clouds of the setting sum.

When the moon rises we dance under the oak, over the heath we glide; but when dawn awakes, like a swarm of bees, a breath cries us away to the lands of the Orient.

The old man is lying under the funerary grotto; beside him sleep his three sons. Ar-Braz had followed the star and he had not returned. Around the ancestors the tombs accumulated and the tents became crowded.

Under a sky always blue, the Master had given to his preferred sons a cradle flowery with irises and vervain.

On the thick grass, like a necklace of pearls, the woolen tents shone; like a river of milk, the white tents descended all the way to the limpid river.

Great russet oaks guarded the gleaming heifers and the slender mares with dappled rumps, while the children, on playful colts, led sheep to pasture in the shady valleys.

The horsemen hunted on the snowy peaks and the women spun.

But around the funerary grotto the tombs accumulate and the tents are crowded; the plain is too narrow.

The plain is too narrow, the flocks have no more grass; the three families will quit the valley of the tombs.

All three will depart; the valley of the tombs will remain the domain of Ar-Braz, the one who had followed the star and had not returned.

The druids throw white sticks on a black cloak. The druidesses pick the sacred herb. Fate is about to speak.

Fate has spoken; for ten weeks, and then for ten further weeks, each tribe will follow its route. The shepherds will go Southwards, the pastors Eastwards and the horsemen Westwards.

They have poured milk over the Father's tomb. They have planted three menhirs. Without looking behind them, they have each followed their route.

If they had looked behind them, they would have seen Ar-Braz and his bride on the tomb of the father, and light forms. They would have seen the fays, neither bodies nor souls, neither flowers nor women: rays of starlight, pearls of the night.

On the green mound of the mute plain, hand in hand with the virgin with the broad brow, the soldier of the Gaels went to sleep smiling, in order to awaken stronger.

They have marched, the sons of the Purs, for ten weeks, and then for ten further weeks, and the sheep stop on the edge of a spring shaded by three huge trees with leaves of reeds, and the cows lie down beside a river without a source, and the horses caper before a pale gulf.

And who have we followed, ourselves? We have followed our queen all the way to the waves of the pale gulf; Ar-Braz was a horseman.

Like dead leaves, a gust of wind carries us away, but we know the future and we have seen the past; the divine Skylark will always sing, over the furrows of the horsemen.

On the beach, silvered by thee kisses of the ea, the horses have grass, but the waves bar the route. What to do?

The druids cast the white sticks on the black cloak. "March!" reply the willow branches, crossing one another.

The waves bar the route. Who will guide the travelers?

The druidess immolates the most beautiful of the foals. In the fuming heart, nothing is written; bleakly, the crowd draws away from the extinct pyre.

But when the sun rises, in a cradle of algae, in the still-warm skies, the druidess finds a child with blue-green eyes.

Neither flowers nor women! What will we be tomorrow?

Today we guide, all the way to the green star, the ardent soul of the poet and the red soul of the soldier. We are the voices of the mute mouths, the voices of the springs, the voices of the rocks, the flowery heaths, the forests and the grass.

In the shadow of the menhirs the child has grown; he is the most handsome and the strongest, and under his clear gaze the virgins blush.

Why do you not choose one, son of the algae? Their arms are softer than the wings of gulls, their lips are fresher than he foam of the waves.

He does not look at the blonde young women; he looks further. Above the pale waves he gazes; he seeks in the mist for the road to the west.

When the old men speak he falls silent, and yet the old men have said to him: "Your voice reminds us of the voice of those who sleep in the valley of the tombs.

One evening he sees a luminous road over the sea, and on that road a woman.

Are we the dreams of a sleeping world? Are we the seeds of a star yet to be born?

Can you see the son of the algae, hand in hand with the virgin with the broad brow? He speaks, and the old men fall silent; he speaks, and the carts move off; he speaks, and the men mount up.

"Let's go!" says the virgin. "Let's go"!" cries the crowd. And the proud horsemen launch their horses into the foam.

Behind the horsemen, the heavy carts move off; the water does not reach the breasts of the horses and does not reach the axles of the carts.

Well in front of the horsemen, on a white stallion, Ar-Braz and his fiancée trace the route through the waves. The sea is crossed, and the Celts sing: "O sword! O great king of the battlefield! O sword! O great king!"

Neither flowers nor women, neither bodies not souls; without amour or tears; perhaps we would like to love like women and die like flowers.

The forests are opened, the mountains crossed. Without allowing themselves to be barred by anything, like a river of milk, from dawn to dusk, the proud squadron marches.

The forests are opened, the mountains crossed, at their feet the Loire shines. "There is my field!" said the Skylark. And Ar-Braz stopped.

Over the fuming swords, when the veins are empty, we soar, and our pale mares carry souls away to the eternal feast.

Flowers or women, bodies or souls, what will we be tomorrow?

ANDRÉ

For whom, friend, are you writing this poem? If you are writing it for scholars, you will prove nothing; if you are writing it for the ignorant, you will teach nothing.

You are the great potter, the bard with the sonorous voice, the sketcher of gods, the carver of granite; you must convince and not charm, and your roses must flourish at the point of swords.

Break the harp and take up the clarion. Let your phrases whistle like bullets and ring like horseshoes. They are asleep; wake them.

THE POET

I'll try; but I'm not who you think I am. If I have already lived in an old château, when a soul animated the marble woman that the moss is now corroding, I was only the curious and loquacious wren. I do not know what he knew.

But why do you want me to be the person of whom that book speaks?

That story, in any case, is only a tale; the author agrees with that.

ANDRÉ

When a remedy is too bitter, the medicine rolls it in a little sugar. The sugar deceives the palate, but it remains on the tongue and only the remedy slides, unsuspected, from the feeble heart to the sick brain.

It is necessary to say to those who no longer want to believe, who no longer want to love, who no longer want to hope: 'Believe as our forefathers did, love for eternity, and die with a smile on your lips.' Instead of putting these truths in a sermon, they have been put into a tale. The bitter remedy has been rolled in a little sugar.

This book has been made to prepare your coming, because you are the one who must announce Ar-Braz.

Sing, as you sang while carving the great gods of Elora.

THE POET

Since I am not saying what must be said, dictate, friend, and I shall write.

ANDRÉ

Since I left you, I have marched a long way, and in the harvested fields I have collected many ears of wheat; it is up to you to make a sheaf of them.

Come, time is pressing; the bloodhounds that are chasing me have a good sense of smell; they will be here tomorrow...

How good that jasmine smells! When I wander in the fields alone, when I knock on doors in the shadow, when I flee, when I hide, sometimes I think I smelled its sweet perfume and I think of you. I think that, hand in hand, leaning on the window-sill in the large drawing room, you are watching the star rise over the big hornbeam, listening to the nightingale sing in the lilacs.

Fortunate are those who love; amour illuminates their route. Before me, everything is dark...

And you, sphinxes, where are your souls? Oh, if I had your cup and your sickle!

It's necessary that they die, the accursed! Come, we need Ar-Braz; summon him!

THE POET

I am not the one who hid poems under the granite brows of the gods of Elora. A poor child picked up under the furze of a sunken path, I only know how to repeat the vague songs that cradled me.

ANDRÉ

You are the promised bard, the bard of France, the one who will sing all her glories, who will mourn all her dolors.

You are the one who will say: forget your passions and your hatreds, your memories and your dreams; love one another, in order that our France, strong and free, will resume her place in the sun.

Tear up all the flags that divide us, chase away all the dreams that lull us, efface all the words that intoxicate us. Give our flag the color of hope; instead of living for the moment, let us live for eternity, and cry: "Vive la France!" on days of intoxication or danger.

That is no longer weeping on a harp, it is crying in a clarion, and if I were a poet, that is how I would speak.

The clover is in flower, the vine-stocks are verdant, and while the beloved is rocking the angel with the blue eyes, André is dictating to the poet the poem of Ar-Braz.

THE POEM OF AR-BRAZ

II

The forests have been opened, the mountains crossed. At their feet the Loire shines and, the skylark having said: "There is my field!" Ar-Braz has stopped.

AR-BRAZ
Horsemen, here is the autumn, and I have said: "The mist will rust their swords in the scabbards, the smoke of the hearth will redden the eyes of their wives, the north wind will dry up the milk of their mares; let us take them, this winter to the lands of summer.

Have I spoken well?

THE HORSEMEN
Let's depart!

AR-BRAZ
I have also said: the daughters of the sun love everything that shines—vermilion wounds as well as gold necklaces—let us take those young women to sword-dances, let us give the fiancés gold for their lovers.

Have I spoken well?

130

THE YOUNG WOMEN

Let's depart!

AR-BRAZ

I have also said: the nightingale has taught my bards all his songs, the grotto has confided all its secrets to them, the cascade has emptied its entire jewel-case for them; let us take them to hear the great mistress, the charmer with the red lips.

Have I spoken well?

THE BARDS

Let's depart!

AR-BRAZ

I have also said: death is the door that opens to life; let us go knock on the door.

Have I spoken well?

THE DRUIDS

Let's depart.

THE SKYLARK

The hive is full; let a swarm emerge!

THE PEOPLE

Let's depart!

THE SKYLARK

No; when hawks depart, crows arrive!

On the shores of the pale gulf, on the banks of the Loire, a hundred people have engraved their names on your breasts, my old companions; but your sons have only felt the weight of the bear's claws again; they are jealous.

Give me those children; I will bring them back to you as men.

THE MOTHERS
Take them!

THE HORSEMEN
Whence comes that stranger? What does he want?

THE STRANGER
I come from the land irrigated by the sourceless river.

AR-BRAZ
In the valley of the tombs the Purs were separated; while our horses marched westwards, you drive your cattle toward the East.

Why, Brother, have you quit the river of the blue lotuses for the land of oaks?

THE STRANGER
Because on the bank of the river a voice said to me: "Seek in the west my laborer, and in the furrow sow my grain.

AR-BRAZ
Are you a druid?

THE STRANGER
I'm a fisherman; but in my bark canoe I love to sing the poems that sleep under the granite brows of the gods of Elora.

The voice spoke and I departed. On emerging from the reeds I found, on this horse, a virgin as beautiful as Cita, the princess with the golden eyes. The virgin said to me: "Mount up before me, you are the sower. I am the one who will winnow the grain."

And I marched, and here I am, and the virgin is waiting for your daughters on the rock up there.

I quit her because I love her.

THE SKYLARK

Salut, Brother; I was expecting you. I am also awaiting the harvester, if the Master does not want the one who has held the plow also to hold the sickle.

But do you want us to take the furrow further forward? My sons have strong arms, and blood flows in their veins.

THE STRANGER

If you wish, let's depart; the Master knows he limits of his field. Where the plow ought to stop, the oxen will lie down of their own accord.

AR-BRAZ

And the druidess?

THE STRANGER

While awaiting the spring, she will sort the divine seed.

THE SKYLARK

You are certainly the bard I was expecting. Let's depart.

AR-BRAZ

I said to myself: The sand of the beach is gentle to the feet of horses; let us follow the Ocean that only has one shore, let us follow it as far as the summer land.

Have I spoken well?

THE STRANGER

Let's depart.

The horses are bridled, let's depart; we are those whom nothing stops, we are the proud voyagers, and our route is long. Let us depart; our route climbs all the way to the stars on high.

The horses are bridled

BLANCHE

What do you want, Monsieur?

THE OFFICER

I'm looking for a man named André. My soldiers are there.

ANDRÉ

I'm André.

THE OFFICER

Are you certain of that?

ANDRÉ

What?

THE OFFICER

If you're not the man we're looking for, we'll look elsewhere.

Be quiet; the windows are open and my soldiers are listening.

This André is a man who believes he can do, alone, what all the others together have not been able to do. He's a man who forgets what is and speaks too loudly about what ought to be. We've been searching for him for a long time. There is a price on his head, and inevitably, his name will soon extend the list of those who have nothing for them but the law.

Excuse us, Madame, we have been misinformed.

ANDRÉ

Have the soldiers come in.

THE OFFICER

No; it's not yet time... We're all with you, but they might not understand yet. Go—go quickly; the victor is watching us. We're only the pack that barks. Go; the hunters will be pitiless.

ANDRÉ
Call your men. I wish it.

THE OFFICER
Come in, all of you. Are you all here?

THE SERGEANT
Yes, lieutenant

ANDRÉ
Lads, you've earned a fine bonus today; I don't know how many thalers, but in sum it makes twenty thousand francs.

A SOLDIER
I'm not a gendarme, I'm a conscript, and if I had been alone in the house I wouldn't have gone.

ANDRÉ
You were afraid that they'd throw your father out, so you joined up? You're a good son.

There are twenty of you. A thousand francs each. That's a tidy sum; you can get a fine pair of oxen for that.

THE SERGEANT
That money would burn my fingers.

ANDRÉ
You're still young, friend; they'll give you an epaulette. Am I to be shot tomorrow or right away?

THE OFFICER
Right away.

ANDRÉ
Well, let's not waste any time.

THE OFFICER
But there's no urgency, if you need...

ANDRÉ
To make my will? That won't take long, and it's you,
sergeant, who'll be my heir.

Here, hide this carefully. On the day of revenge, put it on
your helmet. You'll certainly be a captain then, and if you
command Frenchmen, and I hope you do, say to your men:
"He was summoned, the one who passed, and he gave me his
cockade."

Come on, let's go.

THE SERGEANT
You're the one who...? You've heard mention of him,
the rest of you?

I'll keep your cockade, but I still need wristbands. Isn't
that so, the rest of you?

Lieutenant, we still have to search the village; the man
named André might be hiding there?

By the right, turn.

ANDRÉ
Gently, gently. What if I want to be shot?

A SOLDIER
And what if we don't want to shoot you?

ANDRÉ
You'll be shot

THE LIEUTENANT
And what if that pleases us?

ANDRÉ
Oh, that's different. Do you all have the same idea?

136

A SOLDIER

It's our idea.

ANDRÉ

Well, friends, it's necessary that we don't get shot. Including me there are twenty-one of us; we'll be the first twenty-one. Take these cockades and let's take to the woods. Tomorrow we'll be a thousand...

He had said to the poet: I'll try to be a soldier; you, wake those who are still asleep, write the poem of Ar-Braz.

And the poet wrote the poem of Ar-Braz.

THE POEM OF AR-BRAZ

III

The German wave is beating the Arverne mountains, the horses of the Suebi are browsing the rushes of Morbihan, the daughters of the Teutons are drawing water from the Rhône."

"Many waves have already collided with the waves of the shoreless sea; where are they? The sand of our beaches drinks them, and where they have passed the grass is thicker and the forests are greener."

"In passing, the wave has uprooted the menhirs, the horses have trampled the forests, the daughters of the North have troubled the springs. The German army has passed like a scythe, only leaving the children standing."

"But it has forgotten a druid on an islet of the Loire."

THE DRUID

The German needs robust slaves; he has nourished you for ten years.

Tomorrow he will bind you to the yoke.

Do you want to pull like oxen?

THE CHILDREN

When the German whip whistles, we will break the plow, and then, perhaps, the German will kill us.

Death will kiss, with her cool lips, our streaming brows, and extend under our bruised feet a soft carpet of moss; she will give us for a bed the crimson wave of the sunset.

THE DRUID

Lift your heads, children; your foreheads are too broad for anyone to carve a yoke for them.

Listen to the story of Ar-Braz, the one who is to come, the one who will be reborn in the hour of danger.

THE CHILDREN

Father, it's necessary to go; the Orient is paling.

THE DRUID

My eyes have never seen the glare of the sun and they have never seen the color of the sky, but I know the glare of the sun and I have seen the color of the sky because I have lived before. I have grown old before being a Druid, and now that my bodily eyes are closed, the eyes of my soul can see.

I can see the green star where, like a daisy in the grass, the Gaul above shines, and in the celestial Gaul, on a granite rock, I can see the old man.

O father of the Gaels, part the veil of the past before me; it is necessary that these children know that they are not men like other men. They have grown up among women; it is necessary that they know who their fathers were.

THE CHILDREN

What will the maters say if they do not see us when they wake?

THE DRUID

I am going to talk to you as one talks to men.

A man is a leaf of the divine oak; he is a whole but he is also a part of a whole, and he will not be able to understand fully while the light does not bathe the oak from its crown to its base. Even in the circle of felicity he will not be perfectly happy as long as the sap does not flow equally in every branch. Even in the circle of felicity he will suffer for as long as human suffering exists.

But the Terrible is also the Merciful and he permits the strong to descend again into the arena in order to guide the fighters.

Those men who descend again voluntarily from the circle of felicity into the circle of proofs, those men who, voluntarily, extinguish the torch they have lit, are the Master's beloved. They are reborn human, but they are more than human; they carry a word of the divine science, a radiance of the divine hearth. That word tunes their harps and that radiance tempers their swords.

Children, can you see a large mound nearby, between the Loire and the sea?

I have not seen it myself, and yet I know it; three stones stand on its summit. Under that mound our forefathers laid the long-haired Ar-Braz.

THE CHILDREN
We have grown up among women, but our mothers have told us, in low voices, the story of the invincible guide.

When the proud horsemen launched their horses into the foam, he sang: "O sword! O great king of the battlefield!"

Under the willows of the river the tremulous virgins are slipping and the anxious mothers are searching.

THE MOTHERS
Come on; what will the master say?

THE CHILDREN
Listen to the story of Ar-Braz.

THE YOUNG WOMEN
The master is waiting for us too.

THE MOTHERS
Alas! Alas!

THE DRUID
Tear your breasts, young women; rip out your hair and burn your cheeks with ashes.

THE YOUNG WOMEN
Our breasts are as white as the necks of swans, our cheeks are as pink as apple blossom.

THE MOTHERS
Alas! Alas!

THE YOUNG WOMEN
Our hair is softer than the down of the aspen.

THE CHILDREN
Braid your hair, young women; the children have grown up.

The proud horsemen launched their horses into the foam and the water did not reach the breasts of the horses, and the Celts sang: "O sword! O great king of the battlefield! Ar-Braz is born!"

THE MOTHERS
A head for an eye, an arm for a finger and a heart for a wound! O sword! O great king of the battlefield! O sword! O great king!

THE CHILDREN
Sing of the blue sword that loves the flesh! Sing of the blue sword!

THE MOTHERS

O you who are asleep under the heath, can you hear? Can you hear our sons, O our beloved masters?

For a long time your bed has been cold; for a long time we have been calling you; we were waiting for this day. We wanted to be able to say to you: "Your sons have red blood, large hearts and strong arms."

Come; where the great river foams, our souls are waiting for you.

THE YOUNG WOMEN

Mothers! Mothers!

THE MOTHERS

Work like an ant and sing like a warbler, and you will have handsome sons.

THE YOUNG MEN

Say to the dead without tombs that the cloth will be red at the funeral feast.

The widows are going to rejoin their beloved masters; in its blue shroud, the great river rolls them.

THE DRUID

They have fought bravely; waves, carry their bodies away; gulls, guide their souls.

THE YOUNG MEN

Braid your hair, young women; the men are about to depart. Put on your bracelets, put on your golden necklaces; tomorrow your lips will close our open wounds; tomorrow you will mop our bloody foreheads with your long hair.

Ar-Braz! Ar-Braz! We are ready!

THE DRUID

I am blind, but I want to fight with you. Bring me a horse with a broad breast, in order that it can open a broad furrow; bring me a horse with heavy hooves, in order that it can weigh upon breastplates.

Ar-Braz is born, children! Ar-Braz is born! Strike the blue sword on the shields!

They uproot the oaks, they break the service trees, they seek bronze swords in the depths of lakes.

The young women braid their hair and fasten their golden necklaces.

The Germans are smiling; they find the young women beautiful.

THE YOUNG WOMEN

Our brothers are pruning the ash trees; the sap is about to depart...

Master, let me touch your breastplate...how heavy it is! And your sword...how brightly it shines! You really are the sons of gods...

Empty your cup, master...

To bridle the colts the young men twist willow branches.

In its blue shroud the great river has wrapped the widows.

THE WIDOWS

Gulls, take our fatigued souls on your wings; those who have chosen us are waiting for us up there in their chariots of clouds.

Gulls, take our souls; we shall sleep in the celestial Gaul tonight; our sons have red blood, large hearts and strong arms.

The Germans are smiling; they find the young women beautiful.

THE DEAD

Like ivy you have made the roofs of our houses verdant; like juniper, you have embalmed our hearths; you will always be young, always beautiful, always beloved...

THE YOUNG WOMEN

Our brothers are felling the greedy branches of the service trees.

Your Valkyries are very beautiful, it's said, when they pass by, couched on their black mares... Do you only love them?

Empty your cup, master.

We too, if we wished, could mount your mares, and perhaps we would be more beautiful than your Valkyries...

Empty your cup, master.

Our brothers are fishing in the ponds for the feast. You will never have seen such fish...

Empty your cup, master...

THE SKYLARK

Open on the shady ponds, green nenuphars, your snowy corollas; perfume, violets, the grass of the paths; quiver, clematis on the branches of the birches; sow golden stars on the sunlit heath, rushes of Morbihan; I have found my fiancé again.

THE HORSEMEN

On the cleft mound, a wild stallion is whinnying; would you care to mount him, Father?

THE DRUID

My thighs can scarcely embrace his flanks; he will open a broad furrow.

THE GULLS

We have carried the souls; come, waves come!

On the German mares we have seen the virgins fleeing; pass, waves, pass!

They have uprooted the ash trees; they have broken the service trees; they have taken the bronze swords from the lakes.

Can you see the running on their wild colts?

Can you see the Druid at their head? His white hair is floating in the wind. His stallion is bounding; can you see him?

THE DRUID
Under your hooves the earth trembles; they will not gasp for long.

March faster, march faster; to cut many sheaves it's necessary to enter the field at dawn.

THE HORSEMEN
It is for the good of men that the Master has created the eternal combat; the sword opens the door of the palace up above; the sword cuts the flowers of the gardens of heaven.

THE DRUID
The wheat is dense; the harvest will be good. How many sheaves we shall bind! How many red sheaves!

THE HORSEMEN
It is for the good of men that the Master has created the eternal combat; for bloody souls the feast is smoking; breastplates of azure are being forged on high for punctured breasts.

THE DRUID
To harvest the field labored by the ax, the sweat will flow; but how heavy the sheaves are…!

THE YOUNG WOMEN
Like the Valkyries, we pass on our black mares. Like the Valkyries, we go where souls take flight.

THE HORSEMEN
In the depths of the plain a cloud is running. It is gray ringed with silver.

THE DRUID
For ten years the grass has been thirsty.

THE HORSEMEN
Sparks are stringing forth.

THE DRUID
They will relight the fire extinct for ten years...

THE YOUNG WOMEN
Like the Valkyries, we go where souls take flight. Like the Valkyries, we will be where the swords bite.

THE HORSEMEN
It isn't a cloud; it's a smoking crescent.

THE DRUID
Tighten your knees; it's the Germans.

THE YUNG WOMEN
Like the Valkyries, we will be where the swords bite. Like the Valkyries, we will go where the dead wake.

THE DRUID
It that your chariot, Ar-Braz, that is sounding behind us?

THE HORSEMEN
It is our sisters who are coming, on the Germans' mares.

THE DRUID
When the reapers set forth, the haymakers also set forth; the promised day is dawning.

THE YOUNG WOMEN
We have put on our golden necklaces, we have braided our hair.

THE DRUID
The swords are thirsty; strike the blue swords on the shields!

THE HORSEMEN
Choose your fiancés…!

Do you see that large crescent with scintillating horns? It is the German army. Can you see that dark corner with the trenchant edge? It is the Gaulish army.

At the horns of the crescent the heavy carts resonate; from their bronze shafts three long lances emerge, on their axles, sickles are flamboyant.

At the trenchant edge of the corner one man is alone, his breast bare; it is the blind druid. Behind him, on black mares, two blue-eyed virgins are smiling.

THE YOUNG WOMEN
The swords are thirsty, strike! This evening our lips will dry the streaming foreheads. Strike! Strike; this evening our arms will cradle the open breasts.

THE SKYLARK
The corner is collapsing! The crescent is tightening! The hour has sounded.

Hoe heavy your billhook is, master. I know that the vine-stick will be green again, that the bud will become a branch, but involuntarily. I weep for my handsome fallen branches.

THE DRUID
Children, tighten your knees!

THE SKYLARK
It is not wrens that nest in your branches, hawthorn of the sunset. Open your wings gaily, souls of the brave; your horses are pawing he ground in the green star. Can you hear them whinnying? They are as light as an eagle, as strong as a torrent; their rumps are like a meadow silvered by the spring; their manes are like a plain gilded by autumn...

The sword has cut many blonde braids; the ax has broken many golden necklaces.
Fortunate are those who fall in their strength!

THE DRUID
Tighten your knees, children! Tighten your knees!

THE YOUNG WOMEN
Go; you will still find flax in our distaffs.

"Don't prick yourselves with the spindles?"

"They only had ash-wood spears and service-wood clubs. The colts only had willow branches for bridles."
"Look at the white stallion; he whinnies and the colts stop."
"It isn't the men but the colts that are retreating."
"Look at the white stallion; must have blood all the way to the nostrils. Under his hooves, breastplates are bursting; on his broad breast, squadrons are broken."

THE YOUNG WOMEN
Fear will never knock on the door; the hand of my fiancé is heavy. Hunger will never cross the threshold; the hand of my fiancé is broad.

"Come into the house, warbler, to help me build a nest."

"The swords are whirling! The clubs are resonating! They have red blood, large hearts and strong arms."

"But look at the Druid. He's no longer a blind man with gray eyebrows; he's a proud soldier with blue-green eyes. A double-edged ax is fuming in his hand."

"And on the rump of his stallion... Sharpen your teeth, wolves; open your wings, vultures; weep, daughters of the Germans

"On the rump of his stallion, the beloved smiles; weep, daughters of the Germans."

THE SKYLARK
With a smile on the lips and peace in the heart, go to sleep, my beloved; they have fought bravely.

Sharpen your teeth, wolves! Open your wings, vultures!

THE YOUNG WOMEN
The garden will no longer have a hedge; Ar-Braz is dead! The door will no longer have a bolt; Ar-Braz is dead!

The sky is low, the stars are pale. Over the mute river a gray mist fringes the trunks of the poplars; an insipid vapor trail over the red plain. The veins are empty, the death-rattles have faded away.

Around the scattered fires the victors are sitting.

THE HORSEMEN
Who will guide us tomorrow? He's dead!

THE SKYLARK
On blue lips the souls are palpitating. They are calling; listen, sisters with vermilion wings.

The table is buckling, the cups are foaming; depart, valiant ones; on the ivory bench your swords are glittering, on the nacreous walls your shields are flamboyant.

THE YOUNG WOMEN

Our hair is not wiping streaming brows; our eyes are full of tears, Our lips are not closing open wounds; our eyes are full of tears.

THE HORSEMEN

Through a large wound our soul has flown away; with a flap of the wing it has crossed the steep steps; don't weep, young women.

How the harps are vibrating! How the trumpets are sounding! He is victorious!

THE YOUNG WOMEN

Stand up three stones, there, where the moonlight is shining; let us enclose a bright radiance with him.

Round out a mound, so that it will be high enough for the waves to see it; so that it will be broad enough for our sons to come here and stammer his name on its summit.

They have set up three pink stones, and they have laid the dead hero next to his horse.

"Under the turf that is piled up, only the body is lying; lift the head."

THE YOUNG WOMEN

Look into the sky in the direction of the Orient.

On the horse with a fiery mane, the Brenn is passing. The Valkyries are following him.

On the horse with the fiery mane, the virgin with the broad brow is sitting, and the fortunate souls, in the red shrouds, are smiling at those who must fight another day.

THE HORSEMEN

At the feasts on high, keep places for us next to you, friends.

THE VALKYRIES
The earth tells us: you have a soul. Heaven tells us: you have a body. Are we the dreams of a sleeping world? Are we the seeds of a star yet to be born?

In the luminous confines of the celestial Gaul our mares are rearing up; fortunate are those who can die!

THE SKYLARK
They have fought bravely; victors, make way for them.

THE MOTHERS
While your bones whiten on the heath, our beloved masters, we will make men of these children.

Come! Come! the feast is smoking before the ever-bright fire; in the ever-green enclosure, indefatigable colts are bounding; in the ever-full cowshed, the black oxen are slumbering.

Come! Come! Your distaff will never lack flax; the beehive will never be empty; the chickens will never be cold.

THE OLD MAN
Sit down beside me, Ar-Braz.

They are all my sons, but you are more than my son; all their amours palpate in your heart; all their reams seethe behind your brow. You are the valiant and the sage; you are the good and the strong.

THE SKYLARK
I will always love you.

THE OLD MAN
When will you build your nest, Skylark?

THE SKYLARK
When the bramble no longer grows, when the darnel no longer flowers, when the vulture no longer soars...

But I see in the East a muddy wave that other waves are pushing. I see in the South smoke that is rising. On the trunk of the hawthorn I see a snake uncoiling.

AR-BRAZ
The wave is already growling; the battle is imminent.

THE OLD MAN
O my son, do not forget the oak with a thousand roots and a thousand branches. The sun can gild its crown and the frost can crack its trunk; do not forget her, my son.

The Skylark will build her nest under the hawthorn of the west; in its shadow, you will be reborn; but it will be necessary not to let the accursed wind break the great poplar on the bank of the river. The hawthorn will keep the lightning away, but the ash tree sheaths the sword; do not forget it, my son!

Although the flower of the hawthorn intoxicates, the fruit of the holly shines, and the oil that renders strength flows from the olive tree. Life has dispersed the brothers; under your powerful hand you will reunite them.

AR-BRAZ
I will do that. In the pure granite, my sword will carve a great body with a broad brow, powerful arms and a profound breast, but the rock will be so hard that my sword will break.

THE OLD MAN
Where will you put the heart?

AR-BRAZ
In the nest of the Skylark, under the hawthorn of the west.

THE OLD MAN
You know the Master's secrets; in the sheaf of stars that he has bound for my sons, the green star of the Gauls scintillates brightest of all.

AR-BRAZ

To the great body I will give a heart that will beat forcefully, which will impel red blood to the lips and the arms; but where is the man who will put honey on his tongue? Where is the woman who will light a spark behind his forehead?

Father, where is the eldest of your sons, the bard with the sonorous voice? Where is the daughter of the Ganges, the inspired druidess?

When we left her in the woods of the Pierre-Grosse, she said to us: "Soon." When he died on the bank of the Ebro, his breast open, he said to us: "Au revoir." And the centuries pass slowly, and they have not returned.

THE OLD MAN

Woe betide whoever tries to fathom the secrets of the Master! Woe betide whoever tries to oppose his will to the will of the Almighty!

In the misty worlds the proud man awaits the day when, in order to climb again the step descended, he can live and fight again.

This is the eldest of my sons, Master; let me extend a hand to him. Let me guide him on his route as I guided him on the sand around the woolen tent in the land of the Orient.

When the swords ring, it is necessary that the harps vibrate; O you who love your sons, render them the one who will engrave your name in the granite of Elora.

THE VOICE

Of his destiny, a man is master.

The poet kissed the tender angel with the blue eyes; he had made a song of the poem of Ar-Braz.

THE POEM OF AR-BRAZ

IV

The centuries of the earth are the hours of heaven. On the earth, people were beginning to talk about Caesar.

AR-BRAZ
I can hear the German wave growling. O you whose name I have understood, put a spark in my soul and, stronger, let me go to fight again.

THE SKYLARK
I see blood! I see tears!

Master, I have never fought; I have never lived. I too would like to descend into the arena to fight and suffer; a tear effaces a stain, a kiss illuminates a radiance.

THE VOICE
Who fights rises. Go.

THE OLD MAN
Go, my son, march straight and look up. What does it matter if you fall? The valiant man who falls gets up stronger.

The voice having spoken, the two souls escaped from their luminous bodies. Like two lilies inclining, the two bodiless souls glided over the grass of the green star. But nothing could destroy their eternal beauty; the fingers of death do not marble their cheeks; under an opal veil they sleep. When their souls return, they will wake more gracious and stronger.

The days of the earth are moments in heaven.

"But under that eglantine whose roses are opening, I see another couple whose souls have departed. The woman, who is asleep, has two tears on her cheeks; the man, who is asleep, has a crease on his forehead.

"Why is she weeping, the woman who resembles the statue of the old château? Why does he have a wrinkle on his brow, the man whose hand is clutching an ivory mallet and a steel graver?

"They are weeping because their exiled souls are weeping, and the roses are waiting, in order to open fully, for the nuptial bed of the queen and the potter to be dressed."

But let us follow Ar-Braz and the Skylark.

The two radiant souls float over the green star, and then the wind pushes them into the turbulence that rises from the divine hearth like smoke. In that ardent vapor their radiance is extinguished and where human souls are falling as pale sparks in order to struggle, they fall too.

"Blonde bees of the human hive, carry them on your wings."

THE FAYS
When the Almighty speaks on the waves of the East, we go where souls await.

THE WAVES
In the wind of those wings, our crests hollow out, as in the breath of the Master.

THE FAYS
We take the souls and we slide them where the Master orders, between two kisses or between two petals.

THE WAVES
In the wind of those wings, the Gaulish river ripples and the rocks of Morbihan quiver.

THE FAYS
In our arms, souls forget their past, and yet, where their past pushes them, docile messengers, we go.

Nether bodies not souls, neither flowers nor women, with no tomb or cradle, perhaps we would like to be born like the flowers, and to die like women.

THE RIVER

Stop on my banks. Since my waves have quivered all the way to my bed in the wind of those wings, these souls are mine.

THE FAYS

Where their past pushes them we go; but, our eyes dazzled, we can no longer see the route before us. Where their past pushes us, we go. Southwards we carry the dove.

THE ALMOND TREE

Under the cold sunlight my pale flowers fade.

On the warm shore, if I flourished, the daughters of Ionia would come to sleep under my branches, in order to be loved.

Far from my homeland, my pale flowers fade.

THE FAYS

Where their past pushes us, we go.

Southwards we carry the dove.

Between two petals, between two kisses, into the hard crystal, into the soft nest, we slide the souls; but in our rapturous arms this soul has acquired a body.

She will be our daughter; we shall make her a nest of white daisies; the bees will cradle her and the stream will sing her our rounds.

When the dawn awakes, a breath will carry us to the land of the Orient, but with the stars we will return under the almond tree. Our daughter is our queen; the Voice has told us so.

But why have the fays not hidden the soul with the white wings between two kisses? Is it made of clouds, radiance or perfumes, that beautiful child's body smiling under the almond trees of Narbonne?

"It is made of a little clay of Gaulish soil, the soil that swells when the dew is red, the soil the gilds the grapes and hardens the oaks."

"And the soul with broad wings? Where have the fays taken it?"

"They are gliding northwards; the wind is pushing them toward the beach with green reeds. The field of the Gauls is wide, the Almighty has planted its boundary markers A thief can hide them under a pile of ashes, but to uproot them it would be necessary for the earth to split. When a thief believes that they are hidden under a pile of ashes, and when he has put on that heap, in order to prevent a passer-by from discovering them, his largest flag and his heaviest cannon, the Master flattens the heap as one tramples an ant-hill underfoot, and the boundary-markers of the Gaulish field shine higher."

"How beautiful she is, the daughter of the North; but how sad her large blue eyes are, since Celtill the Arverne has come from the land of the Belges."[17]

IDA

We are not sold for silver; we are not exchanged for the gold of old men who pass by.

---

[17] Celtillus is a king of the Arverni in Julius Caesar's account of the Gallic Wars, allegedly executed by the leaders of neighboring tribes when he tried to unite them under his leadership. According to Caesar, Celtillus' son, Vercingetorix, tried to rally the tribes to unite to resist the Roman invasion, but he was expelled from the Arverni stronghold of Gergovia before raising an army in the country to turn the tables on his adversaries, after which he began a long campaign against Caesar, which eventually ended in defeat. Opinions vary as to the reliability of Caesar's inevitably-biased account, and L'Estoille is by no means the only modern author who has felt free to vary and embroider his story.

I only like the wave that caresses my feet and the wind that unbinds my hair.

THE FAYS
Northwards we are carrying the hawk.

IDA
If I had a sun I would want him to be more beautiful than a torrent iridescent in the midday sun; if I had a son I would want him to be stronger than the north wind that twists the uprooted pines.

Lips will never touch mine; I have given my heart to the breath of our heaths.

THE FAYS
Where their past pushes us we go; on the lips of a virgin we leave the soul with the powerful wings.

IDA
We are not fold to old men who pass by... The wind has caressed my lips! He is as beautiful as a torrent, as strong as a tempest; before the son of the virgin men will tremble.

THE FAYS
When the dawn wakes, a breath carries us to the land of the Orient, but we will return with the stars.

The centuries of the earth are hours in heave; on the impure mud the grass has grown thickly; over the heaped-up cadavers the forest grows green; the sons of the victors have forgotten the Germans and Celtill the Arverne has chosen a beautiful young woman among the Belges.

"Why has he old Brenn not accompanied the young spouse to the lake of Sancy?"

"Since he has returned from the land of the Belges Celtill has not slept under his own roof. Along the road of the unknown an invisible hand has pushed him; into insensate dreams a powerful hand has plunged him; he has descended into the plain with his horsemen; he wants to be a king."

"But Ida?"

"On the shore of the lake, she is smiling at the son of the wind."

THE FAYS

The Brenn with the gray beard has chosen the pale virgin, the blonde lover of stormy nights.

"But Ida's eyes wept on the evening of the betrothal; they wept again the day after and he day after that."

"They will no longer weep today; the breath has passed over her lips... That is the Master's secret.

"She is no longer weeping, but how pale she is! How many months ago did we slip the soul of the hawk between her lips?"

IDA

O my beloved husband, Sylph of the great waves, sustain me with your powerful wing; sweat is moistening my brow... My eyes are troubled... I want to go all the way to the summit, all the way to the bottomless lake; it's necessary that he doesn't catch us. Sustain me.

But he won't catch him; he knows full well that he isn't his son.

THE FAYS

For whom, is that pyre being lit?

"For the madman who wanted to trace routes in the sky for the hawks; for the traitor who wanted the wolves to couple; for Celtill the Arverne.

IDA

I don't want to enter the bed of the man with the gray beard; I'll give your son to the roe deer of the woods; into the bottomless abyss I'll throw my body, and under the somber cloud, O Master, my soul will rejoin you.

But come...I'm afraid!

THE FAYS
Over the snowy peak a breath carries us.

IDA
With you, my husband I shall glide over the green waves. When the stars light up, you will carry me on your powerful wings all the way to the larch wood where the blonde roe deer will nurse him in the raspberry bushes...

He has forgotten! I'm cold...I'm going to die...

Come, our son is handsome.

Your eyes have the color of the waves. You're handsome, but tomorrow the vultures will take you; he has forgotten...

I'm dying.

THE FAYS
He will be as beautiful as the torrent and as strong as the tempest; before the son of the virgin, men will tremble.

"In the green star, wild gull, you are not awaited; come with us. Come with us, you will glide every night on moonbeams all the way to your son's forehead."

"Come with us and perhaps you will know the secret; it is not humans who forged the sword that your son will draw."

IDA
Neither body nor soul, neither flower nor woman, a widow without a betrothal, a mother without a husband, I shall watch over you, my son.

Let us carry him to the roe deer of the woods, my sisters.

I have divined the secret. It's you who slid between my lips that soul escaped from the luminous circle, the brilliant soul that the purest of kisses would have tarnished.

Before the son of the virgin, men will bow down; he carries from above the word that makes harps vibrate, the radiance that tempers swords.

Like fruits hollowed out by a worm, my dreams fall one by one on to the brambles of the path.

"In the midst of madmen who howl: 'Man is only a tooth in the unconscious gear-wheel that the void has set in motion, which rotates without knowing why and which hazard will stop,' you alone said: 'Man is a free whole, knowing whence he came and where he is going, and nothing of him will ever perish.' Having believed you, I felt magnified."

"You don't believe me anymore?"

"No. In the Gaul up above, under the oaks of the green star, the bard will not rediscover is harp, the warrior will not rediscover his horse, and the fiancé will not rediscover his fiancée, since the mother will not rediscover her son there.

"Has not that child who is weeping on the summit of the Sancy already been the victorious druid, the bold pilot of the forests of the Danube, the skilful reaper of the grasslands of the Erbro, the indefatigable horseman of the plateaux of the Arie? At the hearth of heaven, is it Ida or Fleur-d'Épine who will call him her son?"

"How vermilion are the fruits of the vigorous apple tree that your dreams gild at sunrise!

"When the son is reborn the mother is also reborn; if a man is a whole, the family is also a whole. The breath of death does not disperse the ashes of the hearth; it chases away the smoke and reanimates the embers.

"If the echo did not sometimes make words fly in order to sow them everywhere, if a book were not so facile to open, I would tell you why those heroes who are reborn have no family down here. One day, on a high summit, when the children are playing in the valley, we shall talk about this again; but today, remember that Ida was once called Fleur d'Épine, and that, the time having come, perhaps you crossed her path yesterday."

"I understand now why the Brenn with the gray beard no longer returns to the plain."

"Celtill had wanted wolves to couple; he had wanted to trace routes in the sky for hawks; he has mounted the pyre of traitors, and no one can say: "Ida's son is my son.""

Since the death of Ida I believe that the almond tree has flowered twenty times and its buds are about to open; I would like to know what has become of the two souls carried by the fays. Has the dove built a nest? Has the hawk reddened his claws?

"In the flowery branches the fays are twirling, and as they whirl they are singing the forgotten poem; listen and you will know.

THE FAYS

The enemy! Here comes the enemy! Hollow out your bed, Gaulish river, launch your foam to the crowns of the willows; extend your luminous arms over the plain. The Almighty has put you there to guard his domain; crush the thief beneath your overflowing waves

"Who can fathom the Master's secrets? The great river is no more than a stream that the German horses will cross without wetting their manes."

"Arioviste is crossing the Rhine,[18] Caesar is crossing the Rhône."

"You are so high in the sun's rays, divine Skylark, that the sounds of the earth do not rise as high as you. Return to sing in the furrow; they need your voice to guide them. Come back; they have not been able to do drive the crow away from

---

[18] Ariovistus is identified as the leader of the Germanic tribe of the Suebi in the *Gallic Wars*. According to Caesar, he formed an alliance with the Arverni and the Sequani to defeat the Aedui (Duclaux's Eduen) and settled in large numbers in what is now Alsace before Caesar drove them out. The political maneuvering involved is embroidered more elaborately in *Vercingétorix* than it is in the present work.

the walnut tree, and they are showing the wolf the way to the cowshed."

"The dew is wetting our feet, the mist is weighing down our wings; why? The evening is mute and the dawn is mute. Why?"

"The ivory chariot is rolling without a guide in the sky without a voice; on the necreous rumps of the pale mares, the silver queens are floating. Why?"

The waves are growling in the East, the tide is foaming in the south; at the first breath of the storm the oak is already shivering and the immortal guardian of the beloved race has neglected for twenty years the land where the swords are being sharpened in favor of distant worlds. Why? Why?"

"Come back, Skylark, singer over the furrow. They are stronger, they are braver; but everyone wants to go where his caprice leads him. Every brake wounds them, every bridle maddens then; one by one they will fall."

"Neither flowers nor women, neither bodies not souls, we want and do not act. Like leaves fallen from the divine oak, between the closed heavens and the forgotten earth, devoid of tears and power, a breath of wind rolls us.

"The Skylark has not come. The clans are on the march, the Roman army is following them. Arioviste stops, surprised."

"The clarions sound, the horses rear up, the Gauls and the Romans mingle their blood in the cup. The cup is emptied, the horses launch forward... Who will arrive first?"

"The sword of Vercingetorix passes like an iron wheel, and the rut is profound. The rut is so broad that that the Roman army follows it.

"He is as beautiful as the torrent, he is as strong as the tempest, the son of the virgin. He has thrown way the helmet with the heavy wings; over his broad shoulders his long hair is flamboyant. Do you recognize him? His eyes have taken on the somber hue of the irritated wave; from his profound breast a powerful breath emerges; on his sword a bloody foam fumes; do you recognize him?"

"We know the past, we see the future, but who can fathom the secrets of the Master?"

Arioviste is fleeing! The sand has drunk the blood of the Germans! And Caesar says to the son of the fay: 'Will you be my friend and my lieutenant, Vercingetorix?'"

And Strummor, the former companion of Celtill, brandishing the proscribed ensign, traverses the Gaulish nations at a gallop. Can you hear the proud peasant, the rude mountain-dweller? 'You believed that you had cut the hamstrings of the wild stallion! See how he makes our silver stallion rear up now! Your pyre was not large enough to bar our route; make way for the soldiers of Celtill! Make way for the clans of the Monts Dore.'"

And the nations fall silent; the child's sword is so heavy, and Caesar has just said: "Brenn of the Arvernes, you will be my lieutenant and my friend."

"Why has Caesar said that? Will our proud hawk quit his summits for the Roman fist? Will he sell his liberty for a hood embroidered with pearls?"

"He was still an outlaw yesterday, and glory intoxicates him today. Distant worlds are returning, divine Skylark; talk about the fatherland to the Gaul of whom Caesar wants to make a Roman."

"They are not dogs that can be trained, the old mastiffs of Celtill; they have not followed Caesar to Narbonne. Joyfully, they are climbing to the high valley. At their head march Strummor and Vercingetorix. Listen to the worthy laborer and the vigorous woodcutter.

"Today you are a man, Vercingetorix; tomorrow you will pass before your clan on horseback and they will swear to obey you, as long as you love them, and to follow you, as long as you are ahead of them. You are the chief; but I am an old man and I can speak before you. I am the one who found you on the Sancy next to your dead mother; it is my wife who

163

warmed you up, it is her who nursed you; I ought to speak to you as a man speaks to his son.

"You must be good; if you want to be obeyed. You must be just, if you want to be loved.

"Do not forget that you are the sword of your clan; you must also be its shield. But swords of steel are given a golden scabbard, and scintillating flowers are painted on a bronze shield. Let treasure slip through your fingers, let wisdom laugh on your lips."

"He is no longer listening to the old soldier; he is gazing at those two veils that are floating between the holly bushes on the slope. Oh, the two pretty women! One is as fresh as a cherry, the other as golden as an ear of wheat. And their eyes are shining! And their breasts are swelling!"

"That's Ganieda, the ripe cherry of Strummor's orchard, and Moina, the Master's ear of wheat: Moina the druidess, Moina the inspired sister of the laughing Ganieda."

"The old peasant has smiled; he knows that good blood does not weaken and that those children love one another. He takes the bridle of the horse that the chief has left in the middle of the path and, singing a song from his youth, he climbs with the men toward the larch-wood houses."

"But the druidess stops... She sits down on the grass... She is weeping, I think. Ganieda takes her hand."

"Neither flowers nor women, nether bodies not souls, perhaps we would like to loved like women and to die like flowers."

"We do not know how to talk about love; let us be silent, sisters."

GANIEDA

You love him. And why shouldn't you love him? If we hadn't slept in the same cradle, if I weren't his sister. I'd love him too.

See how tall he is, and how handsome!

Can you, when he looks at you, not lower your eyes? I can't, and I'm his sister.

And he also loves you.

When, pale, his eyes partly closed, forehead in hand, you sang what the others have forgotten, I've seen him shiver; I've seen his clear gaze envelop you entirely.

See, he's coming. It isn't for me that he's coming so quickly; I'm only his sister.

Is it for me that you've picked that eglantine, Vercingetorix?

VERCINGETORIX
No, my beloved sister, it's not for you, it's for Moina. Come and kiss me, friend. You've grown, I believe? And how rosy your cheeks are! You haven't wept often for the absentee?

GANIEDA
Moina knew that you'd come back.

VERCINGETORIX
And yet, I'm sure that she has wept.

When you went to see the sun rise up there, you said, didn't you: "As long as that child will be a man."

Well, I have been a man, Moina.

Put your hands on my shoulders, and then, as before, and look me in the eyes. There. Your child has been a man, and a Gaul.

THE FAYS
He is sitting between the two of them, their little hands quivering in his large hand...

"Sisters! Sisters! Perhaps we would like to love like women and die like flowers."

"We do not know how to talk about amour; let us be silent."

165

VERCINGETORIX

Tomorrow I shall be the worried chief, the anxious judge; today I am still only the son of the heath; let us sing, Moina, what the gray lichens say to the old larches, what the heather responds to the flowering myrtles.

MOINA

The gray lichens do not tell the larches the secrets of my heart.

On the island out there, which floats like a dream where the Ocean meets the sky, in the green cup on the granite table, a radiance lights up, and the nine sisters twirl with their hair in the wind. The radiance is illuminated in the green cup and the black serpent slowly rears up. The sword scintillates, the mare whinnies and on the red table silvered by the moon the nine sisters sing, their hair in the wind.

Can the gray lichen tell the larches the secret of my heart?

On the red table they are singing, the sisters. Three of them are looking into the past; they see a blind man on a white stallion. Three are poring over the future; they see the vanquished in a dark cell.

Hair in the wind, they are singing, the sisters. Three are looking into the past, three are poring over the future, three are listening in the present, and all nine are awaiting the vibrant harp and the sword in the golden scabbard.

The gray lichen will tell the larches the secret of my heart.

The radiance lights up, the serpent rears up, the sword scintillates, the mare whinnies; the palest of the sisters takes the stone knife and her blood trickles into the green cup.

Hair in the wind, they are singing, the virgin: "The chain is undone, the circle disrupted, the charm broken; who will take the empty place among the maidservants of the Skylark?

Heath, tell my secret to the flowering myrtles; I am the virgin summoned by the red druidesses.

GANIEDA

Has the heath only told her secret to the flowering myrtles? Respond, brother.

THE FAYS

We would like to love like women, and then die like flowers.

The heath has told Moina's secret, but the chief has departed for Narbonne.

The gray lichens have told her secret, but the chief has found the blonde daughter of the fays under the almond trees of Narbonne and he has not come back.

"How she has wept, the druidess!"

"But she had cradled the man she loves; it is her who has made him a man; she will make him the foremost of the chiefs. In order for her to be heard, in order for her to be the druidess, for all to listen to her, she will go to learn the great secrets on the somber dolmen of the terrible isle."

She already has the red veil of those who must die as virgins; the waves of the sacred isle are already bathing her feet, and yet, like a frightened hind, she is declaring her hopeless love once again to the rocks of Morbihan. Listen.

MOINA

Why do you pass so quickly, clouds? Stop, clasp me in your icy arms; my forehead is burning, my breast seething.

Obey; I am the maidservant of the queen of the sunset, the divine Skylark, Cora the white.[19]

The daughter of Cora! I am only a woman, a woman who weeps. The roe deer is loved, the she-wolf has cubs, but me!

_____

[19] Cora, or Kore, was an alternative name of Persephone, who was a goddess of the spring before her abduction by Hades made her queen of the underworld and a much more ambiguous figure.

But me! I have sworn freely; I must live alone, without desire, without a dream, in order that death may take me entire.

Let lightning strike me! Let oblivion take me! I love him.

IDA

All men will follow him, all women will love him.

MOINA

O Mistress, strike the sacrilegious woman. An impure flame, my soul will crawl over the marsh... I love him! I love him!

Strike, Mistress; I shall love him forever.

IDA

Like you I was a woman; like you I loved. Weep, daughter of the Arvernes; from your tears the flowers will be born that your beloved will pick.

He is as beautiful as the torrent, he is as strong as the tempest; all men will follow him, all women will love him.

Weep, Moina; like you, I wept, and I regret nothing of life but my tears. Weep; your tears will extinguish the flame that is burning you. Weep, but raise your head; the man who calls you his sister cannot love the daughters of earth.

You have smiled over the cradle of the son of the dead woman, you have sung sweet refrains to the son of the fay; in order to make him greater you will throw your heart into the bloody cup; if he were not Ar-Braz he would love you.

You are the chosen, one, you are the fortunate one; you will be the first to give him his name.

MOINA

He is Ar-Braz and you are his immortal fiancée..., Strike; I shall love him forever!

IDA

You will always love him, but you will love him as a sister loves her brother, as a mother loves her son.

Climb into the pilotless boat, Moina; all the way to the holy isle I will guide you. Come; I am the fay who smiled at the child whose mother died; I was the virgin whom Celtill brought from the land of the Belges.

Come; our son will be the Master's sword.

MOINA
And I shall be the victim, whose blood will sanctify the sword.

O you who swell the grapes of the vines of Gaul, swell my veins, Master; let my blood redden the sword from the point to the guard!

Let us hasten, let us hasten! I am thirsty for the red kiss of my beloved.

I would like us to leave children playing in the valley and for us to climb to the summit; you could tell me how Fleur-d'Épine, the Eve of the first day, has become Ida, the fay crowned with iris. You could tell me why, alone among his sons, the Celt beloved by the Master in the celestial fatherland does not have his companion beside him.

"The centuries of the earth are moments in heaven, and the victors will never be completely happy as long as human suffering endures.

To engender her son, Fleur-d'Épine quit the luminous fatherland; in order to watch over him, she wanders with the fays in pathless spaces; but in the heart of heaven her place is not taken and it is the breath of her husband that has passed over her lips when the waves lick her feet in the meadows of the North.

THE GULLS
Over the dolmen the blood will flow. Waves, waves, come! The pilotless boat accosts the holy isle. Waves, waves, pass!

THE GRAND DRUIDESS
Death alone can break the chain with nine links; why have you climbed into the boat without an oarsman, daughter of the Arvernes?

MOINA
I want to be the voice of the past in the harp with nine strings.

THE GRAND DRUIDESS
Do you want this new maidservant, Cora?

For twenty years you have been mute, soul of the oak; for twenty years, white light, you have no longer illuminated the cup. In what star are you dreaming, beloved daughter of the Master? In what skies are you singing, divine Skylark?

As he grass appeals to the rain, as the iceberg appeals to the sun, for twenty years we have been calling you, blonde queen of the sunset.

THE FAYS
For twenty years we have been searching for you; where are you, divine Skylark?

IDA
That is the Master's secret, and that secret I know.

Death alone can break the chain with nine links; the Master has guided her, the boat has carried her, the sword must strike her.

Climb on to the red dolmen, druidesses, before the empty cup that the chosen ring breaks, before the full cup that the broken circle seals for a day.

THE DRUIDESSES
On the red dolmen, let us twirl, sisters.

"It is us who redress the divine balance; our blood falls on to the tray that is too light; our sobs rise from the tray that is too heavy."

"We dream for those who fight, we fight for those who dream."

"We live as virgins in order to render terrestrial amours eternal"

"We die alone, in order that cradles will be filed."

"We are the pyre from which the flame springs, the altar on which the incense fumes."

"We are the voice that falls from heaven to earth."

"We are the voice that rises from earth to heaven,"

"On the red dolmen, let us twirl, sisters."

THE GRAND DRUIDESS
Why do you want to enter the chain, young woman?

MOINA
Under the yoke the bulls are slumbering; I have come to seek the prod.

In the furrow the plow is rusting; I have come to wake the oxherd.

THE GRAND DRUIDESS
The cup is somber, but the serpent is rearing up and the sword is glittering; twirl on the red dolmen, my sisters...

My eyes pierce the azure; I can see...

Take the golden sickle, daughter of the Arvernes; you have forged the sword.

You are not awaited on the green hill; your blood will not fill the cup and the golden sickle will twist in your hand.

Dawn is rising, virgins of the night. The sword is gleaming. The past is summoning you; strike, sisters. The past is summoning you, the future is hers alone.

Take the golden sickle, daughter of the Arvernes; you shall be the vermilion rose that the Gauls will pluck, and beneath our green leaves, the divine Skylark will hide her nest.

On the celestial hill, before the woolen tents, the warriors are waiting for us... But we are waiting for you too... I can read your name in the stars... Come, sisters.

THE FAYS
With the past that is crumbling are we going to fall?
With their souls, are we going to enter the celestial Gaul?

THE DRUIDESSES
Before us the barrier looms up. In our icy bodies, in the land of oaks, our souls await the supreme combat; we shall be the flowers of the next sheaf, the fiancées of the last fighters.

Nine times the blade has been raised; from nine breasts the blood has trickled into the cup. The chain that linked the future to the past is broken; the nine virgins of the bay of Morbihan are dead.

On the bloody dolmen, paler than the dead, Moina hides her head in her hands and does not see the fays who are whirling on the foam of the waves.

But the daughter of the Arvernes knows where her route leads, the void of the gulf does not attract her; she marks her forehead with warm blood and stands up proudly.

A vague form floats in the morning mist.

MOINA
In order to bear the burden I am alone and you are mute, Cora... The cup is foaming...

The serpent is hissing... At your breath I tremble, soul with the powerful wings.

THE FAYS
In the rays of the setting sun we have sought the Skylark and we have not found her. In the flower that is opening, in the passing cloud, we have searched; have we looked hard, sisters, under the branches of the almond tree?

"Like dead leaves, a gust of wind carries us away. The vision glimpsed in the mist is effaced; like dead leaves, a gust of wind carries us away.

MOINA

Why are you hiding under that azure veil, Cora?

I am your maidservant; I have given you my heart entirely... No, I have not given you my heart; when I tried to tear love out of it, I broke it into little pieces.

Here, look! On the track of the roe deer I can hear the pack howling; I am throwing those crumbs to the hungry dogs. Here, look!

Now that I am your maidservant, command, Cora. Do you want me to throw my soul to the pack as well?

THE VOICE

He is waiting for you in Narbonne...

THE FAYS

Like dead leaves, a whirlwind rolls us.

"How pale the dead are on the reed dolmen!"

"The gulls are watching over their bodies; the boat without an oarsman is bearing Moina away."

"When the moon rises, we dance under the oak, we glide over the heath; but when dawn wakes, a gust of wind carries us away like a swarm of bees into the funereal valley in the land of the Orient."

THE GULLS

In order to chase away the crows, we are circling the dolmen, but our wings are stiffening.

"The cup is overturned, the flame is extinct, the serpent is asleep; who will watch over the nine dead women of the holy isle? Our wings are stiffening."

THE TIDE

For those who were searching on the sand under green curtains of algae for the secret of the future, I have carved a bed in the coral the color of blood.

THE ROCK

In the crystal grotto where the leaves that speak unfurl in long festoons, three tombs are hollowed out, three emerald tombs for the savant virgins who read the words of the past in the leaves.

THE WEST WIND

And those who sang to the starlight, who let their long hair float under my lips in my somber domain, where will they hide?

Master, I am the whip of your anger; on the wave I execrate, on the cliff I erode, I hear nothing but plaints; only those mute mouths sang when I passed with open wings.

Change the loosened tresses of those beautiful pale bodies into the sonorous strings of ivory harps.

THE GULLS

Let us go to moisten our wings on the iridescent waves; on the bed of coral three are lying, in the tomb of emerald three are hidden; into ivory harps three are changed.

"To the banks of the Loire the wind pushes the boat. Waves, waves, come! On the somber dolmen, only the harps are weeping. Waves, waves, pass!"

Vercingetorix has found under the almond trees of Narbonne the blonde daughter of the fays, the ward of Caesar, and he has not come back.

"But why is Caesar keeping the young chief beside him, of whom there is already talk around the fires? He has come to conquer; why is he teaching the science of war to the man who will be his enemy tomorrow? Why is it him who is bringing together the immortal fiancés?

"How little a man weighs in the hand of the Almighty! He decides, and the traitor who is going to strike attaches himself the strap of the shield that will ward off his arrow."

"Of his destiny a man is the master; but the One who knows everything makes use of that free will for his own designs.

"Caesar knows that Gaul can only be vanquished by herself, and he wants to put the untamed soul of the north to sleep in the sunlit cup of the south; the Master carves the cup himself, but instead of filling it with the poison that kills, he fills it with the wine that renders strength.

"Listen, and you who know the true names of those who speak will understand."

CAESAR

They are dreaming about Ar-Braz; I shall enable him to be born. I will be the rich man, I will be the master... Then we shall leave, and with them, I shall go further than Darius, further than Cambyses, further than Alexander.

I shall make one body of these thousand stumps; of these thousand tribes I shall make one army; but I need a Gaulish ax to carve this granite; fortune has put him in my hand.

The ax is heavy—if I were not Caesar I would want to be Vercingetorix—but when it has felled the oak, it will want to square it, and then its thinned blade will collide with the Roman sword.

Fortune already smiled on me when Marius had the idea of making a Roman of that Gaulish woman with the soft eyes.

ALAUDA[20]

What do you want of me. Caesar?

CAESAR

To tell you my friends in Rome have sent you to the lions and the gladiators.

---

[20] *Alauda* is the Latin name of the genus of larks that includes the skylark.

ALAUDA

Where are they?

CAESAR

In the circus built for you, my lovely Skylark.

ALAUDA

I'll go see them.

CAESAR

Wait a moment. Would you like to be a queen?

ALAUDA

Queen of what?

CAESAR

Of Gaul.

ALAUDA

And for that, what must I do?

CAESAR

Marry a Gaul and be nothing but the icy cup that pours ardent intoxication. Vercingetorix...

ALAUDA

No, not him.

CAESAR

He alone can dress that altar, but when the incense fumes, I shall return and then you can choose. You are my beloved daughter, Alauda, with the crown I am giving you an altar.

Listen: the Gauls say that a Being, sometimes a goddess and sometimes a woman, watches over their race; they call her the Skylark. Marius knew that when he carried you away in his toga, and that is why he chose your name.

The Gauls also say that in days of danger, that soul is incarnated and an invincible hero, her immortal fiancé, is reborn.

You shall be the awaited goddess and you will make of the man I have chosen for you the hero that all obey.

ALAUDA

He won't want that.

CAESAR

You'll be queen; he'll love you, Return quickly...

It's necessary that he want it; it's necessary that Gaul has but one head, in order for me to be able to sever it with a single stroke.

They can only be vanquished by themselves. In order for me to gain a thousand of them, it will be necessary for me to sacrifice a thousand, but when they're mine. I shall preserve them as a miser hoards his treasure. I have come to Gaul in search of soldiers, not gladiators.

Your veins are fecund, queen of the west; I shall bandage your wounds with crimson and the blood will return red to your heart and your cheek...

If I had not needed him I would have made him my lieutenant, and later I would have carved out a fine kingdom for him in the plains of the Indus or the Ganges. But I need him...

"What does Caesar want, then?"

"He wants what the Master wants; he wants to harness the Gaulish stallion to the Roman chariot. But if he knew who would sit down on the chariot with the sonorous wheels...!"

The centuries of the earth are hours in heaven. How long it took to grease the wheels of the chariot, to bridle the stallion! How long it took to find the coachman!

But the chariot is ready, the route is free; make room for the Skylark of the Gauls!

In order to divine the future it is necessary to look at the past; let us not turn the head yet, and let us listen to the fays

177

who, like fireflies, follow under the almond trees those they call their daughters.

THE FAYS

Why has the hawk quit his aerie?

"Vercingetorix, why have you followed Caesar? The snow is melting; it is necessary to take the colts to pasture, come back. Come back; the young women are sad since you departed."

"Is it Caesar he has followed? The blonde virgin is beautiful, her eyes are as profound as the wave that sleeps under the dolmen of Morbihan."

"She is our daughter; she was born in our arms, but a Roman veil floats over her hair. Why?"

"Draped in her white tunic, on the edge of pathless woods, anxiously, she is listening to the harp that is vibrating in the North and the clarion that is sounding in the South."

"The harp says: 'Remember.' The clarion cries: 'Come, you shall have jewels and marble palaces, wine in full cups and the earth before you into which to push our horse.'"

"Look hard, sisters; is she not the one that we have glimpsed under the azure veil above the dolmen?"

ALAUDA

Vercingetorix... Involuntarily, I spell out that barbaric name.

They almost make me afraid, these tall young men with bright eyes, and I turn round when they pass, involuntarily.

And these poets with golden necklaces and scarred foreheads, who suspend their harps from the chains of their swords, I shiver as I listen to them, and I listen to them, involuntarily.

Vercingetorix... He is also a bard.

When he sang me the somber poem of the virgins of the night, why did it seem to me that I had heard those strophes before, which wept like the winter wind? I no longer want to hear them; during my sleep they take on substance, and when I awake, I'm afraid.

They take on substance…I have seen waves eroding the red dolmen on the island, and I have seen the nine virgins on the dolmen. I have seen them, pale and cold, their eyes open, a knife in the heart. And, their feet in the blood and their arms upraised to the sky, I have seen the living, paler than the dead.

Like the fays of their poems. I floated in a moonbeam, and the virgin said to me: "Where will you sing tomorrow, Skylark?"

I am the daughter of the sin; night horrifies me.

THE FAYS
In the radiance of the sunset we have sought the Skylark, and we have not found her. In the flower that is opening, in the cloud that is passing, we have sought her; have we looked carefully, sisters, beneath the branches of the almond tree?

ALAUDA
I stammered on Marius' knees; I grew up next to Caesar; I'm a Roman. And yet, on waking from that dream my hair seems to me to be impregnated with the bitter perfume of the Ocean.

Among the Gauls, it is said, blonde virgins hide in the forests of oaks. By day the flowers speak to them; by night, a moonbeam carries them all the way to the celestial crescent…I would like to be a Gaulish woman.

I am only a Roman. I shall only be the icy cup that pours ardent intoxication, but I shall be a queen.

No, I won't do that…I believe that I shall love him, the chef with such bright eyes and such a heavy had. When he speaks to me he blushes and trembles; he will be king if I wish it, but I don't want that. I love him, I think.

What will he reply to Caesar?

CAESAR

Vercingetorix does not love you; he has refused the throne that I have offered to him to share with you....

ALAUDA

Oh! I love him!

CAESAR

You did not love him this morning.

ALAUDA

But I love him now... If he had wanted to be your vassal, your lieutenant, I would not have loved him. He will only be your friend, Caesar, and he will love me.

CAESAR

Are you mad?

ALAUDA

All these dispersed clans he would group around him, and when you wanted to go to Rome, he would bring you a fine army. The walls of Rome are thick but the Gauls are strong; with a thrust of the shoulder they would knock them down, and when they had sat you on the ivory throne, when he stood behind you with a bloody sword in his hand, your dream would no longer be a dream.

I too want to see Rome; I would follow him.

CAESAR

Beware, Alauda, my friends are demanding beautiful slaves. I have treated you as a daughter, but I'm your master— have you forgotten that?

ALAUDA

My master! What you have given me, take back; I don't want anything. I've never asked you for anything. Why didn't you leave me in my nest of moss?

I'm a Gaulish woman; adieu, Caesar.

CAESAR
Lictor, take hold of that woman.

ALAUDA
The Skylark has wings.

CAESAR
These somber forests hide strange mysteries; what if what they said were true?

I'm as mad as the sculptor who worshiped the god that he had carved.

It's necessary that Gaul has only one head; let's search for another Ar-Braz.

They're jealous and avid to command; in every clan I'll find an Ar-Braz, obedient and convinced...

She spoke Latin and I believed her to be Roman. She's still nothing but a barbarian; I'll treat her as a barbarian. The people like beautiful Gaulish women.

And you, madman, do you believe that you're of a stature to fight with Caesar? You were alone and you stood up to me; my cavaliers will catch up with you this evening and your head will fall.

THE FAYS
The hour has sounded.

The veil is tearing! Sing, sacred oaks and mossy stones the hymn of the old Gauls to the incarnate virgin.

Awake, blacksmith; we need swords, swords by the hundred; the virgin of battles has shown herself to us.

Under the green birches, bards, awake; we need poems as brilliant as dreams; the white queen has been found.

He has departed, but his soul has remained in Narbonne.

He has marched until sunset without looking back; but before descending he northward-facing slope he has stopped;

the sea breeze brings him the perfume of almond trees, and his heart has remained on Narbonne,

THE FAYS

The almond trees are quivering in the breath of spring and the chilly willows are sowing their golden catkins. In the clear sky the moon is trembling.

In the clear sky the moon is trembling and on the white reeds swayed by the stream an opal veil fringed with sapphires is floating.

In the opal veil fringed by sapphires, broad wings are fluttering silently and blonde tresses are shivering.

The lictor has closed the door of the cell. With his two hands on his ax he is on watch by the threshold, and the slave promised to the kisses of the crowd gazes at her bare feet, bruised by shackles.

The fatigued stallion lying in the long grass sways his heavy head gently. On a reindeer skin near a silver helmet, a greyhound is asleep.

The Arverne is marching slowly in the meadow, but his soul is far away on the marble steps of the palace of Narbonne.

On the marble steps of the palace of Narbonne, the young woman with the azure eyes smiles as she hands him a hawthorn branch

Large tears and drops of blood are dripping from the hawthorn branch...but the virgin smiles and shows him a star.

In the nacreous radiance the blonde fays sway and he cheerful spites twirl... Their wings have touched the bronze door and the lictor on watch there.

The lictor falls, the door opens, the shackles break and the Skylark is free! The blonde fays surround her and the cheerful sprites carry her away.

The stallion whinnies and the greyhound growls, but the Arverne is following his dream.

The Arverne is following his dream, and he does not see the sparks on the road to Narbonne.

On the road to Narbonne, Caesar's Numidians are squeezing the fuming flanks of their black mares.

The stallion rears up, the greyhound bounds, and the Arverne is on horseback, his sword high, his hair in the wind, bare-breasted waiting for the horsemen.

Are there a hundred? Are there a thousand? He charges like a wild bull, head down.

Are there a hundred? Are there a thousand? Mares fall, heads fly.

The blonde fays are surrounding her; the cheerful sprites are carrying her away.

The fays have crowned her with vervain; the sprites have carried her into a large meadow, under the somber dolmen.

There are not a hundred, there are a thousand!

The stallion stumbles; the bloody sword is blunted.

The bloody sword is blunted, the greyhound is gasping; there are not a hundred, there are a thousand.

There are not a hundred, there are a thousand! Heads fly, the bloody sword is blunted.

Cold sweat runs from the forehead of Vercingetorix and it's necessary that his sword empties a circle around him. He recoils all the way to the somber dolmen.

There are not a hundred, there are a thousand! The bloody sword is blunted.

In the clear sky the moon is trembling. I can see long-haired horsemen in the plain, descending from the north.

In the breath of spring the willows are sowing heir golden catkins. The breeze brings me the savage chords of the march of the Arvernes.

Whistling, the javelins tear apart the opal veil. Hold firm, Vercingetorix, Moina is guiding your clan."

MOINA
A head for an eye and a hand for a finger!

THE HORSEMEN
And a heart for a wound!

VERCINGETORIX
Hurrah, companions!

THE FAYS
We have liberated the Skylark, we have guided the druidess; you were not thinking of us, Caesar.
She is shivering under the dolmen, but soon...

ALAUDA
Who has broken my shackles? I don't know whether I'm asleep... I was dreaming; that's certainly the cold wall. While I slept my irons have been removed; the people of Rome don't like women with bruised feet... Caesar, the Skylark has wings,. I'm s Gaulish woman, and I defy you.
But who will warn him, the man who believes in amity? I am a Gaulish woman; death will give me wings and I shall be his fay.

THE FAYS
Don't look at the cold wall of the somber dolmen, look over the plain; we have broken the door of the cell and we have carried you near to your beloved.
"Far from her an invisible hand is pushing us."
"She wanted to be born a woman in order to love better. How beautiful the nuptial bed of Ar-Braz and his bride will be!"
"A gust of wind is carrying us away, but the Numidians are dead. Vercingetorix is looking over there, under the dolmen... The wind is carrying us away..."

VERCINGETORIX

Behold the Valkyries passing; I held the sword but they struck. You arrived just in time.

Luern, find some water; this poor dog is thirsty.

MOINA

Sit down here; your head is bleeding.

VERCINGETORIX

I'm happy; I feel alive; I've become myself again. The amity of that Roman weighed upon my heart and prevented it from beating.

He must be expecting me... Mount up, children, we're going to Narbonne.

Play the march of the Arvernes, Kenrik. Blow with full lungs, so that we can be heard coming; we're not thieves.

How heavy that amity was! Blow, Kenrik, blow more loudly.

ALAUDA

I can hear the march of his clan. Vercingetorix! Vercingetorix! Where am I? He's here.

VERCINGETORIX

That's her voice! Where are you, Alauda?
Who has crowned you with vervain, my beloved?
You're tottering…why?

MOINA

A woman deceives by night, a virgin deceives by day, a foreigner always deceives.

VERCINGETORIX

She's dead.

MOINA

She wanted to bring you Caesar's head herself.

VERCINGETORIX
Which of you killed her? By heaven, he'll die.

MOINA
And what if it were me?

VERCINGETORIX
What if it were you? Why was I not left on the edge of the lake? The vultures would have carried me away.

MOINA
The vultures wouldn't carry Ar-Braz away.

ALAUDA
I love you!

VERCINGETORIX
She loves me. Did you hear, friends? She loves me! Mount up, companions.

MOINA
Lave that Roman woman here.

ALAUDA
Take me with you.

VERCINGETORIX
Come. You'll only have a cabin of tree trunks, but that cabin will have my shield for a door and my sword for a bolt. Luern, your horse.

MOINA
No, this must not be, this cannot be. She's a foreigner and you are Ar-Braz

VERCINGETORIX

Caesar also said: "You are Ar-Braz. She will be my wife.

MOINA

Never! Never! Druidess of Sein,[21] priestess of Cora, maidservant of the Skylark, n this life and the other, I curse her. May those who touch her, those who serve her and those who approach her be...

VERCINGETORIX

Shut up, druidess, And you, come here. Am I a swine-herd or the chief? Come here. Closer, or by my mother's soul, heads will roll on the grass.

Look at her carefully, and when you encounter her, bow down before her.

Now, go where you wish; I am no longer your chief

ALAUDA

You are right, druidess; you don't know who I am, and I know who ought to be the companion of Ar-Braz.

Return to your clan, Vercingetorix. Forget what you have just said; these men love you. You ought only to love the divine Skylark.

VERCINGETORIX

But...

ALAUDA

Only love the divine Skylark; I wish it. Yes I wish it. Believe in me as I have believed in you. Adieu, and may the Master protect you,

VERCINGETORIX

I will always love you.

---

[21] Sein, or Sena is an island off Finistère traditionally associated with Druidism, particularly with an elite of nine priestesses.

ALAUDA

I too will always love you... Go.

VERCINGETORIX

March in your ranks; I want to be alone.

ALAUDA

I love him! I love Ar-Braz, the immortal fiancé of the divine Skylark. Take me, O Death.

He's returning. He loves me.

VERCINGETORIX

Since you have followed me this far, why don't you want to follow me further? Are you afraid that these men will call you foreigner?

ALAUDA

With you, I would not be afraid of anything. I will do what can be done and I will always love you. Believe in me as I have believed in you. Adieu, Ar-Braz.

VERCINGETORIX

Adieu.

ALAUDA

Twice he has come and twice I have rejected him. Why is his horse going so rapidly? Why is the road bending so soon? I can't see him any more... I'll catch up with him at the halt... No, he loves me today, but when he has seen the Skylark he won't love me any longer. But he will have loved me for a day, for an hour... No, no, he won't throw me away like an empty cup, and when he intoxicates himself with the celestial tankard, perhaps he'll think of the frail clay cup. I love him, he loved me; who wouldn't envy me?

Where should I go? In the north they call me foreigner, in the south they call me slave.

But how did I get here? Who broke my shackles? Who opened my prison? Who carried me to that grotto? There's blood... cadavers... Caesar's Numidians! I was asleep; perhaps they carried me away.

Who can tell me? They're all dead.

Since yesterday, I no longer know where I am or whether I'm dreaming. I'm stifling...my head is bursting. Cricket, how fortunate you are to be able to sing!

THE CRICKET

I'm singing because I'm in love.

ALAUDA

It replied to me! I'm afraid! I'm afraid!

THE CRICKET

I replied because you questioned me. But why are you afraid, Skylark?

ALAUDA

I must be the Skylark. He'll love me forever. How can I be sure? Swallow, where have you come from?

THE SWALLOW

From Narbonne, Skylark. Beware, Caesar is coming. Where do you want me to go?

ALAUDA

Can you carry this hawthorn flower?

THE SWALLOW

Its heavy, but I can carry it.

ALAUDA

Fly northwards and place it on Vercingetorix's lips.
I wish I had wings, swallow. Go.
Cricket, do you know who brought me here last night?

THE CRICKET
No, I was asleep; but the willow of the path might know.

ALAUDA
Willows, do you know?

THE WILLOW
The fays crowned you with vervain, and the cheerful sprits carried you.

As they passed, the fays sad: "She's the Skylark. She's our queen, who wanted to be reborn a woman in order to love better."

Here comes Caesar, beware. Would you like to enter into my trunk?

ALAUDA
I want to talk to Caesar. Who is accompanying him?

THE WILLOW
The Eduen Imperadorix.

ALAUDA
Salut, Cesar. Where are you going?

CAESAR
Are you a shade?

ALAUDA
Look at the imprint of bonds on my wrists. The people of Rome must love bruised flesh, since you told your lector to tie them so tightly.

You see this blood on the grass? It isn't that of Ar-Braz. When one launches crows against the claws of a hawk, this is what happens. However, these Numidians were your best cavaliers.

CAESAR
What the Gauls said is true, then? You're the Skylark?

ALAUDA
I'm the Skylark, and Vercingetorix is Ar-Braz.

IMPERADORIX
Vercingetorix is the son of Celtill, the Arverne who my father condemned to the torture of traitors. Does the son want to imitate the father?

Caesar, the Eduens have always been friends of Rome; if you give me this woman. I'll take her to Vercingetorix with a rope around her neck and a distaff in her hand.

CAESAR
If I wanted to punish Vercingetorix I have my legions; but the insult of a barbarian does not rise as high as me.

I came when you called me; if you have no further need of me, I'll leave you to your quarrels.

If she pleases you, take her.

IMPERADORIX
You're beautiful, Alauda; I've loved you for a long time.

ALAUDA
Vercingetorix! Vercingetorix!

CAESAR
The Skylark has wings; be careful she doesn't escape you.

IMPERADORIX
My horse can go faster than her.

You've given her to me. In a month I'll take her to Vercingetorix.

CAESAR

They're jealous and avid to command; I'll be the ally of all those who want to rise and I'll help all those who want to sever heads that are too high.

I searched for an Ar-Braz; I've found two of them. Fortune is smiling on Caesar.

And the Skylark?

The Skylark will be mine, because I love her too.

Caesar sees the wheat that he has sown ripen; half of Gaul follows the Arverne, half follows the Eduen, and the blood flows in floods.

Caesar is about to harvest the grain he has sown; the Roman army raises its pikes over the exhausted fighters.

"Caesar is about to demolish what he has built. When the foreign clarions sound over Gaulish territory, the quarrels are forgotten, the rivals embrace.

"That has always happened ad will be again; you'll see."

"Yes, that will happen. It's for the good of men that the Master has created eternal combat.

"But has the Eduen taken the Skylark away?"

"Listen to what the peasants sad yesterday and you'll know what they will say tomorrow."

STRUMMOR

Your wound is closed, Kenrik, you'll depart at daybreak; the bard ought not to quit the chief.

You'll travel until you're rejoined him, and you'll say to him: "Vercingetorix, your men salute you. They're waiting for you in order to mark the colts; but if what you've commenced isn't foolish, march without looking back.

Depart, my son, and don't forget how your brothers died. Come back with the chief or don't come back.

KENRIK

I'll try to do likewise. Adieu, Father.

192

STRUMMOR

I'm getting old and the house is empty.

When one runs the plain, ax in hand, the days pass quickly and the nights are too short; but when one can no longer quit the fireside and when, before the fire, one sees the circle becoming narrower every evening, instead of sleeping, one thinks. In the dying embers one sees again, as children, those who will not return.

Woe betide those who die on their beds; instead of being mourned, they mourn

Is someone knocking?

Come in, whoever you are; the guest is always expected.

THE BEGGAR WOMAN

Have you, master of this house, a place by your hearth? I'm cold. Have you a place at your table? I'm hungry.

STRUMMOR

Be welcome, Nowadays my hearth is always too large and my table always too long.

GANIEDA

Your feet are bleeding.

THE BEGGAR WOMAN

I've come a long way.

STRUMMOR

You have a kindly gaze.

Ganieda is alone; would you like to help her look after the sheep? I'll give you six lambs ad a woolen cape.

THE BEGGAR WOMAN

I'll be happy to stay in your house.

STRUMMOR

The bargain is made. Come and embrace me; you're my daughter.

GANIEDA

You're my sister.

STRUMMOR

What is your name?

THE BEGGAR WOMAN

When me feet weren't bleeding I sang all day and people called me the Skylark; would you like to leave me that name?

STRUMMOR

The Skylark? You have a pretty name.

When will you sing us the song of the skylark? It's a long time since anyone has sung it.

THE SKYLARK

Your fire has warmed my hands, your welcome has warmed my heart; I'll sing you the beloved song.

Mad is he who weaves a cage for the bird of the sun, for the Skylark of the Gauls.

Who has vanquished? Is it the Eduen? Is it the Arverne? It's the Roman.

Like the crow, he only descends to the battlefield in the evening. Like the wolf, he only comes by night. He only strikes the wounded, that is why he has vanquished. But he has not captured the Skylark. Mad is he who weaves a cage for the bird of the sun.

Why has he conquered all the land from the Seine to the Loire?

Because his tongue is forked like the tongue of a serpent. Because Gaul is not a tree but shoots on a stump, and to each scion he has whispered.

That is why he has vanquished.

But he has not captured the Skylark, the one who sings in the sky when the sword sleeps in a golden scabbard, the one who sings in the furrow when the twisted sword falls from the weary hand.

The chiefs are vanquished, Gaul is not.

They have curbed the heads of the sons of the Brenns, but the son of the virgin, in the snowy valley, is forging a new sword, and on the blade he is engraving unknown words.

STRUMMOR
Who taught you that song?

THE SKYLARK
When the twisted sword falls from the weary hand between the clods of turf, the Skylark sings.

As soon as the snowdrop turns green on the lava, the son of the virgin descends into the plain with his horsemen with tortoiseshell breastplates and starry foreheads.

Straight before him he marches; the Romans are everywhere. Every evening his horsemen have bloody heads and severed hands on their saddle-bows.

The chiefs consult one another. The tribunes threaten. Caesar writes: Your heads will fall if these cutters of the route are not nailed to trees by the roadside.

Owls are nailed to the trees by the roadside, but the hawk cannot be nailed. Listen to the Skylark sing. The immortal fiancée of Ar-Braz the invincible.

GANIEDA
Who are you?

THE SKYLARK
I am your sister; you have said so.

STRUMMOR
If you are only a woman, you have become my daughter. But if you are the one I believe, sing, Skylark; in all those empty seats men have sat who died defending you.

THE SKYLARK
They are good soldiers, the soldiers of the Skylark.

On the saddle-bows heads are bleeding. On the severed hands the rings of knights are glistening. On the thresholds the young women, laughing, are disputing the golden rings, and on the dust of the road, joyful children are counting the drops of blood.

Where the horsemen with the starry foreheads pass, the young men buckle their sword-belts and pick up their striped cloaks, because the young women say: Spin with our distaffs; we will follow the chief with the blue-green eyes in his clan with red arms.

STRUMMOR
A head for an eye and an arm for a finger!

THE SKYLARK
They are vanquished everywhere, always!

The clans no longer have chiefs, the chiefs no longer have soldiers. The wolves have licked the wounds, the snow has blanched the bones.

STRUMMOR
The snow has not blanched the bones of the Eduens, the sword has not touched Imperadorix, the accursed.

THE SKYLARK
Imperadorix the Eduen believed that he was able to catch the Skylark in a trap like a nightingale, but the Skylark broke the trap and flew away.

Has she risen into the sun's radiance? No. She sings on the shoulder of the awaited Ar-Braz; she is perched on the thatch of his roof.

The chiefs are vanquished; Gaul is not. Vercingetorix knows that. While men are bandaging their wounds, while the chiefs are telling lies, he is knotting the green sash of the bards to his cloak.

When the reaper mops his streaming brow, when the haymaker leans on her rake, a powerful voice emerges from the shadow of the walnut trees, a song of the past.

Attentively, the haymakers lean over, and smiling, the reapers say to them in a low voice: "It's the chief with the heavy hand."

And the bard sings the fine battles, the long feasts. And the young women go pale and he men say: "Father, whenever you wish."

STRUMMOR

Yes, whenever he wishes.
You are the divine Skylark.

THE SKYLARK

I am the one you have picked up.

My feet are bleeding, Ganieda; I have walked too far today, I would like to rest.

Watch, Strummor; tonight, the one who is to come might knock on your door.

And You who sees everything, bless this house where the beggar-woman was received as a daughter.

I too would like to hear you sing, Skylark. If you sang, those who quarreled over an ear in the field that the storm has smashed might mingle their gleanings and carry their sickles to the blacksmith. And while the blacksmith straightens the sickles into swords, the men might winnow the wheat and, having taken it to the mill, might say to the miller: "Miller, open the gate of the lock wide, that your mill-wheels might purr gaily; you are milling the wheat of France, for the day of revenge, and for payment you will have your soldier's bread."

But you are soaring too high in the azure, Skylark; only the dreamer can hear your voice. The laborer only hears his neighbors, who are saying: "Why are the ears that that man is cutting heavier than mine?"

"You are seeking her in the clouds, and it's in the furrow that she is singing; those who lower their heads are the only ones heard.

"Listen to what the peasants were saying yesterday and you will know what they will say tomorrow."

STRUMMOR

She is not a woman.

You have blessed my couch, Master. You have given me eight sons, seven have died, struck from the front, and the eighth is brave. You have given me two daughters. Ganieda is as cheerful as a warbler and as laborious as a bee, and Moina is your druidess.

You have blessed my house, Master; the son of the wind grew up here.

Ida wept as she climbed the path; she wept at the nuptial feast, and the next day he old chief departed and never returned.

You are not the son of Celtill, Vercingetorix, you are the son of the wind, you are Ar-Braz.

VERCINGETORIX

I am not Ar-Braz; I am an outlaw

STRUMMOR

Him! She had said so.

Come, my son. My legs are trembling. It's you! It's really you!

Sit down here, where you sat when you were a child. You're a man, my son. You're weeping? Why are you weeping?

VERCINGETORIX

I've come back alone.

STRUMMOR

They were brave, were they not, the seven sons of the woodcutter? They fell beside you, in their place, did they not? When I arrive up there, they will come to meet me, and I shall be proud. The eighth will also be there.

It will not be said that I alone died in my bed; I shall follow you tomorrow,

Ganieda, Ganieda, bring a tankard of wine. Bring it quickly, it's him!

Tomorrow, we will alert the men.

VERCINGETORIX

You'll alert the children; there are no more men among the Arvernes. Those who followed me have not come back.

STRUMMOR

Our sons are yours, and as long as you march at their head, we shall have nothing to say.

VERCINGETORIX

If I'm mistaken...

STRUMMOR

Shut up, Father; you're wrong to talk like that. I can tell you everything myself; the face of the chief ought never to betray his secret.

You're hesitating; I understand. Perhaps you divine a tear in the eyes of fathers, and you have not been fortunate thus far, but it is not necessary that these young men know that. They're children, you see; it's necessary to give them confidence.

You are fighting for a just cause; you are not fighting for yourself but for us; march straight ahead. If you fall, too bad!

If your men fall, too bad! A little sooner or a little later, what you want will be, and you will be blessed.

Ganieda!

VERCINGETORIX

Alauda!

The Eduen said that you loved him; Caesar said that he had captured you.

Strummor, gather the clan. Tomorrow, we depart, the Arvernes are declaring war on Caesar.

THE SKYLARK

Here: empty, my beloved, the cup of betrothal.

Put hawthorn flowers in your hair, daughters of the Arvernes; the Master has blessed your clan. You are the chosen; you are the fortunate. Mingle with the hawthorn the woodland violet; you are the fiancées of the red betrothal. The master has blessed your clan.

Put hawthorn flowers in your hair; hawthorn is the flower of my beloved.

Empty the cup, Ar-Braz; I am your fiancée.

The bard who spoke along the roads, on the threshold of cottages and in the shade of walnut trees has been heard; the clans have sent men to the assembly that is held, on the night of the equinox around the great dolmen of the forest of the Carnutes,

Those men will choose the king of the war, and all of Gaul will rise up at his appeal.

"The Arvernes have not come; why?"

"They have not come, but the Skylark is there and she knows where they are."

Outside the circle the people are waiting. In the evening mist the fays are twirling; around their ensigns the warriors are grouping; under the great dolmen the Skylark is hidden.

THE SKYLARK

The dreams of your philosophers have tarnished the soul of my druids, the words of your poets have perverted the ear of my bards, the lips of your courtesans have drunk the blood of my chiefs, and you think that you are victorious, Caesar? Look there, in the shadows, at the ignorant, the mute and the children; they are the soldiers of Ar-Braz.

To those, whose wounded hands redden the heavy plow, he has not said: "You will be heeded, you will be applauded, you will be feared." He has said: "You will be thirsty and you will be hungry, but those who return with enter under their roofs again free." And they have all followed him.

They are there, more numerous than the needles of the larch, the men of my beloved.

And do you believe that those that you have deceived, those you have seduced and those you have enervated are yours, Caesar? My men are the best, they are the most knowledgeable, and they are the bravest. It is me they seek in your temples, in your circuses and under your tent; when I loom up before them, beware, Caesar!

THE FAYS

In the terrible night the stars are lighting up.

The harps are vibrating, listen.

"Far from our queen, an invisible hand is pushing us."

A BARD

Why are you growling so loudly, voice of darkness? Earth, why are you trembling? Why are you twisting in the clouds, lightning? I am neither your slave nor your son. You have only lent me a cloak of mud, and I will become your master again if you take it back.

THE SKYLARK

I am no long anything but a woman; will you recognize me?

MOINA

Around the enclosure I have circled nine times; the sacred night is commencing, the circle is closed.

Foreigner, what are you doing here?

Roman woman, what do you want?

THE SKYLARK

I want to show you the one who is to come.

He will be as strong as an elk, he will be as beautiful as an aspen; all men will follow him, all women will love him.

You are a woman, my sister.

MOINA

I am the daughter of Cora and you are the daughter of Caesar.

The trumpets are sounding, the fires are being lit. See those weapons gleaming; the circle is closed and I alone can emerge alive from the closed circle. You will die.

I hate you, daughter of the south; you have broken the wings of the wild hawk. You will die.

I hate you; the Arverne is not Ar-Braz, since he only loves you. You will die.

THE SKYLARK

All men will follow him, all women will love him.

You are a woman, my sister, and I am the victim whom the voice will designate to the chief, whose blood will sanctify the sword.

MOINA

You are a foreigner; go away! Take her away.

THE SKYLARK

My people are speaking, Shut up.

THE PEOPLE

You whose throne is motionless above the errant stars, enlarge our hearts and harden our arms; enable lightning to spring from the somber night and may its fires re-temper the twisted sword of the Gauls.

O Cora! Cora the white!

THE SKYLARK

Master, on the holy mountain I was your beloved daughter; do not weigh your hand upon my people. Inspire the one who will speak and enlighten those who will listen.

MOINA

There is a Roman woman here; kill her.

THE PEOPLE

Kill her.

MOINA

I can no longer see her! I thought I saw her.

I see her everywhere, in the smoke that rises, in the cloud that passes, and I believed that my heart had burned and the ashes had been thrown to the wind.

THE PEOPLE

Kill her.

THE FAYS

We have hidden her under the dolmen.

How beautiful our queen is! Her lips have the vague perfume of clearings, her hair has the sweet perfume of furze.

THE PEOPLE

To the mistletoe! To the mistletoe!

The moonlight silvers the vast clearing spangled by armor, and stripes the great shadows of raised stones.

Around the sacred circle that only the chiefs enter, the people growl like a torrent eroding its dike.

On the leaves of the oaks the breeze rocks the fays.

Leaning on the dolmen, the anxious druidess gazes at the stars rising toward the zenith.

MOINA

And Vercingetorix has not come.

The moon is still rising; let us pray, Gauls!

He would have found he foreigner and he would not come. Why has she escaped the mire of the Eduens, that Roman viper?

Let us pray, Gauls!

THE FAYS

Under the dolmen we have hidden the Skylark. But far from the sacred circle a hand rejects us when the fire of midnight is lit on the altar.

"Neither flowers nor women; neither bodies not souls; without hopes and without regrets, why weep like the roses, why pray like humans?"

"What if we were to go to twirl over the sonorous gulf, my sisters, in the white mist of the crazy cascade, with the iridescent bubbles?"

"All the men are there; let us go sit down at the deserted hearths."

"On the idle distaffs we shall mingle with the flax, the fruit of the burdock and the leaf of the holly."

THE BARDS

Peoples, pray.

THE FAYS

A gust of wind lifts us up; a ray of light draws us away; let's go, my sisters.

"The bed is empty... the cradle cold."

"And there…and there…where are they, then, the daughters of the Arvernes?"

"The water has dried up in the bucket, the milk is curdled in the jug, where, then, are the men of Ar-Braz? Where are the daughters of the Arvernes?"

THE CRICKET

For two weeks the fire has been extinct. Two weeks ago, they all departed, the warriors and the women, the old people and the children. They have only taken their weapons.

Daughters of the night, the heather is dry and we are cold. The flame, if you wanted, would rise up roseate and we would sing merrily.

They have all departed for Genabum,[22] the children and the old people. How cold the ashes are!

THE FAYS

At the hearth that you have guarded every night the fire is blazing.

THE CRICKET

The flame is writhing over the black stone like a long serpent.

They were sitting there on the oak benches and the old man said: "He is of our clan; we will follow him everywhere, we will always follow him, and we will all follow him. That is our right."

All the way to the bottom of our holes, the beautiful flame is shining!

---

[22] Genabum or Cenabum was the Carnute city on the site of the modern Orléans. In 52 B.C., according to the *Gallic Wars*, while Vercingetorix was besieging Gorgobina, rebel Carnutes massacred the Roman inhabitants; it was besieged by Caesar before it could be effectively fortified and the town was forced to surrender; it was then pillaged and burned as a reprisal for the massacre.

Then the Skylark stood up, she took a full cup from the table, she wet her lips therein and, holding it out to the chief, she said: "From the hymeneal cup, drink, you whom I have chosen on the green hill, in the land of the sun. Drink, mu husband, my master; you will find on high your wife smiling and your bed flowery."

And they set forth for Genabum, a city guarded by foreign soldiers.

How brightly the flame shines!

The Skylark did not depart with them; she said to them: "I will answer for the Arvernes at the roll-call of the nations; the sword of the king of war must emerge red from its scabbard."

We are crickets, on the road the birds would eat us; but if we were fays, we would go to Genabum to sing the song of the hearth to those who are going to die so far away.

THE FAYS

Will we arrive in time?

Sisters with vermilion wings, mount your black mares; the walls of Genabum are high, and molten lead will corrode their bloody hands...

THE PEOPLE

To the mistletoe; the moon is full!
To the mistletoe! To the mistletoe!

MOINA

He will not come! However, it is him who passed along the roads, who slipped into nocturnal gatherings and said in whispers: "At the assembly of the Carnutes, the blood of the victim will sanctify the sword of Ar-Braz.

THE PEOPLE

To the mistletoe! To the mistletoe!

MOINA

To the ardent pack I have thrown my heart, and it was only a roebuck that the pack pursued.

But the roebuck was handsome and I loved him. I loved him so much that, listening to my heart, I believed that it was him who was speaking.

He was not Ar-Braz, and yet I still love him as I loved him; the pack has not been able to eat my heart; the flame of the dolmen has not been able to burn it.

Cora, I have only given you what he did not want to take; why do you not strike me?

If you pardon, have pity; let your voice designate me and let my blood sanctify the sword of the unknown savior whom the people are summoning and whom I believed that I had divined.

The moon is motionless, the sacred night is commencing, Let the earth be silent; the stars are about to speak.

Why have we gathered?

A BARD

To weep.

THE PEOPLE

To seek.

MOINA

The circle is closed; but the powerful voice of the children rises all the way to the altar.

THE DRUID

Are you all here, chiefs and bards?

A BARD

I have seen many stringless harps on the heather; I have seen many amber and gold necklaces on the paths.

I counted a thousand of them, and my eyes were filled with tears: I have counted ten thousand, and my eyes have closed.

MOINA
I have counted ten thousand and my heart is swollen with joy.

THE PEOPLE
Death is the fecund soil in which the future germinates.

MOINA
Listen, children.
The moon is trembling! The voice is speaking!
Peoples are like a flock without a shepherd; the wolf will eat them. The wolf will eat them one by one, if they do not give themselves a leader whose head is high enough to count them all.

THE CHIEFS
His name.

THE PEOPLE
Ar-Braz.

IMPERADORIX
Why, daughter of Cora, are you letting a voice from outside enter the closed circle.

MOINA
Why are you speaking instead of listening?

IMPERADORIX
The daughter of Cora is also the daughter of the Arvernes.

MOINA

You are the eye of Caesar; may your eyes fill with darkness. You are the ear of Caesar; may your ears fill with terrors.

IMPERADORIX

I am a wise man, who has come to say: "Let us keep our hearts, but let us hold out our hand to someone stronger than us."

THE CHIEFS

It's necessary.

MOINA

Never! Never!

It is not for slaves that I have filled the cup, that the dust should drink it!

The stones will fall, and the tree of the mistletoe will dry up, if the blood of the traitor does not flow.

IMPERADORIX

I am Brenn of the Eduens, Caesar's lieutenant; who will dare to raise a hand against me?

Where are my friends, that I may count them?

Now count yours, daughter of the Arvernes.

MOINA

They are not numerous, the Gauls!

March, children of the oaks, march westwards; there is still a land between the Ocean and the West; it is as green as an emerald.

March, children of the oaks, march westwards; the waves will open before you as they have opened before the long-haired chief. Let us leave this soiled land to the Romans; in the green isle the springs are clear, the oaks are leafy.

Throw away these helmets, throw away these breast-plates, become the men of old again and, breasts bare, hair in the wind, you will pass like a wedge between Caesar's army and the traitor's army.

IMPERADORIX
Like reeds beneath the leafy trees, let us separate; march westwards, and we will march eastwards.

THE PEOPLE
We will march behind Ar-Braz.

Where is the chief with the heavy hand? Where are the horsemen with the starry brows?

THE SKYLARK
The white radiance has reached the altar; the hour is sounding, the victim is waiting.

MOINA
Her! Her again! Her, the inspired victim!

IMPERADORIX
I want her; she's mine,

THE PEOPLE
The victim who offers herself is ours. Strike, druidess.

THE SKYLARK
Strike, druidess.

In the isle of the nine sisters, the virgin, in dying, has said to you: "Take the golden sickle, daughter of the Arvernes; you are not awaited on the green hill; your blood will not fill the cup."

Strike, I am Cora. Strike, I am the Skylark.

MOINA
It was not a roebuck that the pack was pursuing; my heart had deceived me.

Where is the chief with the heavy hand? Where are the horsemen with the heavy brows?

I was the daughter of the night; command, daughter of the sun.

THE SKYLARK

Strike. Let the trumpets sound and the harps quiver! Let the swords be lifted! I am the victim whose blood will speak.

Let my blood swell the empty veins!

Open the enclosure; I want to see all my sons.

They are numerous, the soldiers of Ar-Braz. How handsome they are, my sons! How strong they are!

But why, Imperadorix, do you not have your golden necklace, the necklace that I gave, in the plains of the East, to the father of the Eduens?

My soul is extending its wings!

He was brave among the brave and his sons were worthy to wear the necklace of the Skylark. It was an Eduen who broke the gates of Delphi; it was an Eduen who first crossed the walls of Rome.

The veil is tearing!

Imperadorix, your ancestor was my soldier; you shall be the soldier of Ar-Braz.

IMPERADORIX

Ar-Braz! Ar-Braz, where are you?

THE SKYLARK

Listen.

THE WATCHMAN

At Genabum...

THE SKYLARK

My soul is taking flight!

THE WATCHMAN
The Arvernes have entered.

THE SKYLARK
O my beloved, the harvest will be red, but the bread will be white.

THE WATCHMAN
With Vercingetorix.

IMPERADORIX
We will follow him everywhere. We will always obey him.

THE PEOPLE
Speak, divine Skylark, speak again, the beloved.

THE SKYLARK
The prison is open; my soul is floating free. You are calling me! Close to you I rise, Master; you want him to fight alone, to die alone; you do not want him to share his glory even with me.

But this body that is collapsing, he also loved; daughters of the night, carry it to the hill of the Orient.

To the funereal grotto add three stones; let them be large enough that next to my body there is room for his.

THE PEOPLE
Let the Almighty temper the sword of Gaul!

Under the dolmen of the holy isle. Moina is washing her red hands in the waves of the sea, but nothing effaces the red stain.

On the dolmen, the pale virgins, harps of ivory with bloody breasts, vibrate sadly.

The waves stop; the wind falls silent.

MOINA

I am the daughter of the night, and the dawn has risen.

It has risen radiant. When the sun shines, who still dreams of the pale crescent?

THE WEST WIND

Under the coral grotto three are lying; in the hard crustal three are hidden; but three are changed into ivory harps.

At the wind of my wings, harps of Sein, vibrate.

MOINA

Night, I am your daughter; carry me away.

THE HAPS

Oh, the fine combat!

The sky is whitening, the clarions are sounding, can you hear them? Caesar is showing them Gergovia;[23] they are striking their weapons and shouting: "Attack! Attack!"

"Oh, the fine combat! Three times the she-wolf has leapt, three times she has recoiled. Can you see her?"

"Oh, the beautiful vermilion streams! They are striping the black sand. Can you see them?"

"And the bald man, can you see him, an ensign in his hand? The wounded are getting up; under the feet of the le-

---

[23] In the year calculable as 52 B.C., according to the *Gallic Wars*, Vercingetorix won a significant battle against Caesar at Gergovia, thought to be on the high plateau that is now the site of the town of La Roche-Blanche. It was an important Arverne fortress, from which Vercingetorix had previously been expelled by his own people before they rallied to him. According to *Gallic Wars*, Caesar's forces were troubled because the Aedui violated their treaty with the Romans, and cut the Romans' supply lines, forcing the legions to defeat them and oblige them to switch sides again. Following the defeat, Caesar had to retreat to Aedui territory.

gions the mountain is trembling! Can you see Caesar, an ensign in his hand?"

"Oh, the beautiful coral rocks, illuminated by the moon. The blood is fuming. The Romans are fleeing..."

"Like a galley with broken oars, the Roman army is adrift. It is groaning under the impact of waves with blonde crests and leaving crushed cohorts in its wake."

"But the overflowing Allier is stopping the victor."

"Can you see the horsemen with the tortoiseshell breastplates and winged helmets? Under their gray stallions the sand is giving way, but the yellow water is licking the heavy hooves and the torrents are not as strong as the horses of the Brenns."

"A head for an eye! Blood for blood! The torrent crossed, the Roman army is caught."

MOINA
My lips have not spoken the secret of my heart; the last of the virgins of the past will die in her red tunic, her sickle in her hand.

THE WEST WIND
To the wind of my wings, harps of Sein, vibrate.

THE HARPS
A gliding cloud and a rising turbulence hide the Brenns with winged helmets from us.

MOINA
My lips have not spoken the secret of my heart; I am still the one whose voice stops the wave and agitates he lightning

Of the combats out there, west wind, bring me the echo; to the breath of your wings, which the howling waves drowns, let the ivory harp quiver.

THE HARPS
"The cloud is splitting, the dust flying away."

"The enemy—the eternal enemy, the Northern bear—is moving stealthily toward the wounded she-wolf."

"In the celestial plains, bridle your horses of mist, heroes of ancient days; under the teeth of the she-wolf your sons are bleeding; under the paw of the bear your sons are being crushed.

"The vanquished Caesar has been joined by the van-quished Arioviste, and Gaul is retreating to the ramparts of Alise.[24]

"She is retreating slowly; many have remained on the battlefield. There are a great many; there are as many Romans as Gauls, as many Germans as Gauls."

"The earth is no longer drinking the blood. The aged crows are waiting until the cheeks turn green before descending; the wolves have licked the living wounds and gone to sleep."

"Silence is everywhere; the wounds were mortal and in the furrows crumbled by the horses' shoes, the crickets have been crushed."

MOINA

It is for the good of men that the Master has created the eternal combat; death is the fecund soil in which the future germinates.

But Gaul requires a beautiful funeral. She must not fall under the victor's ax with hands bound; she must die free, her eyes looking heavenwards, her hand on her sword.

You who are weeping on the waves, you who are singing in the stream, you who are dancing on the rushes, you who are sleeping in the oaks, forces without bodies, souls without form, foam of the past, seeds of the future, extinct torches,

---

[24] The modern town of Alise-Sainte-Reine is considered by many, although not uncontroversially, to be the Alesia named in the Gallic Wars as the site of Vercingetorix's last stand; after the battle and consequent siege—a landmark in the history of siege warfare—Gaul became a Roman province.

stars yet to be born, obey the druidess who commands! Transport me to where Gaul is palpitating, on the plateau of Alise.

You will have a fine funeral, blonde queen of the sunset; your tomb will be an altar, your last cry will be a prayer and your ardent shroud will show in the heavens the way to the future, to the old world gone astray.

THE WEST WIND
To the breath of my wings, harps of Sein, weep!

Facing the walls of Alise, Caesar has hollowed out ditches so deep that their horses cannot cross them; he has elevated ramparts so high that they can no longer see the cloudless sky, which refuses them a single drop of water.

Caesar has not quit his camp; who can stop that army, the last dike of Gaul, which has been waiting for the besieged for ten weeks.

VERCINGETORIX
So you have not guided them, my beloved?

And why would she bring them? Why continue the struggle? What must be done is done; in the pure granite my sword has carved a fine body, and the breath has animated it.

What had to be done is done. After a day of sweat, Master, give me a night of repose..

My task is not finished; it is commencing.

Of the thousand Gaulish tribes I have made a united and strong people; but you are not only the soul of Gaul, my beloved, you are the soul of the race of Purs and I am your soldier. My task is not finished, it is commencing. In order to sit down at the divine hearth it is necessary now that I reunite the family that the centuries have dispersed.

Our Gaul is beautiful under her tunic of vines and her crown of wheat; I shall take her by the hand and I shall say to the matron whose hair is silvering: Give your breastplate and spear to your younger sister; her chest is broad, her arm is strong. You will watch, next to the hearth.

And on her rapid mare she will go, straight ahead; she will go all the way to limitless forests, endless sands, and the sourceless river, and all the sons of the sun will shrug off their yokes.

That is what must be done, and that is what I shall do when the Master says that it is time.

Today I am the victim whose blood will seal the pact, but tomorrow...

STRUMMOR
Father, we're thirsty.

VERCINGETORIX
Tomorrow...

STRUMMOR
Tomorrow, we shall no longer be thirsty; I have counted the Brenns; we are enough to fill in that ditch and break through that heap of earth. We are the men of Gergovia, and through the Roman army we will go to demand of the traitors why they did not come.

The chief shakes his head sadly. Those for whom he was waiting are not traitors, but they have not come.

Then a cloud glides across the clear sky and the red druidess stands up before the Brenns, her sickle in her hand.

MOINA
In the plains of the East I have seen them. The wind lays them down, the lighting blinds them; clouds bar their route and torrents cut them.

VERCINGETORIX
Before the man who follows your path, Moina, the sky clears and the wave recoiled.

How did you get through Caesar's camp?

MOINA
I am she who commands; arms have lifted me up and wings have brought me.

In order to be reborn tomorrow, more valiant and more beautiful, Gaul must die today.

It is necessary. I know it. Death is the fecund soil in which the future germinates.

You know it too, Ar-Braz. Gaul died on the dolmen of the Carnutes; in order to sanctify your sword it required all the blood of the Skylark.

It is not the sword of victory but he sword of sacrifice that the blood has sanctified.

To irrigate the exhausted soil a generous blood was required; to drain the Roman mud it required blood to flow from the altar in floods; the Master has chosen Gaul.

The red dew will be fecund; where it falls the flowers will open wide and the ears of wheat will incline heavily

In the gulf with pale waves, Ar-Braz, you have opened the route of the past; on the plateau of Alise, today, you are opening the route to the future.

Freely the victim must mount he altar; buckle your sword-belts, young men; braid your hair, young women; bards, play your harps; priests, build the pyre.

Make the pyre wide enough for Gaul to lay upon it; make it high enough for Rome to see it.

GANIEDA
In the star above the flowers do not fade and hair does not go white.

In the green star, oaths have no wings and dreams no awakening; make your marriage bed, young men,

STRUMMOR

You have kept your promises, we have kept ours; in the celestial Gaul you will still be our chief and we will still be your men.

VERCINGETORIX

I will keep all my promises and you will keep all of yours.

I have said: Between Rome and the German you will be a united and strong people.

You have said: We will follow you everywhere and always obey you.

I have not forgotten my oath, do not forget yours.

IMPERADORIX

We will obey.

MOINA

Where are you going?

VERCINGETORIX

To propose a bargain to Caesar.

The Germans have annihilated the Roman army broken by the torrents and dispersed by the storm; Caesar knows that, and, on the threshold of his tent, he smiles as he gazes at the ramparts of Alise.

"He is gazing at the ramparts of Alise and he does not see the woman with the luminous brow who is in his tent, disdainfully leafing through the pages in which he has lied."

"She is behind him; her hand is about to touch his shoulder.

CAESAR

Gaul has only one head, and that had will fall tomorrow.

THE SKYLARK
The head of Gaul is too high for a human hand to reach.

CAESAR
Always that voice!
Alauda…? The victim of the sacred night!
I'm not afraid of shades; speak.

THE SKYLARK
A man is the master of his destiny; he will be what he wanted to be; but the one who knows everything makes use of that free will for his own designs.

CAESAR
I wanted to vanquish the Invincible, and I have him under my heel.

THE SKYLARK
What the Sage has wished, is; what you would like to be, be.

The vision vanishes. The gate of Alise opens and Vercingetorix appears. The gate closes again; he is alone.

He has his azure breastplate, his helmet with the golden wings. His warhorse whinnies, shaking its multicolored coat, but his sword is in the scabbard.

CAESAR
Have I seen? Can I believe what I see?

These impenetrable forests hide strange mysteries; broad roads cut them.

What does this horseman want? He is coming to ask for mercy. I have retreated before them; all those who have seen that will die.

But the Arverne! He does not believe in death; I shall not have him alive to drag him behind me in the streets of Rome... I want even the name of his clan to be forgotten. I shall throw everyone who has a drop of Arverne blood to the beasts of the circus, and I no longer want even heather to grow on their mountains.

Him!

VERCINGETORIX

I have come to propose a bargain. Would you like, on the day of our triumph, to chain me to your chariot?

CAESAR

And who can prevent me from doing that?

VERCINGETORIX

Me.

CAESAR

Madman, do you think I will let you escape again? Lictors...

VERCINGETORIX

You're forgetting that I'm on horseback and that I have my sword.

I am in your camp because I wanted to come here; the walls of Alise are unbreached.

CAESAR

You will not get out of here.

VERCINGETORIX

That doesn't matter to me; you wouldn't chain me alive to your chariot. My life is my own. But if you accept my bargain, I will give it to you. Have you ever dared to dream of that?

CAESAR

What are you asking?

VERCINGETORIX
The life of my people.

I want you to forget everything. I want my soldiers to mingle with yours. I want my Brenns to climb the steps of the Capitol with you.

CAESAR
I accept.
Lictors, bind him.

And Caesar dragged him behind him in an iron cage, and on the day of his triumph he chained him to his chariot, and while he climbed the steps of the Capitol he had his head cut off.

The poet kissed the tender angel with the blue eyes; he had just finished the poem of Ar-Braz.

BLANCHE
I am only an ignorant woman, friend
Do you really believe in these successive incarnations?

THE POET
Our forefathers believed it, and, no one having proved the contrary to me, I say what our fathers said.

BLANCHE
But these fays who pass? These crickets that talk? In my philosophy course there were no lessons on fays and it was affirmed that only humans talk.

THE POET
Things were affirmed in your course in philosophy?
I am not as strong as your professor; I do not affirm anything.

I have never seen fays, crickets have never talked to me, willows have never indicated my path, the bards of the past have not returned in order to tell me their secrets; but that does not prove that there are no fays, that crickets are mute, that willows are inert and that the dead cannot be reborn. If I have not seen anything, it is because I have looked poorly. If I have not heard anything it is because I have listened poorly. I do not believe myself to be more knowledgeable or wiser than the architect of the Pyramids, the poet of the Ramayana or the legislator of Athens

BLANCHE

If that is true, so much the better. If everything that surrounds me lives, comprehends me and loves me; if, from the stars, friendly gazes reach as far as me, so much the better; I feel magnified and reassured.

I believe you, but others will not believe you, and instead of carrying a stone into the breach, one of these days you will have lost what no longer belongs to you.

Why, in these hours of sadness, anger and struggle, have you written the life of this forgotten hero?

THE POET

Because he was forgotten.

I have not written the story of a hero; I have written the story of the invincible hero, the promised savior. It is in order that belief in the future might be possible that I have spoken about the past

With our old beliefs, our old superstitions and out old dreams, we were the first in the world; with all our science, we are now the last.

Let the scholars shut up; they have said too much.

The day when, like the Gauls, the French love death for what there is afterwards, they will be invincible, as they once were. The day when they believe that a victorious chief always emerges in the hour of danger, they will march without count-

223

ing the enemy and they will be victorious because they will be sure of victory.

Thirty years ago the enemy had only two of our provinces; now he has France entire. Thirty years ago people sympathized with us; today they mock us.

Ar-Braz! Ar-Braz! It is time for you to come!

Rhetors philanthropists, scholars, how much harm you did us when you were mistaken, and even when you were not!

Yes, war is odious and absurd; it ought to disappear and it will disappear, but I do not want my country to be submissive to that dream of peace, I want her to give it.

All peoples will be brothers; I believe that as you do; but at that fraternal banquet I want my people to sit at the top of the table.

Let us first wash away our shame, let us resume our place, and afterwards we shall see. When the tablecloth is clean, when the door is bolted, we shall set up our table and open our drawing rooms.

We are the sons of light; let us shake off this darkness and tear apart these fogs.

Let us wipe our eyes and march! Ar-Braz! Ar-Braz, you are awaited!

BLANCHE
Will they understand?

We have no family; we live alone; we only have one friend, André, and he is no longer here; how will anyone know that what you have said is what you wanted to say?

THE POET
We will know tomorrow. I shall do what André does; like him I shall hide at the doors of workshops, on the thresholds of schools; I shall relate the ancient legend and I will have said what I wanted to say if his troop swells.

BLANCHE
And you'll depart... when?

THE POET

Tonight.

It is a long time since the poet departed. He sang the legend of the past for a long time at the hearths of cottages, and the doors of workshops.

Now he is in the mountains with André's bands.

"When he glides through the shadows, when he wanders in sunken paths, the Voice speaks in his ear.

"It is said that, one night, the fays carried him all the way to the green star; it is said that the Skylark opened the valley of the tombs to him and that he saw, in the plains of the heavens, the heroes of old harnessing their warhorses, and that he saw, under the dolmen in the land of the Orient, the awaited chief buckling his sword-belt."

"His soul has traversed the plains of heaven, his soul has entered the valley of tombs; but he has not seen the awaited chief; he has not seen Ar-Braz.

"Thirty years ago, Ar-Braz quit his funereal grotto; thirty years ago, Ar-Braz was born. If you want to know him, go to the banks of the Allier.

"Under the dolmen there is a chief buckling his sword-belt, but you will not see that chief. He it is who, on the day of the great battle, will command the cavaliers who will fight in the starry plains, in their chariots of clouds, while you fight.

"That chief our forefathers have cursed and our forefathers have loved; that chief is not a Gaul, but he is of the race of the oak and tomorrow, it is not two peoples but two races that will fight.

"In the plains of heaven he has also seen the druidess, with an aureole on her brow. She too, some have loved and others have cursed, but tomorrow, all will love her.

"He has seen the past and he has seen the future; he knows that he is the Potter and that André is Ar-Braz."

"He has seen all that, and he has sung, and men have heard him, and now there is no longer a band, it is an army that André commands in the valley of the Allier."

"But as she cradles the angel with the blue eyes, Blanche is weeping."

"Why?"

BLANCHE
Laugh, my angel; I'm so sad. Laugh, my angel; I'm so afraid.
It is too long since he left.
The nurses have not come back and it is sad in the mountains that the Allier is rolling cadavers. They have killed him.
Who are you? You are not women. Are you the ones who guide the souls with red wings on the route up above?

THE SISTERS
Don't you recognize us?
He recognizes us. Look, he is holding out his arms to us.
Have you forgotten the temple on the bank of the river, then, the crystal hall in which the nacre bed gleamed, the stream under the walnut trees in the ravine of the Fayolles?

BLANCHE
I don't understand you.

THE SISTERS
Queen of the Ganges, you don't recognize those he had enclosed within the granite flanks of the sphinxes of Elora? You no longer recognize the nurses who loved you, Blanche?

BLANCHE
He's dead!

THE SISTERS

I put his head on my breast, as when he was a child.

"He was thirsty; I made him drink, as when he was a child."

"I rocked him on my heart and he went to sleep, as he fell asleep when he was a child."

BLANCHE

He's dead! My heart is dead! Oh, my poor child! What do you want us to do; tell me whether it's necessary to join him immediately? He hasn't yet seen you smile. You'll be better up above.

Death does not return what it takes from us!

THE SISTERS

We are your servants.

"Command; I will obey."

BLANCHE

Why have you touched him?

THE SISTERS

His blood was flowing from a large wound and the veil tore.

"I'm awaited up above," he said. "The cavaliers who are about to deliver the great battle in the starry plains need a bard."

"Blanche will come tomorrow," he said. "The cradle is ready next to the hearth on high. The laughing monkey will amuse her and the storks will shelter her with their ivory wings."

"He put his head on my bosom; I rocked him as of old, and now he is asleep."

BLANCHE

The cradle is ready... Take me to where he died; I want my body to sleep next to is... Come.

The angel with the blue eyes was asleep on the moss; Blanche bent down to pick him up but he woke up and smiled.

His eyes were as blue as the lotuses that open by night on the milky rivers of the distant land.

The mother knelt down and, as she gazed at him, her tears dried up.

As she gazed at him, she dreamed. She thought about the statue that the moss was eating away under the green water of the basin, she thought about the cliff of the bay of Algiers, the grotto in the Fayolles, the temple of Elora, the palace on the bank of the Ganges. She retraced the flowery route of the days of toil and hope. She retraced the stony route of the days of revolt and struggle, and, hiding her head in her hands, she sighed: "Your road is the straight road; I will go where you go, Master."

Then joy shone in the eyes of the two sisters, the two enemies who had become the two nurses; they parted her hands and gently, as they had spoken to her when she was small, they said to her: "His road is the straight road; follow the Master's road."

As she was still weeping, they wept too. They wept so loudly that they did not hear the Skylark coming.

The Skylark placed her hand on Blanche's shoulder.

THE SKYLARK

You don't want me to wait, Sister?

In the plains of heaven the squadrons are forming up, but here men get up slowly.

Sister, I've helped you; help me. I'm no longer a woman; I can only speak to those who love me; tell them what I cannot tell them.

BLANCHE

I will say what must be said. I will do what must be done.

Before my eyes too, the veil has been torn.

228

THE SKYLARK

See those who are coming; if they follow you, my nuptial bed will be dressed on high.

BLANCHE

I know now why we quit the green star. Rejoin André, Skylark; these men will follow me.

Laugh, my angel, your father is up above, can you not hear his harp vibrating? Laugh, my angel; how warm your little feet will be, how soft the grass of the green star will be!

It is no longer a band but an army that André commands, and the victor is moved. His generals are on horseback, his spies are on campaign, his executioners are sharpening their axes; before he expands it is necessary to extinguish in blood the fire that is being lit.

Those whose hearts beat rapidly have already departed. But those who weigh and those who measure are waiting, anxious and discontented. They are anxious because war only likes the strong and laughs at the clever. They are discontented because a voice is murmuring deep inside them: "Are you no more than merchants, you who were once men?"

"They are still Gaul; wait and you'll see. They are steady men, they do not want to have the appearance of acting without reasons; but if they are given a reason, even a bad one, they will soon have joined the others."

"Perhaps that is why, while grumbling, they come into this garden, where voices speak that do not speak elsewhere. Listen."

My son would still be in the house, and my daughter would already be married, if a madman had not come to talk to them about this impossible savior, and if one even madder and

229

more criminal had not tried to put those stupid dreams into action.

You were wrong to bring me here. I'm a peaceful man; but I'm afraid, if I encounter that poet, of saying... of doing...

We have inculcated in our children the precepts of the sanest morality, and we have preached by example, but a stranger comes along to say to them that death is only a transformation, that life is what you want to be, that peoples have a soul, and a thousand other stupidities. They believe that simpleton·and they forget our lessons.

We were born in an unfortunate time; we have already seen defeat and invasion twice, we are now going to see a hopeless revolt and a pitiless punishment.

Why have you brought me here?

In order to know where André is.

Listen, friend. I too am a peaceful man and I'm no longer young, but I'm commencing to find the hand of the foreigner too heavy and I believe, as a good father of a family, that it's better to do right away what our children would be forced to do later.

And you're going to go to war? You're going to enlist with these madmen?

Your son and mine are among these madmen.

I can't obey a man..

Even Ar-Braz?

Ar-Braz broke his sword rather than return it to the scabbard. That's no longer our way.

What does that woman want? She has a singular appearance. Why have you brought me into this garden? One never knows whether one is alive here, or whether one is dreaming.

Her eyes are as blue as the Loire; if it's the woman we've already encountered a year ago, we didn't want to hear her.

Woman, are you the Skylark?

TOINETTE

The Skylark, my good messieurs, doesn't sing in gardens; it's a bird of thatch, heather and furze.

For your information, I'm Toinette and I'm looking for my son, André.

My son is handsome and he will come. You'll see that he is handsome.

Have you come to watch the sunrise? I too have come to watch the sunrise; but the sun I'm expecting isn't the one that you've seen. The one you've seen only enlightens he eyes, whereas the one I'm expecting enlightens the heart.

She's a madwoman. I suspected as much.

TOINETTE

You're laughing? Why are you laughing?

People no longer laugh when I pass by, and no longer laugh when he passes by; he's so handsome and so strong!

He's thirty years old, my good messieurs; if you'd encountered me with my André in my arms, you'd have laughed like the others. Like the others you'd have said:

"Look! Look! It's the child of the furze, what name have you given him, Toinette? Whose eyes does he have?"

And lowering my head, I'd have replied:

"He has the eyes of a little fox; leave me alone."

"You found him under a furze-bush; but who gave him to you, Toinette? Was it a hunter of the plain? Was it one of our lads?"

"It was a little bird who gave him to me: a bird that sang so gaily and to which I listened; a little bird with wings so blue that I caressed it; a tiny bird so tame that it alighted on my lips."

"She's sinned, and she's making fun of us. Ho ho ho! We know them, Toinette, the little birds of the furze. Ho ho! Those blue birds, Toinette, have never sung before Monsieur le Maire."

Until dusk I wept with my head in my apron. "Ho ho!" the trees said to me. "Ho ho!" the stones said to me.

People no longer laugh when I pass by; he's so handsome, and so strong!

How old is your son, Toinette?

TOINETTE

He's thirty years old, my good messieurs, thirty years since Candlemas.

Thirty years ago, where were you? You were with the soldiers, out there, beyond Besançon. I was looking after three piebald cows in the Bois de la Madeleine, and while spinning I said to myself: "If one of those soldiers comes back one-eyed or one-armed, I'll marry him."

I was found one morning under a hawthorn bush, but I spun like a fay and I could have guarded all the cows of Marimbes without a dog.

I said as I twisted my wool: "If the Good Lord gives me a son, he'll go to the land of the Prussians to get his father's hand back."

The beautiful blue bird came and I had that son.

Wait for the day to dawn.

The sun is only waiting for isn't the one that you've seen, but it will rise, that sun. The skylark told me so; the lovely skylark that sings as it flaps its wings, my friend the skylark.

André, André, my beautiful André, the sun is about to rise and you're not yet here. André, André, my beautiful André, the skylark said that you would come and you haven't arrived.

André, André, my beautiful André, have you gone astray? The road from Paris is so long!

André, André, my beautiful André, if by chance you're lost, listen to the skylark sing.

My good messieurs, the skylark doesn't sing in the great woods, it's a bird of thatch, heather and furze. I only come on to the plateau to hear it sing.

If, by chance, André comes, tell him to wait here. He's as blond as an ear of wheat, as handsome as a mossy fir and as straight as a service tree.

You'll recognize him; he reads books in Latin; but it's before a field of wheat, without a hat, with his shirt open and his sickle in his hand that it's necessary to see him, my good messieurs.

He's a bold harvester, the son of the blue bird, and the ears that he'll cut, my good messieurs, will bleed; it's me who assures you of that.

Hush. Listen; the young women are coming.

THE YOUNG WOMEN
And zon, zon, zon!
The dance begins!
And zon, zon, zon!
Where are the violins?
Our clogs are red.
Jump, lads!

That's where one ends up with these stupid stories.

Dull rumbles are descending from the great woods. On the summits, columns of smoke are rising vertically.

"Where are those young women going?"

"They're Gauls; they want to dance the round of words and they pass before every house on festival evenings shouting: "Who's coming to dance?"

THE YOUNG WOMEN
Don't be afraid, Toinette, your André is a good one.

It appears that the Allier was running red yesterday. All our lads are with him.

We've come to search for the lady, and we'll go.

And you, handsome messieurs, have you come to guard our cows? Guard hem, we're leaving.

And zon, zon, zon!
We've brought loaves,
And zon, zon, zon!
For the god lads.
The messieurs from town
Can guard the house
And zon, zon, zon!
Dance, girls!
And zon, zon, zon!
Jump, lads!

On the edge of the round basin, under the great lindens, leaning on a yellow marble vase full of apples and pomegranates, Blanche, her breasts heaving and her nostrils flared, watches the young women climbing two by two, linking arms.

The veil of the past has torn; she is no longer a widow weeping but a druidess dreaming the ardent poems of her beloved.

A crimson cloud descends on the hornbeam arbor and its azure fringes float over the garden.

The young women, astonished, stop; the men look into the scintillating sky to see where that storm-cloud might be coming from. Toinette passes her hand over her brow and Blanche extends her arms toward the cloud, crying:

"Friends, friends! You are Fayolles among the baptized, but you were druidesses when the woods talked."

THE FAYOLLES
That's true! That's true!
Oh mistletoe! Oh mistletoe; the cup is full.
Oh mistletoe! Oh mistletoe, he iron is forged.

The cloud dissipates, the young women utter a cry, the men bare their heads. Toinette passes her hand over her brow; around the basin, on the two rising paths, beautiful young women are crowded.

They are tall and blonde, a golden circlet shines on their bare arms, a black belt tightens their long blue robes at their slender waists.

Blanche goes toward those who are coming.

BLANCHE
We were expecting you, young women. See, the dance will be long. They are my friends.

THE YOUNG WOMEN
We know your friends, Lady. We encountered them on nights of the full moon when we were searching for lost calves on the hills.

What was said was true, Lady, you really are the great fay.

Our lads have been fighting in the Limagne for three days; the Allier is running red; let's go help them.

There are a great many wounded.

BLANCHE
There are a great many wounded.

They've fought like lions and the battlefield is left to them.

If they were commanded by a real general!

But the enemy is awaiting reinforcements; they'll be crushed if we don't arrive.

BLANCHE

You shall have rifles, girls, the rifles of the dead, which still have butts red with blood. I shall have that of my beloved!

THE YOUNG WOMEN

He's dead?

BLANCHE

Yes.

TOINETTE

He's dressing the area up above where God will thresh the wheat that his harvester will reap.

The new area is wide, it's as hard as rock and as smooth as ice; come and dance here!

Who will be the first with her promise?

And zon, zon, zon!
Here come the girls!
And zon, zon, zon!
Take your places, lads.
But their clogs are red;
Embrace them, then.

BLANCHE

Let's go.

And us? While the women fight, do you think we can remain here with folded arms?

You'll care for the wounded; give us the rifles.

THE YOUNG WOMEN

There will be enough for everyone.

They have all departed, the men and the young women.

It was said that the Skylark no longer had any soldiers. It was said that the blood had paled in our veins. Look at the crowd climbing through the flowering heather; it isn't an army, it's a people on the march, with flashing eyes, a song on the lips and faith in the heart.

Sharpen your teeth, wolves! Open your wings, vultures! Weep, daughters of the Germans!

The sun for which Toinette, whose soul is elsewhere, was waiting, has risen today; under its ardent rays the Gaulish soil is seething, sap is splitting the bark and blood is making the veins stand out.

The sun of the morning of old has risen; wolves, sharpen your teeth; vultures, open your wings, weep daughters of the Germans!

Toinette is walking slowly along the grassy pathways. She has been left alone; all the others have gone with André.

The sun is sinking behind the old hornbeam and on the summits columns of gray smoke are rising vertically. A cricket is singing in the grass on the edge of the basin; a vague rumor is rising from the plain; dull rumbles are descending from the great woods; a wren is running through the dry leaves.

The sun is sinking into the valley of the Allier; a warm breeze is shaking the crowns of the lindens; the cricket falls silent; the wren flaps its wings.

Toinette gazes at the rising star and passes her hands over her brow.

The rumor in the plain grows; the rumblings in the great wood swell.

Shrill notes are detached from the vague rumor. Dry clicks mingle with the muted rumblings.

The clarion is sounding! The cannon is speaking!

The moon silvers the canal.

Toinette utters a loud cry: "It's my blood that is flowing! It's my flesh that is being crushed!"

Can you see her, arms raised and breast heaving? Do you recognize her now? She is weeping, the mother of all mothers, for her blood that is flowing and her flesh that is being crushed.

Can you hear her sobbing?

O Master, you have given me fecund veins; have you put enough tears in my eyes? As soon as the meadow is dotted with flowers, the scythe gleams. O Master, have you put enough tears in my eyes?

Who is that man who is coming? Do you recognize him? You don't recognize the old man who went through the vineyards listening to the cicadas sing under the gnarled peach-trees? You don't recognize he man accompanying him, the one who, as a child, he sat on his knees in front of the wood-chip fire? You don't recognize the old man of the green star and the carver of granite in the grottoes of Elora?

In order to lay out, under the apple trees of the green star, the white cloth of tomorrow's feast, the Celt is coming to seek his companion.

In order to tune his harp, the bard of the horsemen is coming to dream until the hour of the battle in the hornbeam arbor where the wren is twittering.

The time has come, the veil is torn. Listen to the old man speak.

"Fleur-d'Épine, our sons are brave, in their veins the blood has not paled. Why weep, my beloved? There are so many empty places at our hearth up above.

"Tomorrow the circle will be wide. Tomorrow Ar-Braz will tell us about his victory, and our bard will sing us the poems that were asleep out there behind the granite foreheads of the gods with a hundred arms."

PART THREE: THE HARVESTER

In the broad plain, it is not two armies but two races that are waiting for the day for triumph or revenge.

Tomorrow will be a day that will not be forgotten.

In the broad plain there are our husbands, our fiancés and our brothers; let us pray!

Tomorrow the great battle will be fought; pray for your fathers, children!

And with the last rays of daylight, the ardent prayer rises to the feet of the Almighty.

I

Next to their rifles in sheaves, around a fire that is going out, twenty young men are sitting. Yesterday they were students, scholars and artists; today they are soldiers.

Look, they are true Gauls; before the somber lines that pale lightning flashes illuminate, when a battery is harnessed or a battalion move off, they talk about their labors or their dreams, about what is great and what is beautiful. They are soldiers and they are poets; they are true Gauls.

"Friends," said one of them, "the water-bottles are empty, the wind is freshening and the fire is extinct; what if we were to sing the song of the Skylark in order to warm ourselves up?

Then a tall young man with a bandaged forehead stood up and he said: "I have the testament of the dead man. Listen to what was dictated to me when the blood trickled, drop by drop, from is punctured breast."

A handful of vine-branches were thrown on the fire and he painter read the end of the poem of Ar-Braz

THE POEM OF AR-BRAZ

Three things diminish continuously and will end up by disappearing: obscurity, error and death.
(The Bardic Mysteries.)

Caesar, triumphant, climbs the Capitol, and in his cell, the head of the Gaul falls.

"A head for an eye and an arm for a finger!"

"Wait until the skylark sings."

The weeder who wants to enter the field before dawn risks leaving the thistles and cutting the wheat.

While waiting for the day that is about to dawn, listen to the end of the poem of Ar-Braz; but if you want to understand, listen with your heart and not with your ears, and do not forget that in the green star, if men are still men, their passions are keener, their amours purer and their hatreds more ardent.

Do not forget that, if they follow the same route, they march more rapidly because they never go astray.

Listen with your heart and not with your ears; it is no longer a man who is speaking but a harp, which vibrates to a breath from above. The breath is powerful, but rust has corroded the strings; you can only hear with your heart the song of the Gaulish lands.

Listen!

Caesar had promised to save the lives of the defenders of Alise, but the clan of Vercingetorix had not wanted to see its chief enchained.

The young men built a pyre, the druidess lit it, and when the victor had the gates broken down he found nothing but a heap of ashes.

That was six years ago. Listen to what is said today on the plains of heaven.

THE VALKYRIES
What are you waiting for, Arvernes?

For winters and summers, in the middle of the road, our impatient mares have been pawing the ground; why are the bronze bits eroding their bloody mouths? Fatigued soldiers, thirsty virgins, old men devoid of hearths, what are you waiting for? Winters and summers ago, the wind dispersed the ashes of the pyre. Where he flame shone, the cornflowers have flourished; what are you waiting for, Gauls of Alise?

They are not looking upwards, they are looking downwards, the glorious dead of Alise.

In the cloud, a form rises. It has a shiny breastplate and a helmet with broad wings; what if it were him?

It is the soul of a soldier, but it is not him.

THE SOUL
On the shoreless sea, in the somber cloud that hides the road to heaven from the death, what are you waiting for, souls with red shrouds?

GANIEDA
At the table of the feast, who ought to sit down first?
We are waiting for the chief.

MOINA
To extinguish the ardent eye, to close he extended hand, to lower the raised sword, he has given himself entirely; in the fog that floats where the Ocean touches the sky, we are waiting for him.

THE SOUL
We are camped near the Tiber.

STRUMMOR

You have gone where our fathers went? You have passed through the breach? You have broken the hawk's cage?

THE SOUL

We have seen the hawk in his cage of iron; but he said to us: "I have kept my word, keep yours. Obey Caesar as you obeyed me.

We have obeyed the father and Caesar has given us tortoiseshell breastplates and silver helmets. On our helmets he has put a skylark with wings outspread. We guard his tent and our Brenns command his finest legions.

STRUMMOR

What have you come to do among us? The Arvernes are not soldiers of Caesar.

THE SOUL

I am not a Roman, I am a Gaul. Through a large wound my soul flew away; I have come to sit down at the feast of the brave.

MOINA

Woe betide whoever want to fathom your designs, Master; your splendor binds the audacious.

In the winds of the earth the leaves fallen from the oak have flown far from its trunk; they have mingled with the thatch of the plain and the algae of the shore. Your wind has risen and in its turbulence they have all gathered, from the Ebro to the Euphrates and from the Thames to the Tiber.

STRUMMOR

But why has the lightning struck the hawk that defended the acorns of the oak against the crows?

You who know the secret, why have you thrown in the fire the branch that the snow could not bend and the East wind could but twist?

You have done that because a man ought to love is clan more than his neighbors, his chief more than his brothers.

When you lit the pyre, druidess, you knew full well that we would never guard Caesar's tent, that we would never learn the Roman language.

MOINA

Don't reach out toward the veil. How do you know that the Roman will not learn your language. How do you know that Vercingetorix has not done what he wanted to do?

A man who is reborn voluntarily carries a word of the divine science, a radiance of the divine hearth; he knows what other men do not know yet. Ar-Braz has ordered what must be done.

Soldier of Caesar you will go before us into the palace of the brave, say that the table is being laid, that the fire is being lit, because the hour is near.

KENRIK

The squire ought to sustain the head of the chief, his bard ought to sing his death song, but in his cell he is alone.

O you whom a gust of wind carries away, whom a ray of light hides, white fays of the torrent, cheerful sprites of the heath, cradle his pale head in your tender arms, sing the battle song in his ear.

Under the bronze bits, he mares are rearing up; over the shoulders of the riders the Valkyries are leaning heir pale heads. For winters and summers the great wings have not whipped with their bloody plumes the ardent mist of battle-fields.

But they are not looking upwards, they are looking downwards, the glorious dead of Alise.

The mares whinny, the Valkyries lift up their blue-tinted eyelids, the riders stand up in their stirrups, the women clap their hands; on the rising route the wind from below pushes a scintillating turbulence.

It is the fays who are coming; the fays, vigilant guardians of the tomb in the Orient; the fays, luminous florets of the black gulf where the Arverne is dreaming of the larches of the Monts Dore.

THE FAYS
We have broken the door with bronze panels; into the funereal grotto, next to the body of the Skylark, we have carried his body. He is coming! He is coming!

In order that he will find them when he wakes, we have put under the dolmen his golden necklace and his heavy sword. He is coming! He is coming!

GANIEDA
It's him! It's the Skylark!

VERCINGETORIX
Salut, friends.

His golden necklace rings, his heavy sword is flamboyant, his stallion whinnies. As on days of battle, he passes.

On the rump of the stallion, the blonde queen is sitting, her hand resting on the shoulder of the chief. She is smiling at her soldiers.

On the azure route, the gray stallion launches forth. Make way for the clans of the Monts Dore!

From the Ocean to the heavens, the green isle rises. All the way to the fuming nostrils the sunlit foam sprigs. Under the ivory hooves the silver sand flies. How uniform it is, the beach of the port without tempests!

Your hooves crush the sand, but the wave is still licking your fetlocks; why are you stopping, white mares?

THE VALKYRIES

At the confines of the celestial Gaul our mares rear up, and like dry leaves, a gust of wind blows us away.

Neither flowers nor women; neither bodies nor souls; between the glimpsed heaven and the disdained earth, we only have the empty spaces for roads.

Will you see us again, Skylark? Will you see us again, horsemen?

THE SKYLARK

With us you have fought; where we are going, come! On the day of the supreme combat you will follow me.

THE FAYS

And us?

THE SKYLARK

You, blonde bees, all day long, will collect honey in the celestial furrows for those who find the cup too bitter at the foreigner's table.

It is bitter, the cup that is being filled for my sons; fly toward the embalmed flowers, blonde bees; tomorrow, in the land of oaks, you will wait for me.

The mares launch forward. The beach is crossed. How large the crowd is beneath the mossy oaks!

THE VALKYRIES

Make way for the king of war! Make way for the clans of the Monts Dore!

THE SKYLARK

They have fought bravely; victors, make room for them.

THE FAYS

O you who have sought, who have sung, who have loved, for a day, take your place among us. We are the vision, the dream, the sought unknown, the intoxicating cup, the eternal kiss. For those who are waiting, let us collect the flower of hope, the flower of patience and the flower of amour.

FLEUR-D'ÉPINE
When I fled on the Sancy the hearth of the chief with the gray beard, you said to me: "Come with us."

Come, you who were my sisters.

THE MOTHERS
O our beloved masters, our sons had red blood, large hearts and strong arms! On seeing them, we thought we were seeing again the evening of the betrothal, the morning of the first day.

Come, on the new tablecloth, the jug is foaming; on the beam, the golden shields are ringing, before the fireplace, great red dogs are sleeping. Come! Under the flowering apple trees your horses are grazing, and in the evergreen forest, herds of fallow deer are bounding.

Come, daughters of the Arvernes; you have sung like the warbler, worked like the ant, loved like the turtle-dove. Come, the cage is full, the flax is soft for your distaffs, and the one of whom you have dreamed is sleeping in the cradle.

Virgins of battle, come too; it is the blood of our veins that crimsons your wings. Come and tell us how our sons died.

He table is large, come too, white fays of the springs, blonde fays of the woods.

Sit down at our hearth, druidess; it is you who sowed the sheaf that our children have bound.

THE WARRIORS
Ar-Braz! Ar-Braz! We too were brave. Do you remember? Have you told them?

AR-BRAZ

The sons were worthy of the fathers. But on the day of the great combat you will be reborn with me, my old companions; to the arms of today our axes are heavy.

Those who have not hesitated to follow him into the waves of the pale gulf press around the chief; those who have twisted the pike of the Teutons on their bare breasts, those who broke down the gates of Genabum with thrusts of the shoulder.

The chief smiles at his soldiers, but his gaze is seeking someone in the crowd.

"Brother! Brother!" Ar-Braz cries.

The crowd parts.

AR-BRAZ

Finally, I've found you, Brother. On quitting the banks of the Ebro, where did your soul go?

THE POTTER

I was a proud man; as an earthworm I crawled in the mud for a long time, a very long time.

Then, in the body of a slave, for a long time, a very long time, I rowed on a river of dull water.

Then, in the skin of a gazelle, on the summit of a rock, naked under the sun, naked under the rain, for a long time, for a very long time, I prayed.

One by one I climbed again the steps descended.

I have been here since yesterday; but has the sin been expiated? Has the Master broken the prison where the proud man had enclosed the innocent soul of his beloved?

THE SKYLARK

I have remounted the stream. The snows of winter and the summer sun have made a little heap of earth of the statue; the prison is open

We shall find the soul of the druidess again, and you shall be my bard, Potter.

That is the Master's secret; but I know where the soul of our beloved is hidden.

You also know where the soul of the queen of the Ganges mourned the potter's sin.

In the old garden you have seen her weep, you have seen her smile; the sin is expiated.

One by one I have climbed the steps descended. And my beloved will rejoin me tomorrow with those who slept and those I have awakened.

My eyes are troubled...my tongue is chilled.... I am only the Master's workman, and his work is done.

On the green mound of the celestial Gaul, listen to the Celt talking to his son. Fleur-d'Épine is smiling to his right, the potter is dreaming at his feet, behind him he druids are leaning on their white staffs, before him the warriors, as on the day of battle, are arranged clan by clan.

THE OLD MAN

Before the day ends, you come home, laborer, and the furrow is dug; you must be weary; sit down, my son.

Sit down beside me, Ar-Braz; they are all my sons, but you are more than my son, you are the valiant and the sage, you are the good and the strong.

And you, daughter of the white foam, divine soul whom death has made a woman, sit down next to Ar-Braz on the mound where I am dreaming about the Master's promises.

What have you done?

AR-BRAZ

I have broken my sword on the hard granite.

THE SKYLARK
But in the formless rock he has carved a great body, with a broad brow, powerful arms and a profound breast.

THE OLD MAN
You hear, potter? In the formless rock he has carved a great body with a profound breast; in that great heart, which was beating yesterday, sow the grain of the Almighty with full hands.

THE POTTER
I wanted to work for myself; the Master would still like me to work for him?

THE OLD MAN
Between the future and the past the veil falls...

Master, I do not try to fathom your designs; I trust your word. With closed eyes I put myself in your hands, sure that your powerful hand will guide me to port.

As on earth, in the green star to live is to struggle, to struggle is to learn, to learn is to climb; live, children, seek and love.

THE BARDS
It is necessary to struggle for a long time in the cold crystal, under the rude bark, in the profound lair. It is necessary to struggle for a long time before becoming human.

THE DRUIDS
The human soul will struggle for a long time; it requires a long time to comprehend. In order to comprehend, it is necessary to grow old many times.

THE OLD MAN
Between the past and the future the veil lifts...

Time has no more measures, space has no more limits. In luminous rings the future and the past are welded together, from the abyss to the summit the steps extend.

How slowly the crowd climbs on those steep steps!

How slowly the crowd is climbing! The arms of the strong no longer sustaining her, the son of the Skylark no longer announces the dawn to it.

On those steep steps, how slowly the crowd climbs! Here, it slips in blood, there it trembles in darkness!

How heavy your hand is, Master!

Fleur-d'Épine, the mother of all mothers, clasps the hand of the Skylark between her own hands, and her heart whispers: "The Almighty has given me fecund veins, but has he put enough tears in my eyes?"

"Death," the bards sing, "is the beautiful bride."

"Ar-Braz," cry the men, "if the axes are heavy in the arms of our sons, call and we will come."

But the Potter is getting up; listen.

THE POTTER

The battle is won, the circle is crossed.

Like dry leaves, dead earths whirl in the breath of the abyss, and new suns light up the radiant beacon of the summit.

The route is straight to the realm of light, it is flat and it is shady, but it has no end. One sun pales, thousands are ignited, and, ever more knowledgeable and ever more liberated, the crowd always rises toward the new stars.

THE OLD MAN

My sons are numerous, and they march at the head.

MOINA

Before my eyes too, the veil is torn...

While the hungry sons of the night, leaning on the shafts of their great empty carts, gaze at the wheat in the valleys and the vines on the hills, the insouciant sons of the sun display their treasures and, like cocks intoxicated by amour, blunt their swords on their dented breastplates.

THE WARRIORS
When the wine is red and the cup is golden, it is necessary, druidess, that men show their blood and their amours. Our hearts are pure; let them be seen. Our veins are full, let the blood be drawn from them. You, who can see the future, see the enemy binding its bulls; so much the better, or sons will fall in their strength.

THE MOTHERS
On the new tablecloth the pitchers are foaming, on the equal seats at the round table, come and sit down, Arvernes.

The young women have braided their hair; enameled belts are ringing over their striped skirts, amour is shining in their eyes; cup in hand, they are waiting beside your seats; come.

Potter, come too; the guest ornaments the table as a fleuron ornaments a shield. Friend of the chief, come and sit down with us; at the table of the Arvernes, the stranger's seat is higher than all the others.

Under the leafy oaks, the table is set up, round and immense.

AR-BRAZ
Come, Brother; we have not talked for such a long time before a full cup.

Do you remember the feast on the banks of the Ebro when you said to me: "Laborer, unhitch your oxen, the furrow should finish here."

It was a fine feast. The circle was so great on the flowery lawn that at the center, in the chariots of the vanquished, the pile of weapons rose higher than an oak. Around the bloody trophy, the crouching prisoners groaned. Before us, our horses were eating oats from the golden cups of the Iberians. Behind us, the unkempt virgins were extending their bound hands over our heads to protect us from the sun.

THE POTTER
It was a fine feast. The Ebro, like an azure serpent, meandered over the plain; on the hills, olive groves embraced mossy rocks with their silvery arms; in the distance, the sea growled dully in the gulf.

AR-BRAZ
You're a good little sister, Ganieda; how often, when I drank the insipid water of the Tiber in my prison, I thought of the fresh beverage that you brought me in the beech-wood bowl when I returned from hunting.

Taste, friend, the wine of myrtles.

IMPERADORIX
I wager that he'd prefer the wine of the Eduens.

Nothing is as good as the wine of the Eduens, not even the wine of Athens,

When you were asleep on the bank of the Ebro, Ar-Braz, I was jealous of you, jealous of your glory, as I was jealous again yesterday.

Touch my cup, friend; I am no longer jealous.

So, when you were asleep on the bank of the Ebro, I gathered those who loved changing place and we departed.

Every morning we marched to the point where we had seen the sun rise, and every day our troop swelled. One evening, it was necessary for us to stop; we were on the bank of the flooded Euphrates.

THE POTTER
And what wine did you drink on the bank of the Euphrates?

IMPERADORIX
The wine of reeds, in cups of onyx.

STRUMMOR

The cups were beautiful but the wine was bad. My ancestor spoke of that reed wine often, during evenings by the fireside.

IMPERADORIX

It was bad, but it gave odd ideas.

We drank in an immense hall, the porphyry ceiling of which was supported by painted columns; we had attached the master of the palace—a priest or a king, I no longer know which—to a bronze ring sealed n the wall, and he was trembling.

He was facing me, and I cannot bear to see a man tremble. I lifted my spear...and he trembled more forcefully.

Then I said to him: if you can make me tremble I'll return your place to you.

"Go in there," he said to me, showing me an iron door.

I opened the door, but I closed it again very quickly.

GANIEDA

And did you return the palace to its master?

IMPERADORIX

Yes, and I made him sit down next to me.

But the reed wine had given me an idea; I said to the men: "There are lions behind that door; what if, without deranging ourselves, we were to give ourselves the pleasure of a hunt?

They all clapped their hands and the door was opened.

There was a troop of them; it was a fine hunt.

AR-BRAZ

And the master of the palace?

IMPERADORIX

He was eaten by his lions.

GANIEDA

And the palace?

IMPERADORIX

As it was no longer mine, I set fire to it.

STRUMMOR

Fill the cups, Ganieda; we have nothing to hide.

Bards, tune your harps; the hall is sonorous.

Put the pitchers on the table, young women; your fiancés are waiting.

Kenrik, take your white bagpipe and play the dance of the Monts Dore.

The horns circled with gold are no longer more than half-empty, the bards are only drawing vague chords from their harps, the young women are pressing their hearts, which are beating too rapidly; Kenrik wipes his swollen lips, and the mothers leaning on the smooth trunks of the oaks indicate, while smiling, the stars lighting up in the deep blue sky.

It was a fine feast. The chief had shaken the hands of all his men. Moina had put her forehead on the knees of the Skylark and the daughter of the foam was caressing the heavy tresses of the druidess with the bright eyes.

It was a fine feast, at which the men were talking about the battles of old. But the chief lifted his cup.

AR-BRAZ

To your amours, friends! To the past, companions! To the next battle, comrades!

When the hour sounds, I will come to fetch all of you, and it will be fine, the final battle.

Repose is not made for us; let's depart, Skylark.

THE VALKYRIES

Impatiently, our mares are pawing the ground.

THE SKYLARK
When the hour sounds, you will come.

THE FAYS
Let's depart; we are carrying a ray of sunlight on our wings, the celestial dew is pearling in our hair, an ever-fresh rose is shining in our hand.

Let's depart; we shall be the vision, the dream, the sought unknown, the intoxicating cup, the eternal kiss.

Let's depart; we shall be the flowers of the last bouquet, the fiancées of the last fighters.

MOINA
Where are you going, Brother? Where are you going Skylark?

AR-BRAZ
In the praetory outside Alise I had not only given my life to Caesar, I had given myself entirely; I must wait in the tomb until he comes personally to say to me: "Do what I wanted to do."

I am going to the funereal grotto in the land of the Orient.

MOINA
You swore that! But he will never wake you. Why did you swear that?

THE SKYLARK
Those who are reborn carry to the earth a radiance of the divine hearth; they know what others do not know. Ar-Braz did what had to be done.

THE OLD MAN
It is for the good of men that the Master has created eternal combat; it is war that labors his field.

Druidess, the man you call Caesar, the man you hate, has played on the sand before the woolen tent between Ar-Braz and the Potter. He is following his path, follow yours; all roads lead to the same goal.

MOINA

But I have promised nothing, I have sworn nothing. Free, I lit the pyre. Free, I died.

Vercingetorix, I shall avenge you. Ar-Braz, I shall drive into the grotto where he believes that he has walled you up the man who was devoid of pity.

I was your servant, Cora; Master, I was your druidess; let my soul wander between heaven and earth; I shall be the messenger of good news, the torch of sleepless nights, the flag of days of battle.

Between heaven and earth let my soul wander; I shall go where hearts beat strongly, where large tears fall. Master, I will be the sword of your justice. Cora, I will be the sword of your vengeance.

Then, the voice to which the echo dares not respond spoke in the silence of the azure plains.

When it had spoken, the souls flew confidently along the route that they had chosen freely.

On the Gaulish heaths, a moonbeam deposited the fays; all the way to the funereal grotto, a cloud carried Ar-Braz and his fiancée.

In the meadows of the green star the Valkyries hobbled their mares with great wings, and before her hearth, Fleur-d'Épine sat down between the Celt and the Potter.

"Mother, Mother," said the Potter, "they are all departing and I must stay. When will the sin be expiated?

And the mother of all mothers, Fleur-d'Épine with the golden hair, Ida with the periwinkle eyes, took the rude hand of the Potter between her slender hands, and the Celt, indicating the ivory cradle shining by the fireside, said to the youngest of her sons: "The centuries have not yellowed the wings of the stork, smoke has not dulled the eyes of the laughing monkey; the sin will be expiated and you shall sing the poem of our race between two kisses when the sons of my grandsons have forgotten it."

And Moina?

On the steps of the Capitol, can you see that woman clad in mourning who parts her veil when the senators descend? That's her.

And when they descend the marble steps two by two, the senators whisper in one another's ear: "That's Liberty weeping. If we dared…?"

One day, the woman clad in mourning followed into their houses two of those who were said to be brave, who were said to be scholars, who were said to be wise, and the two men dared.

She kept her oath, the druidess; through the door, left open, rays of moonlight enter the empty hall; look.

"Like the snow of a glacier, the steps shine; like the rock of a torrent, between his bronze spurs, the tribune of speech shines; but how that red patch on the marble pavement shines!"

"It's the blood of Caesar."

Her feet in the stain, a woman crowned with vervain is brandishing a golden sickle; do you recognize her?

Through the door, left open, rays of moonlight enter. Through the white light a form glides.

Before the one who is coming, the druidess bows and says: "He is avenged, Skylark."

"The circle of the past is closed," responds the Skylark; "you shall no longer redden, druidess, the golden sickle."

The cadaver of Caesar is bleeding before the crowd, and his maddened soul floats above the turbulent city.

Where is it going to go? It only loves the earth; like thistledown, it drifts at random from the fogs of the Tiber to the dust of the Forum.

It has never looked heavenwards; before it, no route extends, no signpost looms up, no beacon is ignited.

Maddened, until night it drifts, from the dust of the Forum to the fog of the Tiber, and, not knowing where to go, it descends again next to its stiffened body

"I do not know where to go," it said, "Why should I not sleep for one night beneath that forehead where I commanded? And if, tomorrow, the flame of the pyre can consume me... I should like to revive and be nothing but this soldier... I am no longer anything at all!"

But the soldier who was guarding Caesar's cadaver was a Gaul, one of those Gauls who had kept heir oath in obeying Caesar as they had obeyed Vercingetorix.

Caesar had given the Gaul a tortoiseshell breastplate and a silver helmet; he had paraded him from combat to combat, he had never confiscated his booty, and the soldier loved his general.

Leaning on his javelin, the Gaul gazed at that broad bald brow. He was thoughtful.

"Why did they kill him?" he said. "He had always been victorious. It's not him for whom I feel sorry but them; they have broken the bolt of their door, the key of their treasure, and instead of felling you they have magnified you. The breastplate was beginning to weigh you down, you needed help to mount a horse; you were too brave not to have the right to fall in your strength. A man is the master of his destiny."

The soul heard.

"A man is the master of his destiny! Is that Gaul right? I wanted to curb all heads, drink from all cups; but now I'm dead and I don't know what I want. If someone commands shades, let his hand push me."

Then a wind rose and carried away the soul of the man who had been Caesar.

Do not listen with your ears to the harp with the slack strings, listen with your hearts and you will hear the voice of heaven.

What I tell you is true. What good would it do me to lie? I am going to die.

Believe, like your forefathers, in eternal life, in eternal activity, in eternal liberty, and you will understand what appears to you to be incomprehensible, and you will find good what appeared to you to be bad, and you will find just what seemed to you to be unjust.

A man is what he wanted to be; he will be what he would like to be, life is not a goal but a means; life is an expiation and a recompense. Every man carries within him his paradise and his inferno.

In order to climb the summits, the harshest routes are always the shortest; fortunate are those whose feet bleed!

When triumphant Caesar dragged behind his chariot the defeated of Alise, if anyone had said to the crowd, "Of those two men, which is the most fortunate?" the crowd would have cried: "Caesar."

The crowd would have been mistaken. With the triumphal chariot, Caesar was going under the dagger of Brutus, Vercingetorix under the lictor's ax; but the dagger plunged into darkness the man who only loved life and the ax opened the luminous door to the man who only loved death.

Believe as your forefathers did and you will find just what seemed to you to be unjust.

Before the muddy flood driven by the East wind, the disunited Occident recoiled, and the flood passed over, as rapid as a torrent, leaving behind nothing but rocks and sand.

"It is necessary," said the Master, "in order that the flood can deposit its mud on my exhausted land, that a dike dam it, and that that dike should retreat slowly.

Then he found a Gaul who said: "Let us make of the jealous clans a strong and free people, of which I shall be the bard after having been the soldier."

Then he found a Roman who said: "Now that Gaul only has one head, let us sever it and make of the west an empire of which I shall be the king..

As the Gaul had done what he had dreamed of doing, the Roman did what he had dreamed of doing, and what the Master wanted was done; a straight dike was built from the Thames to Carthage.

The highest waves could not raze the dike, but the waves battered it.

A man is the master of his destiny, but the One who knows everything makes use of that free will for his own designs.

What I am saying is true; what purpose would a lie serve? Where its destiny pushed it, the wind carried the soul of the man who had been Caesar.

As rapid as lightning it passed through the night. It stopped on a grassy plateau.

"Where am I?" it said.

Then the ray of light that had made the red stain shine on the paving stones of the Capitol illuminated the grassy plateau.

"It's Alise," said the soul; "there are the ashes of the pyre that melted the golden sickle. It's there that I was victorious."

"It's me who was victorious," a voice replies.

Caesar turns round, and he sees Moina and he sees the Skylark.

"Them again!"

"Always them," responds the druidess. "While you were enchaining the Gaul, your lieutenant were listening, in the Celtic forests, to the voice that once spoke in the plains of Latium, and you have fallen as Tarquin fell. It's here that I was victorious."

Then the Skylark says: "You have killed your brother; what did you want to be?"

"The first—and I was."

"And now what are you?"

"Nothing."

"If you had wanted, with Ar-Braz, tomorrow you would have gone further than Darius, further than Cambyses, further than Alexander, further than Caesar."

"I kept my oath, let Ar-Braz keep his; I hate him. He will not emerge from the tomb unless I go to fetch him; you will never see the man you called your fiancée alive again, Skylark."

"He saw you flee and you hate him. I too have seen you flee and I hate you. But I have sworn nothing; Caesar, you will find the druidess in your path again."

"Sister, the path of the man is only the path of the Master," responds the Skylark.

A cloud veiled the ray of light and a gust of wind carried away the soul of the man who had been Caesar like a wisp of straw.

Where the flame has shone, the periwinkle has flowered; the grass of Alise is green.

The victor has passed the plow over the bleeding city, but under the leveled ruins, how green the grass has grown! Look; by the pale light of the moon, in its circle of high ramparts, the sacred mountain resembles an emerald cup mounted in a silver circle.

It is the cup of the betrothal of Gaul to the future. The fiancée has held it out full; sing, bards, the husband's response to his beloved.

The bards are dead; the cup is empty, and alone, with her head on the shoulder of the druidess of the past, the fiancée dreams of her beloved.

As she dreams she sings; listen.

THE SKYLARK

When the snow has melted, when the wheat hides the earth, under forgotten heather the Skylark will build her nest in the furrow of the land of Gaul.

"But the winter is long, Skylark; until spring you will be cold. Huddling under the grassy turf."

"Until spring I shall sing in the clear sky, in the beautiful sunlight. Winter cannot veil my beautiful sum in the sky of amour.

"The sower, his hand raised, passes back and forth in the plain; his sack is full, his wheat heavy; under his feet the earth fumes; the Gaulish wheat will be thick."

"But the East wind has pushed heavy clouds over Gaul; mad waters will stripe your field. Why does your laborer not take up his pick-ax?

"Water runs in sheets over the field; my field is a good field of clay. When the sun has drunk the water, you will see the ashen mud that will glaze my long furrows, and he wheat will grow thick from the fertile mud."

"The water that runs over the roads, draws grains and seeds. They have slumbered all winter but spring wakes them; look at your field, Skylark, thistles are mingled with brambles. Stifled, your wheat is yellowing; why has your laborer not take up his harrow?"

"My laborer's harrow is a heavy harrow; it would break the wheat in breaking the plants. We shall take a workman, and for the price of his day's work, we shall give him the plants."

"Choose well, Skylark; good laborers are rare."

"I have chosen my worker; he will believe that he is working for himself and will do the work well. He is a solid worker who does not shirk his task when he thinks he is working for himself.

"When he has burned in a heap the thistles of the land of the Franks and the brambles of the Burgundians, I will say to him: 'Have you sown the wheat that will grow here? Go away, planter of furze; if you want to reap, sow.'"

"Who, then, is this worker, who will labor without a salary?"

"He is the one who wants to earn too much."

"I know that worker; he comes as soon as he is called, but when it is necessary to pay him…don't forget Caesar, Skylark."

"What my druidess has done before, my druidess will do again, and on the furrow cleared of weeds the Gaulish wheat will flourish.

"The wheat is sprouting on the plain but it has not yet flowered. From their great leafless woods the crows have not yet returned; they will come in flocks, they will eat your wheat. Let your sower take up his arrows."

"It carries too far, my beloved's arrow. Above the crows the white storks are soaring; it might wound them. I know an avid hunger, for whom all prey is good; I shall say to him: 'Come on to my land, the dead prey will be for you.'"

"The odor of blood attracts hungry wolves. The wolf will come upon the hunter when his quiver is empty."

"The wolf will come, I am certain of it, and when he bites the neck I shall say to him: 'Vanquished, do you remember the druidess? Caesar, do you remember Alise?' And he will respond: 'What I could not do alone, the two of us will do; let us wake my brother.'

"And in his funereal grotto, Caesar will go in search of his brother Vercingetorix, my beloved Ar-Braz, and, the hawthorn being in flower, I shall wed my fiancé."

By the white light of the moon, in its circle of high ramparts, the sacred mountain resembles an emerald cup set in a circle of silver.

Like a wisp of straw, the wind carried away the soul of the man who was Caesar.

At the hearth of the Celt, the Potter talked about the land where the flowers are alive, where the mountains sing, and where the blue gods bathe in rivers of milk, Fleur-d'Épine listened.

When he had finished speaking, Fleur-d'Épine, indicating the two empty seats, said: "What if they were here? Ar-Braz will return, but the other?"

"Mother, I have already returned," replied the Potter. "The other will also return."

The door opened. Caesar was on the threshold.

"My son..."

When day broke, Fleur-d'Épine was weeping.

Into an unknown world, like a wisp of straw, the wind had carried the man who only wanted to work for himself.

The centuries of the earth are hours in heaven. They crawl like black serpents on earth but they pass on high like blue birds.

"What are the English doing in the field of the Skylark?"

"The wheat has been mingled with rye; they are cutting the ears of the rye."

"But they will crush the wheat! Who will summon the Skylark?"

"The Gaulish fays are watching. Over the funereal mound in the land of the Orient they are whirling. Listen.

THE FAYS

The hours of heaven are centuries here. The hours that glide like blue birds on high crawl like serpents here.

"Skylark, the grass is green, the sky is pure, wake up! The grass is green, the sky is pure, the apple trees in your orchard are snowing, the hawthorn is flowering in your hedge; Skylark, Skylark, wake up!

"Next to her fiancé in the somber grotto, she sleeps. On the stone that we have rolled, a cedar has germinated, then grown, and then died. The hours up above are centuries here."

"The foreigner is breaking the flowery branches of the apple tree; Skylark, wake up. On your hawthorn the foreigner wants to graft the northern bush; Skylark, wake up!"

"The heavy stone is shaking. She has heard."

THE SKYLARK

The man who wants to earn too much has burned the thistles and the brambles; let him take the ashes, they are his; but he must not harvest the wheat that he has not sown.

You believe that you are working for yourself, but you are the worker of the Master who only pays those who ask for nothing. Briton, remember Caesar.

The sword of Gaul cannot be broken; her soldier can be bound by an oath, but the celestial sickle cannot be broken, and when the druidess raises her arm, the chains fall away.

Return to my trampled meadows and my crushed woodlands, blonde bees; tomorrow the flower that will give honey will be reborn.

Since the death of Caesar, the druidess has been waiting for the day of the Almighty.

Between heaven and earth her soul is floating; she is seeking and she is waiting. Today, she is dreaming under the dolmen when the ivory harps vibrate on the sea breeze.

But the sobs of Gaul, which is gasping under the English foot, fill her ears; she is not listening to the harps, she is listening to her heart weep.

THE HARPS

In the infinite void we have seen the immortal souls, brilliant sparks of the great heath, all equal, fly away.

And the hearth was no longer anything but a whirl of sparks.

"But where the flame seemed extinct, a voice spoke. That voice said: 'You are me and I am you, and yet, between you and me, infinity has been hollowed out.'

"You are because I am. and yet, emerged from myself, I still remain entire."

"We have seen that in the infinite void; but the more the sheaf of sparks grew, the higher rose the flame of the hearth."

MOINA

I have heard mention of the one they command; his tongue is forked, like Caesar's.

Why did my handsome roebuck allow himself to be put in a cage? Why did he lock that cage with an oath?

THE HARPS

Life flows like a river between the shores of time.

"On the sand she sleeps today, tomorrow she will foam on the rock."

"From the abyss to the summit life seethes; in the granite a soul is asleep, in the moss a soul is dreaming, in the swallow a soul is waiting."

MOINA

On the ashes of the pyre of Alise the Skylark said: "When my field has grass, it is Caesar that my Master will send to weed it."

Is this Briton Caesar?

He is not weeding the wheat, he is uprooting it! He is crushing it

She does not hear the harps vibrating; she is listening to her own heart weeping.

She does not see the Skylark coming; she is gazing into her own heart.

THE SKYLARK

Sister, I have need of you.

MOINA

When the East wind blew I said to you: "Have you heard, Skylark?"

It replied to me: "She is asleep?"

How long I found the night, Mistress!

Here you are; the dawn is imminent. In the ardent sunlight, your ears will ripen.

THE SKYLARK

What Ar-Braz could not do, it is necessary for you to do. Will you?

MOINA

In the hands of a woman the sword of Ar-Braz will be heavy, but I will do my best.

Into a cottage in Lorraine the fays took the soul of the druidess, and Jeanne was born...

If you fall in your rank, if you die with hope in your heart and a smile on your lips, you will see Jeanne tomorrow in the celestial fatherland.

I have seen her myself. Was it a long time ago? Was it yesterday? The centuries of the earth are hours in heaven.

I have seen her in the green star. Grouped around the mound, the soldiers of Ar-Braz were listening to me—they love long stories—when a crimson radiance striped the azure sky. That radiance descended from the world of light, the word without frontiers, the world without swords. In that radiance a female form was gliding.

Dazzled, the soldiers put their hands over their eyes.

It was not a woman who was gliding in the radiance she was no longer a woman, but the person who was called Moina on the pyre of Alise but who was called Jeanne on the pyre of Rouen.

She it was who said to the Gauls: March!

She it was who said to the French: Believe!

She it is who says today: Love! Love everything that lives, love everything that grows, love one another.

When she appeared over the mound was the pyre of Rouen still fuming? I don't know; the centuries of earth are hours n heaven.

But in touching the stars she said "Why put your hands over your eyes? Look at me, Gauls, I am the druidess of ancient days; I am your daughter; I am your sister. It is the flame of the pyre of Alise that shines on my brow. And you who fell under the walls of Orléans, do you no longer recognize your Jeanne?"

Then the soldiers replied: "We recognize you. Do you have need of us, Jeanne? We will follow you as we have followed you before."

A long time ago, a very long time ago, the wind had dispersed the ashes of the pyre; I remember now. A long time ago, a very long time age, the knights who have just spoken were sitting among us.

The Gauls of Vercingetorix had also recognized her.

Then she said: "Would you like to know my name? Potter, make your harp vibrate; my name is the first syllable of the name of the Almighty."

The Potter made his harp vibrate. "Liberty," sang the strings, "you bring the good news; you are the swallow of the promised spring, the primrose of the dreamed garden."

Then she said: "Like the swallow, I would like to twitter on your roofs; like the primrose, I would like to shine on the breast of brides; but I am still Moina the druidess, Jeanne the warrior; prepare your swords, companions."

"It is for the good of men that the Master has created the eternal combat, in the blood his grain sprouts; take up your swords, companions.

"The struggle will be long. The swords will pass like scythes, but afterwards, how green the meadow will be!

"I am the swallow of the promised spring, the primrose of the dreamed garden. On the land of the west, who wants to be reborn in order to dig my garden?"

All the men followed her.

Perhaps yesterday, perhaps a long time ago, I saw that in the green star.

I would have liked to follow her too, but the sin was not yet expiated, and I remained alone.

Sadly, I dreamed. Then a woman approached and she said to me: "My name is Agnès[25] and I am a friend of Jeanne. Lend me your harp; at the court of France they find my voice sweet; to put your sadness to sleep I will tell you the legend of the valleys of the Mont-Dore.

And the valiant friend of the king without courage sang.

The moon is paling, the Orient is silvery; listen.

---

[25] Agnès Sorel (1422-1450), the chief mistress of Charles VII.

THE PERIWINKLE
I have seen nothing; as soon as the sun hides, my stem inclines and my calyx closes.

THE HEATHER
The man had entered between the two women; they were walking slowly. A gold necklace was gleaming on the bare breast of the man; a long sword was hanging at his hip. He was taller than those who pass by day.

They were walking slowly; they were not women like those who pass by day.

THE ROE DEER
The one who was holding a sprig of lily-of-the-valley said to me: "Take me, roe deer, to the spring where you drink; the flame has dried my lips." And I led her to the spring.

She was not a woman like those who pass by day; she spoke our language.

THE PERIWINKLE
She was a fay.

THE HEATHER
No, the fays have no tears and I saw tears in the eyes of the woman with blonde hair.

THE ROCK
The one you saw weeping I have seen laughing, when the tall larches were no higher than the grass. Then the man with the golden necklace was sitting beside her, in my shadow. For a long time I thought that they loved one another; then the woman came alone and wept for a long time in my shadow.

THE ROE DEER

And the other, the one who was smiling? I saw the great larches bow down before her and I saw the raspberry bushes moving aside from the path.

Why, raspberry bushes, did you move aside before her?

THE RASPBERRY BUSHES

We don't know.

THE TORRENT

I know. I saw her glide down the radiance of a star; it was a long time ago, a very long time ago, when the forefathers of those who descend bent double with bundles of wood on their shoulders passed by with flashing eyes, ax in hand.

She isn't a woman and she isn't a fay; she's the Skylark.

THE PERIWINKLE

The Skylark? By night I sleep, but I sometimes dream and my soul has wings; I soar over the blue lake, I pass over the great woods, and I circle over the heath, but I have never seen that divine Skylark, whose song is the echo of the voice of the Almighty.

THE LAKE

I have seen her, by night, sitting on the granite, when the opal crescent was mirrored in my waves.

The virgin with the blonde tresses as hugging the warrior to her, and the warrior, standing and smiling, was listening to her.

She said: "Further away than the green star, closer to the divine hearth, an immense scintillating globe floats in the cloudless azure; there, Jeanne, you will go.

"It is the world of light, the world without frontiers, the world without swords. It is the bay without tempests, where the human rivers mingle for a day. It is the forgotten heaven, the dreamed fatherland, the hearth of the dusk.

There, in the bark of the oak, three words are engraved; you will read them, Jeanne, and then you will come back

Then a gust of wind passed over my surface, and in the gleams of the dawn, it carried Jeanne, the Skylark and the warrior away.

Then, the one who has only loved too much sighed: "I too would have liked to follow her, but the sin is not yet expiated.

Tomorrow, if you fall in your rank, you will understand what the periwinkles say to the roe deer of the woods. Tomorrow, if you die with a smile on your lips, you will find the periwinkle of the dreamed garden in the green star.

Huddled around the fire of vine-branches, the young men are listening to the poet's song of death; but the one who was reading, placing the crumpled pages on his knee, said:

"For a few moments his voice faded away; he asked me for something to drink, and then he closed his eyes and I thought he was dead.

I placed my hand over his heart. He raised his eyelids, but he did not seem to recognize me, and he spoke about himself.

He said: "I remember; as in an open book, my past is there before me. Death is turning the pages. What I dreamed is true, and what André dreams is true; he is Ar-Braz and I am the Potter.

"Death turns the pages of the book; I remember. Thirty years ago, under the flowering eglantine of the green star, we were talking with the beloved about the sphinxes of the old garden when the great army arrived. Ar-Braz and the Skylark were marching at the head.

"I remember. The one whose name we pronounced yesterday in whispers, the Primrose of the dreamed garden, was with them.

"Then he primrose said: 'The man who was Caesar is lying, vanquished, in the funereal grotto, on the bed of Ar-Braz; sing, Potter.'

"And Ar-Braz said: 'The men of the East have come, the army of Gaul is dead; sing, Potter.'

"'And the Skylark said: 'But the dead will be reborn; sing, Potter.'

He closed his eyes and he sang in a low voice, in a language with soft and guttural syllables, and I thought he was going to die.

I moistened his lips. He raised his eyelids; but he did not seem to recognize me and he talked about him.

He said: "I am the second son of the father of our race, I am the brother of Ar-Braz and of the one who only wanted to work for himself.

I also wanted one day only to work for myself.

When I worked for the Master I engraved poems on the granite foreheads of the gods of Elora, I sang to the Gauls the true name of the Creator. When I wanted to work for myself I was only able to ripen in a prison of mud the soul of my beloved.

Woe betide the bard who only wants to work for himself; his harp breaks, his dream fades away and his torch is extinguished.

The one who had guarded his heart like a miser turns in circles, mute, so long as one better than him does not come to find him on the stony road, and does not come to put, in order that he might re-climb the step descended, a bleeding heart under his feet.

If the old man had not put his heart under my feet, I would still be turning in the endless circle, mute.

But in that heart there were all our memories, all our dreams, all our amours and all our hopes, and I found myself so high that my heart has vertigo...

He was speaking slowly, mingling the present and the past. He said: "I was the wild child of the old château and the

273

grandfather was the Celt who had followed the friend of the Skylark with the vanquished of Alise.

"Celestial messenger of the good news, I was not worthy to salute your coming, to mourn your dolors; but today I am your bard, and with the forest for a harp, I shall sing your triumph to the reconciled brothers.

"Mossy firs, vibrate! Sing, elders! Sing, service trees."

He seemed to be listening to a voice and he said: "Tomorrow you will rejoin me, beloved, and you will take away the child; his cradle will be ready. With their golden hair the fays have woven his curtain and the peris have hidden in his rattle the cricket that knows all the songs in the world.

"You will rejoin me tomorrow; I am departing today because a bard is needed by the cavaliers who are going to deliver the great battle in the starry plains..."

He believed that he could see her and he said: "I will always love you; but I will not love you any more than I love you today, than I loved the Statue, than I loved the Druidess, than I loved the queen of the river of milk. In the green star we shall sit down in our place; I am dying struck by the sword that I have brought out of its scabbard.

"Sing of the blue blade!"

The he passed his hand over his brow and he got up, pale and covered in blood.

"The Gaul dies on his feet," he said in a loud voice. "Write, soldier."

And I wrote. Listen.

In the funereal grotto, his hand on the sword that the centuries were tarnishing, Ar-Braz was dreaming.

He pricked up his ears and he said: "Through the thick vault I can hear a clarion sounding."

THE SKYLARK

That clarion is sounding the good news. Jeanne has descended from the world of light.

The hour is imminent, friend.

Let us talk about the past; in looking at the past, one sees the future.

They talked about the past, fine battles and long marches.

"Skylark," said the chief, "I can hear something like the sound of swords."

THE SKYLARK

The crows are about to fall on the fruits of Jeanne's garden, the Master has put his bow in the hand of the hunter, and the frightened crows are circling; the ground is black with their cadavers.

In their fall they have crushed the wheat! Those who followed Jeanne are dead; but this time, they have fallen victorious, the vanquished of Alise.

AR-BRAZ

And Gaul has no more soldiers?

THE SKYLARK

There remain those you gave to Caesar; you kept your oath. They have kept theirs.

AR-BRAZ

How far we could have gone together, if you had wanted, Caesar

Then a radiance filled the cavern and the priestess of the pyre of Alise, the victim of the pyre of Rouen, appeared.

She said: "A warrior had come. Like you he said: "I want Gaul to be united.

"All women loved him, all men followed him; in the vague light of the dawn I mistook him for you and I showed him his route, and I gave him my soldiers.

"When the sun appeared I saw that my soldiers were dead and that the man was not you.

"But those who followed him worshipped him like a god; when I wanted to talk they said to me: "Go away."

They have effaced the words that I had engraved; what is it necessary to do, Skylark?"

THE SKYLARK

Wait; the hour is imminent.

All three of them spoke about the past; but the chief listened and he said: "I can hear something like a death-rattle."

In the depths of the funereal pathway, a vague gleam has appeared.

What is that armed shadow? Who is that chief with a bald forehead?

In the night of the tomb, for whom are you searching?

THE SHADE

You.

THE SKYLARK

A man is the master of his destiny; he will be what he wanted to be; but the one who knows everything makes use of that free will for his own designs.

AR-BRAZ

Where have you come from?

THE SHADE

From the blazing reef. From a cage of lava lost upon the Ocean.

Like a bolt of lightning the Almighty threw me; where I shone the ash is smoking.

But I fought bravely, soldier, give me the bed from which you are rising; I'm weary.

I wanted to kill you, Vercingetorix; I only opened your path. I wanted to take your place; I shall take it in the night of the tomb.

AR-BRAZ
Who are those who are following you?

THE SHADE
Don't you recognize them? With them I have done more than Cambyses, more than Darius, more than Alexander. They're the men you gave me on the plateau of Alise. I'm returning them to you.

THE ARMY
We're ready for battle; but if you want to sleep the eternal slumber, make room for us at your sides.

THE SHADE
They kept the oath that you swore; all the way to death, they wanted to follow me.

They do not want to climb without me the route from which my past bars me; take them, as I took them once.

As you came to the plateau of Alise, I have come; render a soul to that dead army and...

In exchange for your people, on the plateau of Alise, you enchained yourself freely, and I am no longer anything but a phantom with a bloody forehead... Leave me the bed from which you are rising.

AR-BRAZ
Brother, do you remember our games before the woolen tent in the land of the Orient? I have forgotten all the rest; sit down beside me.

In the grotto illuminated by reflections of steel, they talk about their battles. The one who was Vercingetorix and the one who was Caesar, sitting next to one another, listen.

"But where, then, is the Awaited? Where, then, is the Skylark?"

277

The Gauls had said to the Awaited: "Go away!" She returned to the land of light, the land without frontiers, the land without words. She will come back when she is called; she will only come when she is called.

The Skylark has remembered her promise. In the plains of the Ebro she had said to the bard: 'I will help you to recover your beloved.'

The bard is searching today, she has gone to help him.

Without help he will succumb; he is nothing but a man like other men; the old man has returned to sit at the hearth of heaven. The Skylark will guide her bard because the two enemies will break their shackles is his heart goes astray.

If the two enemies break their shackles, matter will resume its empire over mind and the steps climbed will crumble.

The Skylark loves her soldier, but she needs her bard.

Like the oak, their emblem, the sons of light only touch the ground with their feet; but the shadow of the oak etiolates the bushes, and its roots plunge all the way to the great heart that beats within the living earth. That is why the sons of darkness are jealous of the sons of the sun, that is why the earth is jealous of heaven.

And since the commencement, the struggle has endured, and since the commencement, the German armies have collided with the Gaulish armies, and since the commencement, the voice that impels has been seeking to stifle the voice that thinks.

The envious have bumped their heads on the heavy sword of Ar-Braz; but caressant nature, the snake with the golden scales, which, order to see the flower again sooner, kills the fruit as soon as it is ripe, is always young, always beautiful and always seductive.

To vanquish her, it is necessary to prove to her that those who struggle against her are those who love her the most. To vanquish her, it is necessary to prove to her that she ought not to be neither a mistress or a slave, but an ally.

That is the goal that the older brother of Ar-Braz and his proud companion, whose soul descended from the summit on the brilliant foam of the overflowing Ganges, have been trying to attain through the centuries, under the magnolias or under the oaks, in the caverns of Elora and on the banks of the Loire.

In the forest of India, where sensuality and death ruled without division, the couple descended from the snowy valley of the mountains of the North had said: "Death, why are you trying to kill the souls along with the bodies?"

And Sensuality replied: "Because death is my sister. I love what is beautiful, and only youth is beautiful."

The couple replied: "Kill our bodies, like the flower, when they have withered, but do not touch our souls, for their youth is eternal. Hymn of embalmed nights, song of days of sunlight, tell our sister not to knead human souls with their bodies; the greater the soul feels in a obedient body, the more it will put flames in the eyes and intoxication on the lips."

And the two sisters responded: "If what you say is true, prove it. If you do not weary of my caresses, if you do not tremble under my hand, vanquished, we will obey you."

And the struggle commenced.

It the Potter has vanquished they would have rotted the trunk of the oak in order to sow the fecund earth with azure clematis and emerald scarabs.

When the Potter says: "True amour is an eternal bond that nothing loosens and nothing wears away," he enchains the sensuality that shreds the human soul. When he says: "The tomb is a bed in which the soul ought only to lie down in order to repose before continuing on its way," he enchains the death that, of the unconscious debris fallen from the lips of her sister, makes butterflies or roses.

If he forgets the queen of the Ganges, if his amour goes astray, the chain is broken and, as in the first days, under terrestrial caresses, the human soul is enervated, and, as in the first days, the human soul lingers, rocking itself in the wave and intoxicating itself in the flower.

That is why it is necessary for the bard to find his beloved again. That is why the Skylark has quit her fiancé. That is why she has gone into the garden of the old château.

"I am weary of the whinnying of horses, the clicking of iron; let us go into the garden where he narcissi are chatting and the wren is gossiping."

We have come too late; look.
On the moss near the round basin, in the shadow of the lindens, he is dead.
The soul that animated the garden has gone; we can no longer hear the narcissi chatting and the wren gossiping.
"Has the soul departed? Listen."

THE NIGHTINGALE

When the kébir with the gray eyes passed by under the palm trees of Boghar, gazelles, you moved aside your veils.

When he has passed you told me your troubles. I remember them; you said: "We are asphodels; if you wished to embalm your tent tonight, kébir, you only have to lower yourself.

But the kébir had an eglantine under his tent, gazelles. I told you so, I remember. The perfume of the white eglantine was so sweet that, when the eglantine faded, the kébir went to the green garden where beloved eglantines are reborn.

Weep under the palm trees, gazelles! Weep also, turtle-doves of the blue mountains! Weep, all those who loved him; like a gladiolus broken by the wind, he is lying on the grass.

THE SPHINXES

We were the turtle-doves of the blue mountains; what you say is true.

Weep, nightingale, instead of singing. Don't weep for him, weep for us, the disdained.

THE WREN

Who spoke? In the breath that brings these voices, I am palpitating as in spring, but I am also trembling… why?

They are not two monsters who are dreaming, they are two women who are weeping on granite pedestals.

I recognize them; they are the women she called "maid-servants" on the evening when the stranger talked about amour to her on the terrace.

THE NIGHTINGALE

I recognize them too. I saw them on the cliff in the clump of pomegranate trees, where the perfume of the bean-fields mingles with the perfume of laurels.

They are the sisters of the bank of the Nile; there is Aïchouna and there is Meyrin. Look, they are as beautiful as the rising moon, as the star that is going to sleep,

The one whose hair has coppery reflections is Meyrin, whose dark eyes emit sparks when the perfume of the bean-fields rises up to the pomegranate wood.

The one whose heavy tresses, like two black snakes, writhe over her bare shoulders, is the caressant Aïchouna, the beauty with the sapphire eyes; Aïchouna the indolent, who, in the pomegranate wood, preferred the odor of the laurels to the perfume of the bean-fields.

THE SPHINXES

You recognize us, nightingale, but you are not speaking our true names.

Aïchouna is Death; Meyrin is Sensuality.

Weep, nightingale, instead of singing; weep for us, the disdained.

Do not weep for him, weep for us; he has vanquished.

"Today he has vanquished, but tomorrow he might perhaps succumb. I can hear heavy cavaliers coming from the East; the Skylark has descended again to her furrow; he will not leave Ar-Braz to struggle alone against the envious; he will want to be reborn as man, and this time, I shall make myself so beautiful that, in my arms, he will forget his queen."

"Then I shall make myself so tender that he will say to me: 'Before my dream ends, take me.'"

"Weep, nightingale, instead of singing; the kébir will forget the beloved eglantine."

Not knowing how to weep, the nightingale fell silent. Huddled under a dry leaf, the wren listened; something like a flutter of wings could be heard, like a sound of kisses.

Then they emerged from the hornbeam arbor and descended, hand in hand, the path bordered by box. However, his body was lying on the moss on the edge of the basin, and her body had been in the little cemetery in the midst of the vineyards for three days.

The Skylark followed them.

The two women who were weeping, leaning on the granite pedestals, shivered. Head downs, arms folded over the breast, they went before the woman who was coming.

"We are your slaves, command," they said, without raising their eyes.

"Why are you not where you ought to be?" replied the queen of the Ganges. "Return to these flanks of granite and, as in the time when I was queen, lie down under the bed of nacre in the crystal hall."

The Potter smiled as he looked at his beloved, and she blushed. Why?

Then the Potter said: "Under the eglantine always in flower we shall have for a nuptial bed a cloud crimsoned by the dusk; why do you want to send these two to the crystal hall where the bed of nacre is tarnishing, my queen?"

The beloved blushed. Why?

Then the Potter bent down and, taking a lump of clay from the stream shining under the irises and cress, he kneaded it between his fingers.

The clay was fine and white, like the clay on the bank of the Ganges under the magnolia of the enclosure; the Potter made a rose with it.

As he modeled the clay he said: "Why is this rose not turning crimson under my fingers?

"Maidservants, in the immense reservoir from which you believe you can draw life with full hands, search for a soul. When you have found it, you will be free. Search."

The two sphinxes responded: "Since we have been your servants, freed souls have escaped the bodies that we kill; freely, they chose the bodies that we created. We can no longer retain them, they slip between our fingers; but if, for a day, you render us the ever-full cup and the ever-sharp scythe, we will intoxicate the most beautiful of virgins; body and soul she will give herself to us, and in your flower of clay we will hide her soul, still fully embalmed by the first amour, blushing at the first kiss."

"I render your weapons to you, but only for one day. Tomorrow you will rejoin me in the green star."

And they departed.

Then the Skylark said: "Bard, what have you done? My sons wanted to look the celestial light in the face and their dazzled eyes closed; when they see those two flames shining in their darkness, they might believe they are seeing the lighthouse once glimpsed, and they will run on to the reefs. They were your slaves; why have your released their bonds?"

"By shaking her chains the slave ends up breaking them. I want to make those two enemies into two associates."

"O my bard, remember the past; only be the Master's worker. I do not know where your route will go; I can neither follow you nor aid you. O my bard, the struggle is imminent, do not break the harp when the sword is about to be raised."

And, the Skylark having disappeared in the crimson of the dusk, the Potter said:

Between your women and our guards, in your crystal palanquin, on your huge elephant, like a bird in the sky you passed on high, my queen, when, among the beggars on the threshold of our palace, the Potter crawled like a lizard in the mud. And yet, the queen loved the Potter.

In the sunlight of the first day, on the mountain of the Orient, the daughter of the white foam saw the face of the Master; I only heard the voice of the Almighty in the plaint of the waves and the song of the woods, and yet, the voice told me what it had not told the Skylark.

Evil was not in God; it was only created by him in order to permit humans to grow by means of the struggle; in trying to vanquish it, therefore, I do not rebel. Evil will not be eternal, since it will no longer be necessary on the day of victory; in trying to bring forward the hour of the supreme repose, therefore, I am working for those who suffer and those who cause suffering.

Let there be light, and the enemies will see that they are striking themselves. Let there be light, and the enemies will blunt of their own accord the weapons that the Master's wisdom put into their hands sharpened. Let there be light, and the enemies will see that it is necessary to magnify instead of debasing, to unite instead of breaking, and instead of being my slaves, they will be my associates.

When, naked under the sun, naked under the rain, I prayed for centuries on the holy mountain in the distant land, the wind that came from the Ganges brought me the echo of the voice of the Almighty.

That voice said: "Human beings have been created equal, and everything has been created for them. When they have relearned everything they have forgotten, they will all be equal before me, and in them, all will be melted."

This is what the voice also said to me in the land of prayer: "When the time has come, in the infinite void, like a mirror shining in the face of its creator, only humanity will remain, and souls without shades will have for bodies stars without clouds. And matter and spirit will only make one whole. And death will be the sun of that radiant world, of which love will be the dew.

"In the green star, go to wait for those who believe that they are crumbling an immense soul at their whim, when they are only giving a nest to a bird as yet without wings.

"Go and wait for them, they will return with empty hands; every soul builds its own house to its dimensions, cottage or palace, and in order to animate that rose, it is necessary that my soul hide within it.

"They will return with empty hands and they will know then that souls go where they want to go, and that although they can slow them down in their path by intoxicating them, they cannot make them trace new ones. They only change the location of that which they thought to destroy and that which they believed they were creating.

"Then, light being created, we shall have two associates."

While the queen listened to the Potter, whose body was stiffening on the grass, the nightingale sang the amorous plaints of the white asphodels to the date-palms of Boghar, and the wren said to the dry leaves: "I knew that he would come back to the hornbeam by night in order to speak to the blonde stars about his friend the wren."

Over the dormant plain, over the mute city, two gleams glided, and a warm breeze gilded the green leaves of the vines of the plain, and in closed rooms the curious crickets fell silent.

Over the dormant plain, over the mute city, in the rustle of leaves, in the quiver of curtains, if one lent an ear, one could have heard two voices responding to one another. Those voices falling from the two distant gleams said:

"I have the smile of a virgin and the rump of a lion; I am the imperishable image of amour such as God has made it. I am the immobile sphinx with the broad brow and the lowered eyes."

"Under my swollen breasts my claws are hidden; I am death and I am life. I am the immobile sphinx with the broad brow and the lowered eyes."

And in closed rooms the curious crickets fell silent, and in the clusters of the vines the grapes reddened.

The voices falling from the two gleams said:

"The softness of my lips attracts, the milk of my teat intoxicates; but after the given kiss my claws tear the heart to pieces and the wind scatters the crumbs."

"Lying on the crumpled flowers you see, young men, the rump of the wild beast, and you stop, trembling; gaze at my soft smile, gaze at my swollen breasts."

"Love, and you will die."

"Die, and you will love."

But the flutter of gilded wings falling over the vines, mingling with the sound of kisses, over the dormant plain, in the mute city no one any longer hears the voices...

I can hear the voices, they are calling me... Let's go, I'm ready... Ar-Braz is born, Gaul! Ar-Braz is born!

It is not yet them who are calling me; my task is not finished. It is the fays, weeping in the swirling snow, that I believe I can still hear. Listen.

You have not seen that, young men; you are not thirty years old. Myself, I have seen it from on high. In the snow that fell thirty years ago, my soul was weeping with the fays, and I forgot that I was a bard, and I wept like a soldier.

In those who recoiled thirty years ago, I recognized those I had commanded the day before and those who had commanded me the day before, and I wept like a soldier.

I recognized my old chasseurs of Africa and the Crimea, but when, a soul without a body, I leaned over those who were dying with blasphemy on their lips, I did not even stop the snow that was marbling their emaciated cheeks.

When I said to them: "You are still the brave men of Malakoff and Zaatcha;[26] you have been commanded to do the impossible," they did not hear me.

---

[26] The Battle of Malakoff in 1855 was a French attack on Russian forces during the siege of Sebastopol, in the Crimean War. The raising of the French flag by a zouave above the Malakoff redoubt became a symbolic turning point in the siege

Until death they heard nothing but that clarion sounding the retreat. Forever! Forever!

You have not seen that, young men, you are not thirty years old. You have not seen the victim fall bleeding under the mass; myself, I have seen it and my heart is full of hatred..

But what you have seen is sadder still; you have seen the butchers cutting up the great cadaver. And who were the butchers…?

I have seen that, as you have; from the world of light I have descended again in order to struggle and suffer with you.

When the scattered parts were quivering on the butcher's stall, when the idiot butchers were smiling at their work, the man from the East came and he said: "That meat is mine."

And the butchers dared not even raise their voices.

What you have seen, what we have seen, is sadder than what your forefathers had seen; they had seen defeat, but we have seen shame.

We have a stain on the forehead; will our blood be red enough to efface it?

Listen, and let your hearts fill with hatred.

Listen; this is what I have seen, and what I have heard, while my soul was weeping with the fays in the swirling snow.

It is no longer the dying man who is speaking, no longer the bard who is singing, it is history that is dictating; write, soldier.

The wind is blowing, the snow is falling and on the plain they are dying, alone. Does France no longer have any doctors? Does Gaul no longer have any women? Do these soldiers

---

and in the war. The siege of Zaatcha in Algiers in 1849 was a crucial phase in the conflict between the French colonial forces and he resistant Arab and Berber forces commanded by Sheikh Bouziane, whose dogged refusal to surrender and eventual execution and beheading might have reminded neutral observers of Vercingetorix's last stand.

no longer have any chiefs? Do these men no longer have any sisters?

They are dying; the wind is whistling; in the white swirls the fays are passing. Listen.

THE FAYS

The moon is rising, here we are. For those who are dying we have hidden a ray of sunlight in our hair, and we are carrying a warm caress from the land of the Orient under our wings.

How cold they are! Why are you blowing so strongly, winter wind. Why, pale cavalier, are you letting your icy cloak trail over these bleeding wounds? They're children; look.

Toward the sea with gray waves turn your thin mare and we shall follow you under the northern fir trees. We shall build a sapphire palace there, a luminous palace with crystal vaults and ruby gates.

THE NORTH WIND

I am the grave-digger; I am bringing the shroud.

THE FAYS

We have our sunlit scarves, our long veils of mist; we shall make shrouds of them; all this blood would stain your cloak.

THE NORTH WIND

They are lifting your scarves, they are parting your veils, and they are getting up again.

A WOUNDED MAN

With my broken hand, what would I do at home? It's better to stay here.

Slumber is coming...I shall have fine white sheets in which to sleep.

THE NORTH WIND

I'm extending the shroud; lie down.

THE WOUNDED MAN

They could have me killed; that was their right; but why are they letting me die of hunger?

The bread was black at home but the crumbs were large. There was enough for all of us, for the chickens and for the dog.

THE NORTH WIND

Lie down! Lie down!

THE WOUNDED MAN

Give me back my clogs; my feet are bleeding in my shoes without soles! Have me killed; I'm hungry!

THE NORTH WIND

Lie down! Lie down!

THE FAYS

The frost has stiffened our hair, the snow has made out wings heavy, and our lips have no breath with which to warm their hands.

They wandered free, the proud bulls; you have come and they have extended their necks meekly to the yoke. Why have you not been able to make them follow the path? Since when have the oxherds, instead of marching ahead, marched behind?

THE WOUNDED MAN

Perhaps my hand might be healed? Oh, if I could only move the snow away...!

THE FAYS

Souls without bodies, a ray of light traverses us, a breath lifts us up. Thistledown is too heavy for our arms.

THE NORTH WIND

Now, sleep.

THE FAYS

Sisters with vermilion wings, you have not descended from the green star. Who will guide these souls on the route up above?

THE SKYLARK

Me.

Up there, the sun is scintillating in the azure! Up there the feast is fuming. Come! Come!

Fortunate is the first harvester to bind his sheaf. Come! Come!

THE FAYS

Tears make flowers grow on tombs; weep, sisters.

"In the furrows of the green star we have picked the flower of hope; let us plant it on these tombs."

I was with the fays; with them I wept on the snow reddened by the blood of sacrifices.

But around the Skylark, on the route up above, those who were rising seemed so happy and so proud that my tears dried up and I followed the fays, who were carried toward Paris by a gust of wind

The white fays said: "Let us weep for those who remain.

"A child is calling us, come."

And I entered the room without a fire where the child was wailing with the fays.

Listen, the child is scratching the frost on the window panes with his fingernails, and the grandfather is wrapping his old mantle of blue cloth around his knees.

THE CHILD

The doors are closed, one can no longer go out, but the fays have no need to go through doors.

You love good little children, good fays; I'm very god, Mama says. I never ask for anything, and I left the last pear for grandfather, but bring me some milk. The bread is too hard; it scratches my mouth and burns my neck; bring me some milk, only a very little pot, and I'll give some to grandfather.

THE FAYS
Thistledown is too heavy for our arms.

But we give beautiful dreams. Close your eyes, darling. Close your beautiful blue eyes, darling, and houris will bring you the oranges of paradise.

THE GRANDFATHER
Do you hear? Another victory!

THE MOTHER
Yes, Father.

THE GRANDFATHER
Is that the cannons of Les Invalides?

THE MOTHER
Yes, Father,

THE FAYS
Close your eyes, darling. Close our pretty blue eyes.

Take the bowl from the dresser, the big bowl with the butterflies and come into the grounds quickly; the black cow has good milk.

Close your eyes, your pretty eyes. Close your pretty blue eyes.

THE GRANDFATHER
It's the cannons of Les Invalides. I recognize their voice. There are some in there that I helped to capture.

Is there a review? I want to see it.

My feet are dragging, my head shaking and I'm his conscript, but he's still there, steady on his legs, his hands behind
his back...it's necessary to see how he bears arms; he sees
everything

Child? Child, do you hear?

THE CHILD
I heard the black cow calling her calf.

THE GRANDFATHER
And you didn't hear the salvo? The cannons of the twen-
ty-four fired. But that isn't ringing; they're conscripts who are
loading.

THE CHILD
It's the Prussians.

THE GRANDFATHER
Oh. it's the Prussians who are receiving it, this time!
To the devil with the tisane; give me a bottle of old wine.
And biscuits.

THE MOTHER
Wait a while, Father, the key to the sideboard has gone
astray.

THE CHILD
You know full well that there's nothing in the sideboard
but siege bread.

THE GRANDFATHER
Siege bread! But that's a bullet whistling! What's hap-
pening children?

I've slept for a long time, then? Oh, my head! My poor
head" Let's see, let's see; where's your father, child?"

THE CHILD

On the ramparts. The gates have been closed and we can no longer get milk...my throat is burning, Maman.

THE MOTHER

What's the matter, my dear? What do you want?

THE CHILD

The beautiful ladies have given me milk is a big bowl...give the rest to grandfather.

THE GRANDFATHER

Present, *mon empereur*.

THE CHILD

No, no, I'm afraid.

THE MOTHER

Oh my God, have pity on me

THE FAYS

Don't be afraid, darling; look, your grandfather is with you. Come, we have beautiful meadows full of black cows, which you can milk yourself, into the bowl with the butterflies.

Come with us, old man, we know where the companions of your youth are waiting, we'll take you to them.

But who will console her?

THE SKYLARK

Me.

I did not follow the fays who carried away the soul of the old man to where the soldiers of the man who had been Caesar were waiting, and I did not follow the fays into the meadow where the black cows were grazing; I leaned over the bereaved mother with the Skylark.

A spirit without a body, the mother cannot see me, but the Skylark is more than a woman, when she wants the cloud to model her a body, the sun weaves her a mantle; she takes the trembling hand in her own hands, and the mother sees her.

THE MOTHER
He's dead, Madame. What do you want with me?

THE SKYLARK
He is still too small to do without you. I'm not a woman, look. Do you want to die and rejoin him?

THE MOTHER
What about his father, who loved him so much?

THE SKYLARK
He's my soldier; we'll bring him too.

THE MOTHER
Wait for me, my child, wait for me!

THE SKYLARK
He is with my fays, the little one. Let's go find his father.

THE MOTHER
I'm no longer cold, I'm no longer hungry, I'm no longer afraid. Why don't you take all the children who are suffering and all the mothers who are weeping?

A shell has smashed the window and its shards have crushed the three cadavers; but what does it matter? The souls had already departed.

The grandfather was already talking about the siege to the artillerymen of the *grand armée*; the child had already filled the butterfly bowl with milk and the wife was going into a smoldering house on the bank of the Marne with the Skylark.

I followed them, but on seeing again, black with powder, the flag that had guided me in the Lombard plains and the Kabyle mountains, I wept at no longer being a soldier.

They had fought bravely, my chasseurs, one against a hundred. The small nucleus that remained blocked the street proudly, and the Bavarian column writhed at each discharge.

In the smoldering house they had all fallen at their loopholes; there was no longer anyone alive except a trumpeter and the sergeant who had once picked me up from the shingle of the beach.

The wife pointed to the trumpeter.

"I know him," replied the Skylark. "Before being a soldier he was one of those who went to listen to the last of my druids talk about the past.

A clarion sounded in the distance.

"Always, then," sighed the commandant, replacing his saber abruptly in its scabbard.

And, slowly, the little troop drew away in the avenue of poplars.

No one emerged from the smoldering house.

They had heard, however; listen.

THE TRUMPETER
They're sounding the retreat.

THE SERGEANT
I don't care. How many have you got left?

THE TRUMPETER
One.

THE SERGEANT
Pass it to me.

THE TRUMPETER
No. This cartridge is mine.

THE SERGEANT
You're only a conscript. A bad soldier.

THE TRUMPETER
I have a broken arm. Take my rifle, Sergeant. Don't hurry; it's necessary, for the last shot, to bring down a fine prey.

THE SERGEANT
The blood is blinding me

THE TRUMPETER
Well, that's it. Sit down here, Sergeant. That's it. It's all right. You can have the appeal sounded. The whole section is here: the lieutenant, the sergeants and the corporals, the whole section. That's nice, isn't it?

THE SERGEANT
Yes, that's nice, lad. When someone said to me: Blavet, you'll have that married man for a trumpeter, I wasn't content; but you haven't dishonored the uniform.
Are they all dead?

THE TRUMPETER
They're all dead, and we won't be long delayed. We'll all arrive together and the eternal father will pass us in a fine review. The door's opening…it's time. A woman!

THE SKYLARK
Give me your rifle.

THE TRUMPETER
What a handful! Wait, I'll get up; I want to see.
Touché! Sergeant, our last cartridge has killed a general. Now go, there aren't any more. And hide well, these fellows kill women.

THE SKYLARK

I never hide, and no one can kill me. Have you a message for your homeland?

THE SERGEANT

No. I quit my homeland too long ago, no one knows me there any longer. But this conscript has a wife and child.

THE TRUMPETER

My son will do what I have done, and my wife won't forget me. Tell them what you've seen and watch over them— I've recognized you.

THE SERGEANT

You've recognized her?

THE SKYLARK

I'm the one whom you have loved, and whom you love. I'm the one for whom you're about to die. I'm France. Do you want to carry my flag, Sergeant? Do you want to sound my orders, Trumpeter?

Your wife is here, look.

THE MOTHER

Come, the little one is waiting for us.

THE TRUMPETER

And Father?

THE MOTHER

He's also waiting for us.

THE TRUMPETER

When one does one's duty, everything works out for the best. Paris, do your duty!

And Paris did her duty.

You haven't seen that; you're not thirty years old; but I've seen that myself, from above.

I've seen the beautiful city, in her girdle of smoke, under a dome of lightning.

They said: "She's a courtesan with greedy lips and languid eyes."

They found an amazon, and when the peace delivered it to them, she had such a proud bearing that they didn't even dare touch her bruised breast under her dented breastplate.

When you see her in her festival jewelry, think about that.

Myself I haven't seen her again since that evening of battle, but tomorrow, when the victory is won, when I have all the strings of heaven on my harp, I'll descend during nights of vigil to lean my elbows on the tables of her poets, and in order that she should always be the most beautiful, I'll teach those who love her all the secrets.

Paris did her duty; the Skylark smiled at her and, in the starry night, and a gust of wind carried us all the way to the funereal grotto in the Orient.

The mound is open. On the two sides of the gaping vault the Valkyries are gathered, hands raised, in long tightly-knit squadrons.

We are in the hall that is vaguely illuminated by steely reflections.

THE SERGEANT

We should have brought the whole section. We went too quickly; they'll never catch up with us.

Here's the barracks. The vault is dark, but how big the courtyard is!

THE SKYLARK

We've arrived. Play, trumpeter, the march of the Skylark.

THE TRUMPETER
The march of the Skylark? Don't know it.

THE SKYLARK
Sound the charge. That's my march.

THE SERGEANT
Oh, what fine soldiers!

THE SKYLARK
Well, Sergeant, have the appeal sounded.

The clarion sounds; they are all standing up.

Davout! Lannes! Ney! Murat! Hoche! Augereau! Moncey! Without stopping, the sergeant calls the names and all those named rise to their feet.

They get up in their turn, they summon their regiments, their brigades, their divisions, their armies.

Listen! Santons! Ruthènes! Séquanes! Carnutes! Eduens! The army is in battle order. No one misses the roll-call.

THE SHADE
And me, why have you not called me?

THE SKYLARK
You have only labored for yourself. You are your own soldier, not mine. Sleep, Caesar.

Ar-Braz, this is your army of tomorrow.

The chief, having got up, picked up his golden helmet with the broad silver wings and buckled on his heavy sword. Then he approached the one who had been Caesar and he said: "Brother, come with me."

"No," replied the Skylark, "my soldiers are not your soldiers."

Then, the one who had commanded the legions said:

"Ar-Braz, I shall wait for you as you have waited for me."

The army is in battle order, the chief is on horseback.

The clarion sounds, the army moves off.

Like a black whirlwind, it rises into the fog. Ar-Braz, his sword bare, guides it.

At the summit of the green mound, between her two soldiers, the Skylark smiles.

Uttering hurrahs, the brigades file past. Here are the battalions of Arcole, the grenadiers of Jemmapes, the chasseurs of the Pyramids, the hussars of Elhingen, the batteries of Montereau, the voltigeurs of Iéna, the dragoons of Austerlitz, the cuirassiers of Eylan.

Into the fog they rise, their weapons glinting and their horses prancing.

The sergeant calls out his bronze list.

The last squadron passes at the gallop. "No one is missing," says the sergeant.

Into the fog the army rises. The chief extends his hand and it stops; a somber troop is approaching from the West.

"Where have you come from, soldiers?" cries Ar-Braz.

"From Reichoffen, Sedan, Metz, the Loire, Paris and the Vosges."

"Where are you going?"

"We have fought bravely; we are going to sit down at the feast of the brave."

"Trumpeter, sound," says the Skylark. "Forward! Add them to our list, Sergeant.

"For my soldiers, the tomb is only a bed of sweet dreams! As soon as my song rises in the heavens, they awake smiling, smiling and proud.

"See the diadem of lightning and steel that my soldiers have forged for me; I am the queen of the sunset, the queen with the bright eyes, the queen with the golden scepter, the queen with full hands."

The two troops mingle and the breath of the Master pushes them all the way to the green star, where the clan of Vercingetorix has been waiting for its chief for twenty centuries.

This happened thirty years ago, on the day when, hunger having done what the Prussians had not been able to do. Paris lay down on her flag in order to receive the mortal blow.

Those armies are no longer in the green star; they only stayed there for one day. Ar-Braz is no longer in the green star; he only stayed here for one day.

In order to expel he enemy, those souls have returned to request earthly bodies.

Those armies are here... Ar-Braz commands them...

What I am saying is true.

The poet slid on to the grass. He was dead.

Around the blazing fire they are dreaming about what they have heard.

"Who goes there?" cries the sentinel.

The young men are on their feet; the sound is heard of the footfalls of a crowd.

"France!" responds a voice; and the crowd emerges from the shadows.

They are the young women who have come to pick up the reddened rifles of their lovers; they are the sensate men who have come to join the madmen.

"But where are the Fayolles? Where is Blanche?"

"Perhaps we shall find them later; now let's search for the chief; I want to see again the man who was Vercingetorix, who was Ar-Braz, and whom the soldiers call General André."

"He is passing under the beeches. Follow him."

The moon is shining between the beeches; he mounts the path of the Pierres du Jour, the rocks that loom up roseate between the slope of the Loire and the slope of the Allier. From their summit he can embrace the battlefield where the Germans and the Celts will fight tomorrow, where the enemies will settle their quarrel of thirty centuries, in which the vanquished race will lose even its name.

"In the spring, André was only an outlaw who went into the mountains with twenty deserters. In the autumn, he is the leader of a million soldiers. Why?

Why have these men, who broke an idol every day in order to have the pleasure of carving a new one every morning, followed him?"

"Because he was the one who was to come, and his hour has come. Because he is the harvester, and the Master's crop is ripe.

Since the hour that had no commencement, tomorrow's victory has been written in the eternal pages; he is only the sword that has pointed to the goal; he is only the voice that will cry: "Charge!"

That which is, must be. A man is the master of his destiny, but humanity is marching toward a fatal goal. To attain the supreme good there is only a road bordered by two abysms, into which the malevolent fall when they try to bar the route, or into which the mad fall when they want to broaden it.

The strong are the humble who search in the heavens for the traced route. The crowd believes them, and follows them, because they march straight.

Like those stars of summer nights that glide, brushing the earth, they trace a luminous furrow, and then they disappear without leaving behind either ash or smoke. Having come from the sky, they return there

André, have no doubt; tomorrow you will be victorious.

But the strong doubt their strength; with his forehead applied to the mossy stone, he says, joining his hands: "Give me confidence, Master."

"Your path is the straight path; march, my beloved."

André lifts his head; a woman is before him.

"You really are the one of whom I dreamed! You really are the one I love! Since you have come to me, my path is the straight path. Skylark. Look down there at that shining stream; tomorrow, when my horse crosses it, the battle will be won.

The Skylark puts a kiss on the forehead of the chief, and disappears.

"Tomorrow," said André, "it is necessary that my eyes are not troubled; the clarion, sounding the *réveille*, will wake me up."

He lay down at the foot of a beech and went to sleep.

The moon is trembling, the stars in the sky are scintillating, the breeze is singing in the beeches, the curlew is whistling in the rushes, thyme is perfuming the heath, the firs are embalming the clouds; the land of Gaul is ornamenting herself like a bride.

In the two armies the fires pale and the noises die down.

André is asleep.

Between the two dolmens, in the circle carpeted with myrtles, shaded by the leafy oaks, on a bed of flowering gorse, the soldiers had laid the body of the poet. Uttering plaintive cries, a nightjar that is passing back and forth caresses the mute mouth with its silky wing; fireflies are buzzing around the pale forehead; glow-worms are shining like candles, and like the marble greyhounds of Gothic tombs, a huge wolf lies down at the feet of the cadaver..

The moon rises above the fir trees, the circle is illuminated and the widow parts the crawling branches of the oaks. The orphan is smiling in her arms; the two virgins are guiding her, the Fayolles are following her.

The widow lays the orphan on the bloody breast; then she kneels down and, pressing the cold hand against her heart, she says:

"I have done what you wanted, friend, what should I do now? Summon me; I would like to sit on the rump of your horse tomorrow, as of old."

Then the virgin with the dark eyes lifts the forehead of the dead man to the widow's lips; then the virgin with the blue eyes touches with her white finger the widow, who is weeping, and the orphan, who is smiling, and the souls of the wife and the child, free, open their wings.

On the carpet of myrtles the Fayolles twirl, and like the gazelles on the tombs of distant lands, a roe deer emerges from the wood and lies down beside the huge wolf, at the feet of the dead woman.

In his sleep, André smiles. In the two armies, before the extinct fires, the mute sentinels watch.

Like a steel necklace, the Allier glitters; like a silver ring, the Montoncel shines; like a gauze veil, a fine vapor floats from the hazel-nut trees of the Bèbre to the service trees of Crèches, and like a silken mantle, the heaths of the Tombérino, from Rochefort to the Sapé, extend their long stiff pleats. The land of Gaul is ornamenting herself like a bride.

The moon descends behind Montoncel, the shadows elongate; a luminous mist blurs the dolmen. Arms enlaced, the Fayolles stop; the wolf raises its head; the roe deer listens, and one of those voices that humans do not hear resonates under the somber vaults of the beech forest. It says:

"From my sonorous hand into the blue gulf, your hours fall slowly, God!

"It was a day of tears, the day gone by! What will the day that is about commence be?"

From the depths of the sky a voce responds:

"It will be the day of justice, the day of my sons.

"Let the barriers be lowered, let he abysms be filled in! The earth belongs to my sons; let the earth aid them!"

Then the angel of midnight, the one who had spoken under the beeches, cried in his clear voice:

"Do you hear? Hidden forces, veiled souls, voiceless lips, wake up. The barriers are lowered, the abysms are filled in; enter the open list."

Then a rain of sparks crackled on the leaves, ran along the trunks, filled the hollows in the rock, streamed over the moss and, like a necklace of rubies, the immense round-dance garlanded the forest and the heath with its glittering folds

As they spun, the Gaulish fays sang:

"The barriers are lowered! Like women we are going to live, struggle and love.

"We shall be the flowers of the last bouquet, the fiancées of the last fighters.

"The abysms are filled in; sing, sacred ebonies and mossy stones, sing the hymn of the old Gauls to the virgin incarnate."

And the rocks responded:

"Sing the song of the blue blade that loves the flesh! Sing the song of the blue blade! A head for an eye, an arm for a finger, and a heart for a wound!"

And the oaks responded:

"O sword! O great king of the battlefield! O sword! O great king! O blood and fire! O iron and fire! The sword is king!

"The sword is drawn, the fire is lit! The lists are open! Enlarge out hearts and harden our arms. From the somber night, enable the lightning to spring, and may our fires retemper the twisted sword of the Gauls."

Then a crimson radiance writhed in the blue sky.

The fays disconnected their rounds; the Fayolles hid under the leafy oaks; the roe deer shivered; the wolf howled dully, and the great dolmen trembled under a cascade of flame.

The mares with bloody wings scratched the granite with their ivory hooves. The awaited hour chimed; the Valkyries descended from the green star.

White, their breasts erect, their hair loose, their nostrils quivering and their arms raised, on their horses that are rearing up, can you hear them?

305

"The sword is drawn, the flame lit, the lists are open, here we are!

"Flower, violets of the woodland paths; bouquets of red betrothals are required.

"Flower, eglantines of the roadside bushes! Flower, buttercups on the banks of streams! We shall collect betrothal bouquets for the soldiers of the Skylark with sword-thrusts.

"Do not chew your bronze bits any longer, impatient mares; your ivory hooves will no longer be reddened by blood already cold; we no longer have flowers, we have swords, and it is in the first rank that we are going to fly.

"The barriers are lowered, the abysms are filled in; we are going to fight like men and we shall be loved like women!"

The angel of midnight cried in his loud voice:

"From my sonorous hand into the blue gulf, the hours have fallen; the past is closed, the future is open. Let the tears dry; blood is about to flow."

Then a great silence fell and the old fir trees shivered, all the way to their roots. Between her two soldiers on the table of the dolmen, the Skylark smiled.

"Are we ready?" she said. "Trumpeter, sound the *réveille.*"

And the trumpeter blew.

A cannon shot vibrated in the German camp; a resounding appeal shook the Gaulish camp, and André, waking up, said:

"What I dream is just; come what may."

The morning mist hid beneath its silky folds the clearing and the dolmen.

In the Orient the stars were paling, the horses are saddled, the cannons are harnessed and the battalions are aligned.

It is not two peoples but two races that are about to settle their quarrel, three thousand years old. It is not only two races that are about to settle their quarrel, it is right that is about to struggle against force, light that is about to struggle against darkness.

The Gauls have with them the souls without bodies, ardent daughters of their bards, pensive daughters of their druids, chaste daughters of their soldiers. The Germans have for allies that which is not in God, but which God created in order that humans could grow by means of conflict.

Wolves, sharpen your teeth! Vultures, open your wings!

Weep, daughters of the Germans! Evil, which was not in God, could not be created eternal and three things diminish continually: obscurity, error and death. That which once gave you strength will no longer give it to you today.

Weep, daughters of the Germans! While your brothers were looking down, the great Potter was looking up. While your brothers, scalpel in hand, were searching for the sensitive fiber, the thinking nerve, the creative lobe, the poet was searching in the heavens for the divine why.

Through the centuries, in the caverns of India, under the oaks of the west, he searched, and when he had found it he said: "Spirit is the master, matter is the slave, my people will not perish."

Weep, daughters of the Germans! While your brothers said to matter: "Take us, we are yours," the great Potter said to it: "I am your master; I know the secret and the two forces that move you obey me and love me."

Weep, daughters of the Germans! The one who causes birth and the one who causes death have nourished with their milk in the garden of the old château the one who sharpened the weapon that the soldier had drawn, the one called the bard, the poet, the friend of André.

They nourished him with their milk because he said to them, when he was able to command:

"Friends, why continue a struggle that must end in defeat, since you have only been created in order to be vanquished? Instead of weighing upon the soul that wants to climb, why do you, who know how to give a shoot to the seed of an ash-tree and feathers to an eaglet, not give wings to human souls? Do you not know, then, that the day of defeat will also be the day of triumph? Do you not know that on the day when humans have achieved their goal, when they will no longer have to struggle, but when they will still want to learn and create, they will call upon you to animate their dreams and broaden their brows?"

They believed him, and they are with us.

The horses whinny, the cannons thunder and the earth trembles. Wolves, sharpen your teeth! Vultures, open your wings! Weep, daughters of the Germans!

The sun appears. Its golden arrows tear apart he veil of mist; the battlefield, with its broad plateaux, its steep hills and its encased river, is illuminated; and against the harsh blue sky the great dolmen in profiled, scintillating.

The armies are deployed. Squadrons appear on the crests and disappear immediately. Like two snakes watching one another, two thin lines of smoke undulate over the gorse. One by one, isolated batteries open fire on the hills and their shells cross paths in the alders of the ravine.

On the dolmen, motionless in a sparkling nimbus, between her two soldiers, the divine Skylark, an eglantine in her hand, watches. Leaning on his flagpole, the old sergeant leans over in order to get a better view, and the attentive chasseur, his clarion raised, does not take his eyes off the lips that will command.

Like a wall of steel, the Gaulish army cuts the plain in two. Between its divisions, the batteries are unharnessed; on its wings, the squadrons gather. The woods hide the German army; its batteries are no longer firing.

The thin lines of smoke glide over the gorse. Only the river separates the sharpshooters; the battle commences.

In the French army, fire is ignited to the right and the left. Bullets riddle the branches, shells search the ravines; the Prussians will have to show themselves...! Then a yellow light sets a beech-wood ablaze; the earth trembles; a hundred guns have spoken simultaneously, and a large section of the steel wall collapses on the plain.

The Skylark goes pale... The breach is filled... But at equal intervals, the volcano ignites and breaches are hollowed out.

"Trumpeter," says the Skylark, "sound the charge."

And the clarion sounds. But the breaches are broad... How much time it takes, how many men it requires, to fill them!

Breathless the old sergeant leans over. The battalions hesitate... "Conscript," he says, in a harsh voice, "blow harder."

And the clarion sounded so loudly that the trees quivered and the rock trembled. Then a cry sprang from all breasts, all the trumpets vibrated, all the horses whinnied and, like their great rivers when they break their dikes, the Gauls launched themselves forward in impetuous torrents.

Smoke fills the valley.

"I wish I could see," says the sergeant.

"Look," responds the Skylark.

The great dolmen, ripped from its base, rises into the blue sky on a crimson and gold cloud.

It is higher than the smoke, and it is still rising into the blue sky.

"What can you see, Sergeant?"

"Before me, between the stars, I see a limitless plain, and on that plain, an immense crescent, and facing that crescent, a sharp wedge."

On the crimson and gold cloud, into the blue sky, the dolmen rises.

"What can you see, Sergeant?"

"In the sharp wedge, in the immense crescent, I see soldiers, men with bare chests, cannons, chariots, wolf-skins, mantles, bayonets and pikes. There are two strange armies, the like of which I've never seen."

Into the blue sky the dolmen rises.

"What can you see, Sergeant?"

"I can see other armies around the plain. Their last ranks rise all the way to the stars. Before the crescent, on a horse without a saddle, I can see a man brandishing an ax. His beard is white and there are two bulls' horns on his helmet. At the point of the corner, I can see a horseman with a short sword in his hand; a crown of laurels partly hides his bald head. There are two strange armies, the like of which I've never seen."

Smiling, the Skylark says. "The enemies are numerous, but my sons are also numerous. Trumpeter, sound the charge!"

And the clarion sounds, and like a dragon waking up, the crescent writhes, and like a hawk spreading its wings, the wedge opens.

The clarion sounds and the battle commences. The chariots resonate, the cannons fume, the arrows fly, the bullets whistle, the sabers slash, the axes crush, and naked horsemen pass like waves over the smoky lines of haggard grenadiers.

"What can you see down below, Sergeant?"

"I can see the river, which is filling in. How deep the ravine is! How rapidly those cannon are firing!

"Sound, conscript! Sound louder!"

And the trumpeter blew and breathless chests leaned on red-hot cannons, and in the bloody river, gun-carriages crushed disemboweled caissons.

Behind the thickets the Prussians stand up; they have not yet fought. They empty their full water-bottles, pass their thick cloaks over their shoulders and, with a sure foot and a firm hand they crown the plateau with a dark wall.

Their heavy rifles lower, and like grapes under hail, streaming brows burst where the volcano had smoked.

"Sound, trumpeter; the river is full, our cannons can pass over."

The clarion sounds. The batteries descend at the gallop, traverse the valley at the gallop, and launch themselves at the gallop over the palpitating causeway that bars the bloody stream.

The horses sink all the way to the withers in breasts that are still warm, wheels sink in all the way to the axles; but the clarion sounds so loudly that the horses get up... The cannons have passed over.

With a dark wall the Prussians crown the plateau; from their lowered rifles lead flows in a gray sheet. The trees tremble. The vegetation is scythed.

To the wheels, cannoneers; the slope is steep! Hold firm; the horses are baulking! They are falling back on the caissons... Hold firm; the guns are slipping back! The battle is lost....!

The old sergeant hides his head in his hands; the chasseur crushes his trumpet on the stone; but the Skylark, smiling, raises her eglantine branch.

Then a heavy cloud rises from the forest and crashes down on the plateau.

In the blue sky the sun scintillates.

Then a gust of wind impregnated with the sweet perfume of hawthorn passes through the valley. In the branches of the birches the foliage is motionless.

The horses get up, the cannons move forward. One might think that they were no longer crumpling the vegetation; one might think that the wounded lying crosswise under their wheels were smiling when they had passed.

The slope is climbed. On the plateau, the batteries are aligned. The blinded Prussians retreat...

"What can you see, Sergeant?"

"My eyes are too full of tears! I can hear our cannons... Conscript, do you think we can be beaten twice in succession? Look, this is what we can do when our generals do as we do."

"I can only see a vermilion cloud. But what a loud voice our cannons have!"

"Those cannons could not have climbed he hill on their own...You still love your soldiers, then, Skylark? Love them; only they love you.

"But why are those two armies battling in that limitless plain?

"I recognize the breastplates that we were once made to oil, and which we found too large. I recognize the general crowned with laurels. While the sons are fighting the fathers wanted to fight too. I want to fight as well. Come on, conscript."

And the Skylark, indicating the titanic battle, said: "You too, go and fight."

It is a beautiful battle; while their sons are fighting for the earth, all the Celts whose swords have opened the celestial barrier, and all the Germans who have given red shrouds to their souls, are fighting for heaven.

All those who had once aided them, like judges in duels, had come, armed, in order to see the quarrel settled. But could their swords remain in their scabbards? Could Cyrus, Alexander, Hannibal, Marius, Tamerlane and Mahomet watch the battle without taking part? Their troops launch forward into the melee...

Oh, what a fine battle! The Germans are retreating! Oh, what a fine battle!

The ardent mist descends from heaven to earth and rises from earth to heaven. The Germans are fleeing, the Prussians are fleeing. Oh, what a fine battle! a fine battle!

But then, louder than the noise of the battle, a savage voice makes the sky tremble.

That voice cries: "I am the hammer of God! Attila! Attila!"

And yellow horsemen launch themselves forward over the exhausted fighters...

"How heavy your hand is, Master!" sobs the Skylark.

They run like flame in a field of furze, the Mongol archers, and the Skylark weeps as she wept in the prison of Narbonne.

But a broad radiance falls from the green star, and in that radiance a cavalier glides. His delicate mare, with the eyes of a gazelle, shakes her curly mane, and on her silky rump, a woman with a luminous brow and a green tunic sown with golden reeds, is shredding lotuses, lilies-of-the-valley and roses.

"It's the Potter! It's the queen!"

The savage archers pass back and forth over the exhausted fighters. They cry: "We are the scourge of God, the whip of his wrath! Attila! Attila!"

In the thickest part of the melee, the white mare rears up, and, harp in hand, the great Potter sings. Listen:

"The indolent colts are lying on the shaft; the whip whistles, and they are on their feet. The grain germinates in the ear; the scourge falls and the hard and bright wheat spring from the threshing area. You hold the whip, I hold the plow; you were only the Master's aides. You have crushed the ears, but the basket is full.

"As for me, I am the harvester."

Then a red furrow striped the limitless plain; Attila had heard, under his quivering knee, his stallion bounded..

He said: "Who speaks before the king? Is that you, Potter? Do you want to know how heavily the hammer of God comes down?"

Before the white mare, the savage stallion looms up.

The Potter responds:

"You are the hammer that has forged the steel. The earth was the anvil..."

"In forging the steel, see whether the hammer shatters!"

The ax rebounds from the bronze harp and its double blade slashes Attila's forehead.

Like a wounded lion, the king of the Huns roars. The bard draws his sword.

The sword flashes, the ax whirls. Steel grates... The ax was too heavy, the sword broke, and Attila smiled.

He raises his hand. The queen of the Ganges extends her bare arm over the Potter's head. As a daisy falls under the scythe, the arm is severed; but the bard plunges the stump of his sword into the king's throat.

The stallion falls backwards, the king gasps... Who will have the bloody trophy?

Cries overlap, arrows collide, breasts are crushed, cannons thunder, chariots swerve, flesh fumes, blood flows... Oh, what a fine battle!

"Victory! Victory!"

Like a swarm of flies, it is the fays who are rising up.

"Victory! Victory!" cry the Valkyries, wiping their swords. "Victory! Victory!" The Prussians have fed before André.

But the grim fighters do not see the fays rising and do not hear the Valkyries. Around the fallen Attila the bodies pile up... Who will have the bloody trophy?

Before the common enemy, the Germans and the Celts have forgotten their hatreds; it is the day of the great battle of darkness against light, and it is the Potter who commands Arminius and Caesar.

Who will have the bloody trophy?

"Victory!" cry the Valkyries. "Battle!" cries the Skylark. And before the vermilion squadron, on her foaming mare, with a golden sickle in her hand, she enters into the ardent melee.

Who will have the bloody trophy?

Then two forms with broad wings descend from the starry sky; one is holding a full cup, the other brandishing a scythe; Germans and Celts get up again, and like the leaves of the ash-tree when the icy wind blows, the savage archers fall over the body of their chief.

On the bank of the stream the victors have laid André down. Sadly, they crowd around him; he is going to die.

The first star is rising; he indicates it to them and says:

"Love one another and we shall see one another again."

"Where are we?"

"In what was yesterday still celestial Gaul, in the green star."

"I can no longer see men on the beach, I can no longer see houses on the hills, I can no longer see horses in the meadows. On the day after the great victory of the Celts in the star, I can no longer see any Celts."

It is for the good of men that the Master created the eternal combat; the ruder the battle is, the longer is the forward step taken. Yesterday the Celts were defeated; today France is more beautiful and the celestial Gaul is higher.

All men have been created equal, all peoples have been created brothers; the promised day will dawn when all men have become equal again, when all peoples have become brothers again.

The Germans and the Celts, the two primary peoples, have grown by virtue of their conflict. Yesterday they were enemies, today, in a star greener than the celestial Gaul and brighter than the Germany on high, they are mingled at the table of the eternal feast.

They are in the world of light, the world without frontiers, the world without swords.

"Why, then, instead of showing me that new fatherland, have you brought me to this deserted star?"

"We do not yet have the wings necessary to go so far."

But the pearl of the Ocean of the heavens is not deserted. Under its great trees of flowering reeds, do you not recognize that woolen tent?

It is the tent that the son of the oak erected on the mountain of the Arie.

In the meadow, near the spring, do you not recognize the father of our race, and his companion Fleur-d'Épine, and Caesar, and the Potter, and Ar-Braz? Do you not recognize in those two smiling women the queen of the Ganges and the Skylark?

"I recognize them."

The brother who marched alone for such a long time is between the two brothers; Fleur-d'Épine is dreaming, and the old man, extending his hand over their heads, with his eyes raised toward the sky, says:

315

"You have blessed my couch, Master; you alone can count my lineage, and the first-born of my sons have traced your route straightly. You have blessed your servant, Master; like a green nenuphar on an azure lake. My green star is floating on the ocean of the heavens; but I want to rise closer to you, Father; I am thirsty for light.

"Children, empty in peace the full cup; the battle is won."

"You are those who seek the unknown routes," said Fleur-d'Épine, "you will catch up with us rapidly. Love; amour is the torch that illuminates the route."

Fleur-d'Épine put her hand of the shoulder of the old man and they both rose up into the cloudless heavens, toward an unknown world.

Then the one who had been Caesar said: "The sin is ardent, and springs are scarce on the unknown routes. If I go astray, as I have gone astray before, it will be necessary, Mother, to show me the spring. The Almighty launched me like a thunderbolt; I have left nothing behind me but ashes. Mother, it is necessary in the night to take me by the hand; personally, I have no amour to guide me.

"Adieu, Brothers."

"Stay with us," said the Potter.

"Come with us," said Ar-Braz.

"No; my heart is like the forest, the wind of solitude blows there and its sadness rises to my lips. Until the day of danger, adieu, Brothers."

And alone, he climbs the snowy mountain.

Ar-Braz follows him with his eyes, and when he disappears behind the cedars of a ravine, he sighs: "When the sword is rusting in the scabbard, one likes to talk about the days when it shone in the sunlight."

Then the Skylark leans toward his ear and says to him in a low voice: "The wheat is ripe and the hawthorn is flowering."

The sun so long waited has finally risen; frontiers are effaced and the fighters are reposing after their terrestrial battles.

The proud soldiers will not descend again from their scintillating star; the time of weapons has passed here, the time of the spirit is beginning.

They are waiting for us up above, where there are still battles to be won.

"And the Skylark?"

"Between her soldiers and her bards, she is waiting for us too. But she is like an exile, she is always dreaming of the beautiful country where there forests are green and, when her friends are asleep, she descends again under the oaks of the land she loved so much.

There poets have sometimes encountered her and she has reminded them of the forgotten songs that lull like the waves, embalm like the heath and shine like flowering gorse.

Sometimes she has encountered, in solitary paths, old soldiers at whom rude laborers laughed, because they pass by idly, their gaze extinct and their backs curbed; to them she says: you will rediscover hordes and weapons up above, and you will fight again for those who forget that it is the sword that has cut the brambles of the path."

But the divine Skylark does not only love the soldiers and the bards; she loves all the sons of Gaul, and when, from the world of light, she goes in search of the one who has to watch over the human races, it is in the land of oaks that she makes her pause.

It is from the land of Gaul that the messenger of the good news will depart.

On the plateau of Alise they touch the earth; listen.

THE SKYLARK

Look; my harvester has finished his task.

He was a robust worker; look at the thrusts of his scythe.

How gilded the ears of wheat are in the fields of Gaul, how white the straw is!

317

It will be necessary for you, Moina, to bind the sheaves, and when you have bound them, it will be necessary to say to the oxherds: take the sheaves to the threshing area.

Then you will say to the beaters: go to work gaily; this wheat has no tares; the flour will be soft and it is you who will eat the bread that the flour has made.

That bread will be the bread of the strong, and the table will be broad and the seats equal.

THE AWAITED

What will it be necessary to say to the oxherds, when the beaters have taken their seats at the table, Skylark?

THE SKYLARK

You will say to them, Moina: "Love one another."

On winter evenings, around the fire, when the old men are chatting, when the young people are blushing while whispering in one another's ears, when the children, with half-closed eyes are seeing animals in the embers, you will lift the latch of the door gently and you will say to them: "Gauls, I have come from far away, I know many new songs; make room for me at the hearth."

Then you will talk to them about the fine battles and long marches of Ar-Braz and the Potter, about all those who have divined you and all those who have loved you. You will not forget the Skylark.

You will say to them: it is necessary to struggle, as your forefathers struggled, and never forget that the steel of your plow was once a sword that was wielded by the valiant."

You will say to them: "It is necessary to dream, as your forefathers dreamed; it is in dreams that they found the first three words of the secret for which the Master has told us to search."

You will say to them: "Love, as your forefathers loved. Love everything that lives. Love everything that grows. Love one another."

They will believe you, Moina, and you will be the messenger of the good news.

I have to stay up above with my old soldiers—we fought together for such a long time—but I loved the mild land of green woods and rosy heaths so much that I am almost an exile.

I only had a little corner of this vast earth, but how flowery that corner was! How beautiful my Gaul was!

Liberty the Master has given to the entire earth; sing the sacred hymn to everyone, but to the Gauls, sometimes sing the song of the Skylark.

To Alphonse Lequeutre[27]

Friend, you ask me why I have written this book.

Because I wanted to give substance to an idea that has haunted my brain for twenty years, in a hundred different forms.

For twenty years I have made and broken many molds; some were too large, others too small, all were deformed. The last is worth no more than the others, but the years pass, and in handling the plow and the ax one obtains a heavy hand. I feared no longer having the time and, slightly lame, slightly hunchbacked, with poor eyesight, I have sent you my sketch. The head is too large, the legs too frail... but I have done what I could.

"Let us pass over the form," you say to me; "but the foundation... I cannot see your idea very clearly."

I have tried to read in the past the history of the future. I have tried to console those who are weeping, to enlighten those who doubt, by showing them that they were the sons of Gauls, that the allies of their forefathers always had virtues, and that they had only to want it to be the strongest, the happiest and the wisest.

My work is vague and incoherent, I know only too well, but I am certain that tomorrow... or later, I will end up saying what I wanted to say, what I have to say being true.

Life is short, but for the Gauls, life has always had a tomorrow.

"Then why show this sketch?"

---

[27] Alphonse Lequeutre (1829-1891) was a mountaineer with a passion for the Pyrenees; he was the first to climb many of the peaks, and he wrote two guide-books of his own as well as contributing to the noted series of Joanne guides. In 1878 he moved on to explore the peaks of the Central Massif, and it was presumably then that he formed his friendship with L'Estoille.

In order that its faults can be pointed out to me. My statue is in clay and not in bronze, I can and I want to remake it and correct it.

Les Bonnéveaux, 1 November 1880.[28]

---

[28] The commune now known as Bonneveaux is adjacent to Renaison, Duclaux's birthplace; the plural is still employed locally, and is retained by the local wine.